THREE BRIDGES

RJ COONS

9/5/15

To Trisha,
Enjoy the
Adventure.
RJ Coons

ISBN-13: 978-1511853125

ISBN-10: 1511853123

Dedication

To Bobby and Justin my sons.

Acknowledgements

I would like to express my appreciation to all the people who helped in the research and structure of this novel. I am deeply grateful for the police, fire, and park personnel for their insight and first-hand knowledge they brought to the story.

A special thanks to my family and friends who were supportive and gave valuable advice.

Photograph of the author by Carol Malott.

Chapter One

The clock on the dashboard read 7:55 when the black Hummer turned onto Serpentine Lane; the driver switched off the headlights and slowly maneuvered his vehicle down the tree-lined street towards the third house on the right. The driver knew exactly where to go, having practiced many times before. If he had to, he was confident he could make the drive blindfolded, but that was only in the movies; tonight was for real, no Hollywood retakes, only one performance. At 204, the driver eased the truck to the curb, shifted into neutral and pulled up the parking brake. The engine kept running.

A moonless black sky added an extra darkness to the night. The only light, a pale yellow glow from a streetlamp at the end of the block flickered in and out of the tree branches with each gust of wind. A damp mist crept in off the Gulf and clung to everything with cold drizzly hands. The driver stared at the rivulets of water building along the top of the window until the windshield was completely covered with a cloud of mist. One drop raced down the windshield and disappeared below the hood, an apt metaphor of a life that now raced out of control. *How was he sucked into this insane scheme*, he thought to himself. *Oh well, show time, Happy Birthday Blaine Sterling.*

The street was deserted, not a soul outside playing, walking a dog or taking the garbage out. All the neighbors were either inside watching television or at Blaine Sterling's birthday party at the end of the block. He was not invited, but he heard about the big birthday bash all week long from the other rangers. The extra large shrimp from Publix, steaks from Herman's Meat Market, the signature strawberry shortcake birthday cake from Upper Crust Café, and a jump castle for the

1

kids, a fireworks extravaganza and to add a touch of mystery to the occasion, a surprise guest. Every day a different ranger would post a new suggestion for the `name the special guest contest` at the Nature Center: Sarasota's favorite son, aerialist Nick Wallenda, just back from his Chicago Tower spectacular, will wire-walk across Serpentine Lane; an Elvis impersonator; a Chippendale male dancer; the Governor; or maybe a dancing bear were all bandied about. The only thing the rangers agreed upon, knowing Lou Bravo, the special guest had to be someone or something outrageous. About thirty people, co-workers, neighbors, friends of Blaine Sterling, were all celebrating her special day down at Lou Bravo's house, but not him.

He liked birthday parties, the driver thought. He never forgot his tenth birthday. His father hired Spiderman, not Toby McGuire, but a Spiderman performer. He rode up to the house on top of a car, jumped the chain-linked fence, past Buddy his dog and climbed up the chimney to the roof. He ran along the peak, jumped down to the front porch and then to the ground. He was spectacular. He showed all the kids how to climb up the swing-set in the backyard, balance on top of the support pole and how to jump and roll to the ground without hurting themselves.

Finally, everyone had a picture taken sitting on Spiderman's shoulders. He had a Spiderman birthday cake, Spiderman birthday hats, Spiderman masks, but the coolest present of all was a Spiderman glove that shot out gooey spider web stuff. He got a little carried away shooting people; his dad took it away until the party was over. After the cake, everyone watched a Spiderman movie. What a great party.

Since the driver wasn't a friend, co-worker or a neighbor, he wasn't invited. But he did have a surprise—a special present for the birthday girl.

Carefully, the driver reached over to the passenger's seat, opened the small blue Igloo cooler and took out his gift. He pushed opened the driver's side door and quickly walked up the sidewalk in front of Blaine's house. He took out a Zippo lighter and lit the rag that stuck out of the gasoline- filled coke bottle in his left hand. A single flame spit black smoke and a burning orange-yellow glow silhouetted a young man dressed in a black hoodie, blue jeans, black tee and orange sneakers. In one fluid motion, the Molotov cocktail sailed through the air across the front lawn, shattered the front dining room window and exploded inside. Fire engulfed the room as angry red and yellow flames shot out the broken window and clawed their way up the side of the house. The brilliant flames lit up the entire front of the property, two neighboring homes and the interloper. The bomber reached for his cell phone, snapped a picture and immediately e-mailed his handiwork to a pre-arranged cell phone number three hundred miles away. It was eight o'clock in the evening.

The repeated high-pitched beeps from Sterling's home smoke detectors and outdoor fire alarm speaker fractured the evening's silence as the Hummer pulled away from the curb. The driver glanced in his rear view mirror and smiled. Shadows of people running into the street danced back and forth in the glass. The black Hummer drove away into the night.

Chapter Two

Johnny West, a convicted murderer coughed out in a low raspy voice from his bed across the room, "What you got there Charlie?" Too many years of smoking finally caught up with him and took one of his lungs. Unfortunately, that wasn't the only thing that caught up with him. For fifty years he outsmarted the law. Johnny changed his name, moved to New Mexico, got married, had a job, kids and played the role of model citizen. Thought he was home free until that damn Most Wanted Show put his picture and story on television. A week later, the cops knocked on his door, handcuffed him and extradited him back to Florida. New DNA forensics confirmed he raped and murdered the thirteen-year-old girl and to avoid a death sentence West pleaded guilty. Three days later, he was cleaning out toilets at Union Correctional in Raiford, Florida. At seventy, he understood that he'd be spending the rest of his life in prison. "So what's that on your cute little pink phone?" Johnny asked again and spat into the toilet leaving another green-brown mass of phlegm floating on the top.

"It's a birthday present from my son, Thor." Charlie Boltier laughed and held up the phone he bought last week for three hundred dollars from one of the inmates, Big Willie. Big Willie had connections; if you needed something, Big Willie was the go to guy. At 6' 6", three hundred pounds of evil, and tattoos from head to toe, Big Willie was the baddest motherfucker in the joint. Nobody crossed Big Willie. Five years ago, one guy tried to muscle in on Big Willie's operation. He had some gang connection from LA, and tried to throw his weight around, a real big talker. Two weeks after he arrived, the big talk stopped. The guards found him hanging in his cell. Ruled a suicide, nobody said anything, but everyone knew you don't mess with Big Willie and live for long.

"It's not your birthday, Charlie; I remember you said your birthday was in June and what kinda birthday picture is that, a house on fire?" Johnny coughed and spit into the toilet just before he began to urinate.

"Man, this is better than sex, check it out."

"Sex, Charlie, what do you know about sex? Your old lady walked out on you months ago. You haven't been laid in almost a year and you're not what I'd call an expert on the subject," Johnny said, and zipped up his fly.

"I didn't say it was my birthday numbnuts. It's a birthday present for Blaine Sterling, Assistant Park Manager at the Osprey State Park. The bitch who sent me here for thirty to life. Just because I drove the fucking boat at the Venice Boat Parade, while a friend of mine, Remi Cole, shot her, but ended up killing some old lady. An accessory to second degree murder, because I was there and made no attempt to prevent the crime. Can you believe that crap?"

"Listen Johnny, just look at the fucking picture before I flatten your skinny little ass." Boltier shoved the phone up against Johnny's face.

"So, Charlie, what's with the picture? I see a house on fire. What kinda birthday present is that?" Johnny asked and stepped back.

"Today's her birthday. She's at a friend's house celebrating, having a good time and that's her house burning down. Just a little payback," Charlie hissed and e-mailed the picture along with a text greeting: *Happy Birthday. Sorry I missed your party, but I am a little tied up at the moment. This is only the beginning.*

Chapter Three

Two hours earlier, Blaine Sterling's daughter, Brooke, was dressed and ready to leave for her mother's birthday party down the block at Lou Bravo's house. All week she listened to neighbors' gossip and pontificate about how grand the party was going to be. Trucks delivered tables, chairs, flowers, boxes, and lumber, while workers hammered and moved around the property all week long. The anticipation was too much for a seven-year-old girl to endure, she had to get some air or she would explode.

Brooke opened the front door and standing at the end of the driveway was a big red stagecoach hitched to two spirited gray stallions. Holding the reins, high up on the driver's box, dressed in full cowboy gear, Stetson hat, red flannel shirt, leather vest, jeans, chaps, buckskin boots and a six-shooter sat Lou Bravo. He waved his black ten-gallon hat high in the air and shouted," Howdy partner, where's the birthday girl?"

Brooke couldn't believe her eyes. A red Wells Fargo stagecoach, two gray horses and a crazy cowboy parked in front of her house. She closed the door and called," Mom, are you ready? You have to come here now! You're not going to believe what's outside."

"Just about, sweetie, I want to check one more thing." Standing in front of the bathroom mirror, Blaine took one last look. Her new birthday present to herself, a white, high-waisted cotton pencil skirt with a floral print and a white sleeveless blouse fit her slender, well-toned 5' 11" frame perfectly. Her straight blonde hair, pulled back in a ponytail by a matching scrunchie, complimented her outfit and her bright blue eyes. "Well, birthday girl, let's go party and celebrate number twenty-eight, but who's counting, not me." Blaine turned off the light and walked into the living room. "Okay, sweetie, I'm ready. So, what am I not going to believe?" Blaine said, as Brooke opened the front door.

They stood there in awe, gawking at the unbelievable sight before them. At the same moment, Lou Bravo pulled at a string attached to the luggage railing, and a white and blue banner unfurled down the side of the stagecoach. In bright red letters, "Happy Birthday Blaine" welcomed them.

"Don't just stand there ladies, hop in," Lou Bravo called. "Everyone is waiting for you at the party, giddyap girls."

Walking down the driveway, Blaine asked, "Is that the stagecoach from outside the Wells Fargo Bank on Venice Avenue? The paper said that Wells Fargo was a sponsor of the Arcadia Rodeo and the stagecoach was sent from their corporate headquarters in San Francisco to march in the opening day parade this weekend."

"Mommy said the stagecoach is over a hundred years old. How cool!"

"So if this stagecoach is in the opening day ceremony this weekend, why are you driving it?"

"Well, birthday girl, that's a long story and we're late for a very important date. Let's just say that my good friend, Whitney Crumb, the manager at Wells Fargo, owed me a favor. He had an overdraft problem from our Thursday night poker games and decided to clear the books with this little birthday ride. Anyway, they won't send this old beauty up to the event until tomorrow, so here I am buckaroo. Plus, this stagecoach fits perfectly into the Country and Western theme for your birthday party and everyone knows how much you love country and western music, right darlin'?" Lou Bravo leaned down and pulled open the compartment door. Two white cowboy hats rested on the black leather seats. The ride down the block to Lou Bravo's house took only about four minutes, but the jostling back and forth was uncomfortable. Blaine could only imagine what travel back in the 1800's was like, not pleasant by any stretch of the imagination.

"Mommy, take my picture. We're studying transportation in school and I want to show my class what a real stagecoach looks like." Brooke moved close to the window. "How do I look?"

"Great." Blaine reached into her pocketbook and took out her phone, "One, two, three, smile. It looks fantastic. Here look," and handed Brooke her phone between jerks.

"So cool, the kids will love it and the hat fits perfectly. Let me take your picture."

"Ready, smile, one, two, three. Wow! You can even see the leather padding against the door. What's that for?"

"Probably to protect the passengers from all the bouncing around, like we're doing now," Blaine said and grabbed the leather strap against the window. "I have a feeling we'll both be black and blue by tomorrow morning."

Everyone was out on the front lawn and cheered when the stagecoach pulled up. A worker from Windsong Farm, where the horses were stabled, grabbed the bridles and steadied the horses while the passengers disembarked and joined the party. Lou Bravo ran over to Blaine, took her arm and said, "Close your eyes. I have a surprise for you," and walked her down the driveway to the backyard. Like everything in Lou Bravo's life, when he put his mind to it, surprises always turned into extravaganzas and Blaine's birthday party took the cake. "Okay, open them, birthday girl!"

"Oh my God, I don't believe it. It's amazing," Blaine cried out as tears of joy rolled down her cheeks. "All I wanted was a simple little birthday party."

The entire backyard had been transformed into an old country and western town and hummed with excitement. Along the perimeter of the property, wooden facades of a saloon, jail, train depot, bank, horse barn with corral and a general store set the authentic old town spirit. Under an old oak tree, covered with lights, smoke rose from a chuck wagon where a cowboy grilled steaks and burgers for all the partygoers. A blackened pot of beans bubbled at the end of the grill, no doubt Lou Bravo's famous baked beans everyone loved, adding another savory aroma to the night's air. Three cowgirls walked around with trays of shrimp, pigs-in-a-blanket, meatballs, cheese and Cheetos for everyone to enjoy (Brooke loved Cheetos). Tables with red and white checkered tablecloths circled a small campfire in the center of the yard where all the guests waited for Blaine to arrive. Finally, old gas lampposts, placed around the yard, added an old fashioned glow that put everyone in a festive mood. Lou Bravo walked Blaine and Brooke over to a large table where Marybeth Maiello, Charlene and Ken Brecht and Mary and Bob Travers sat. "Here, Blaine, why don't you and Brooke sit next to Marybeth. I have one more surprise," and waved his hat.

A spotlight lit up the front porch of the saloon and through the swinging doors stepped Patti Highland singing happy birthday. Patti Highland was Blaine Sterling's all-time favorite country and western singer. Religiously, Blaine and Brooke would go to Buddy's Pizzeria in Venice, almost every Thursday night, and listen to her sing all the old Patsy Cline hits. They would order the house special: antipasto salad, large pepperoni pizza, a pitcher of pop and for dessert a free cup of chocolate gelato from an old ice cream machine in the back dining room. For hours, Blaine and all the patrons would sing along to such favorites as "Walking after Midnight," "I Fall to Pieces," "Sweet Dreams," and Blaine's all-time favorite, "Crazy." Poor Brooke, she grit her teeth and bore through it all. She would rather have been at a Britney Spears or Bruno Mars concert, but she knew her mom loved Patti Highland and Thursdays at Buddy's was a tradition; that is until it closed and bummed out everyone in Venice. Patti sang all night long, but before the cake and coffee arrived, she sat down with Blaine and invited her to the Shamrock Café on Thursday and Saturday to hear her sing at the new venue.

"Brooke, did you hear Patti say she is now singing at a little restaurant on Shamrock, Thursday and Saturday nights? Maybe we could go next Thursday and start a new tradition!" Brooke just rolled her eyes.

At precisely quarter after eight, the music stopped and all the lights in Lou Bravo's backyard went dark. On cue, the back door flew open and the two cowgirls rushed out carrying the three tiered, strawberry shortcake birthday cake aglow with colored candles flickering in the wind to Blaine's table. Everyone gathered around singing happy birthday and snapping pictures. "Blow them out, mommy, blow them out."

"I will, sweetie, but first I need to make a wish. Who put all those candles on the cake? There must be a mistake; I'm certainly not that old. How many candles are there anyway?"

"I cannot tell a lie. I did," Lou Bravo said. "Twenty-eight and one for good luck."

"Okay, I'm ready, Brooke. Please help me blow them out. One, two, three, blow!"

Chapter Four

All the candles blown out, the lights went on, Patti Highland started to sing, and Blaine's cell phone rang. She looked down at the text message: *Happy Birthday. Sorry I missed your party, but I am a little tied up at the moment. This is only the beginning.* Confused, she opened the attachment and froze. All happiness drained from Blaine's face, which suddenly contorted with fear and disbelief. Trembling, she handed the phone to Marybeth and ran from the table. Once out on the street her fear turned to panic. The siren blasts from fire engines, ambulances and police cars shattered the silence as she turned onto Serpentine Lane. Flashing red, blue, orange and white lights lit up the night while the flow of rescue vehicles crisscrossed the street blocking all access to 204 Serpentine Lane. Firefighters attacked the flames with water, while police cordoned off the area with yellow caution tape and set up a perimeter to hold back the gathering crowd of onlookers.

"What's going on? Is there a fire?" shouted Lou Bravo, who was first to catch up to Blaine.

"Yes, it's my house!"

"How do you know it's your house? There are so many trucks and cars all over the road. Maybe it's the empty lot next to the Traver's house?"

"Trust me, I know," Blaine shouted and started to run.

Thunderous blasts from sirens brought out concerned neighbors, who with the party guests converged towards the fire. Red and orange flames still raced up the front of her house when Blaine, Lou Bravo, and the rest of the crowd reached the yellow caution tape. Firefighters struggled with the pressure of their hoses as water streamed from the two pump engines parked directly in front of the burning building. Water exploded into the flames, hurling back a cloud of black smoke that hung over the property as firefighters raced into the house with fire hoses and axes. Smoke bellowed up from a hole in the roof as water pounded down from the aerial boom. Blaine ducked under the yellow caution tape and walked towards her burning house. "Stop, you're not permitted here. Stay behind the yellow caution tape," the police officer shouted and raised his hand.

"This is my house! Is Detective Beale here?" Blaine screamed. "I need to see him now!"

"He's on his way, but you and your friend need to wait here." He turned and walked behind a row of police cars and disappeared.

Chapter Five

Three minutes later Detective Beale and his partner, Detective Stan Hordowski appeared on the scene. Side-by-side the two made an odd partnership, Justin Beale 42, 6' 2", 185lbs, thick wavy brown hair with a muscular physique, and Stan Hordowski 32, eight inches shorter, chubby, a bit out of shape, with thin spiked brown hair. Appearances aside, they worked well together. They escorted Blaine and Lou Bravo to the police command area off the driveway along the side of the house. A block of cameras recorded and monitored every section of the fire, which was also linked to police headquarters and the fire department. A computer tech handed Beale a printout. "Hordowski, take a look at this. A firefighter said he saw shards of glass from a broken soda bottle when he first entered the house. We may be talking arson."

"Maybe this fire is connected to that wilding incident last week up in Sarasota. The one where a group of teenagers ran down Bamboo Lane and smashed every car window on the block. Five cars were destroyed. What a mess."

"I remember, behind the Verizon building in Sarasota. The sheriff had some leads, thought it could be a gang initiation or maybe a high school prank. I'll give him a call and see what he thinks." Beale took out his notepad, wrote call sheriff, and drew a picture of a fire.

"I'll see if the fire marshal arrived, if he has, I'll follow up on the arson theory."

"Say hello to old carrot top for me," Beale shouted as Hordowski walked towards the house.

"Arson! There's an arsonist running around Venice! What are you going to do about it, Detectives?" Lou Bravo barked out and stepped in front of Beale.

"Wait just one minute, sir. No one said it was definitely arson. That's for Fire Marshal Cavanagh to determine. I don't want to panic the neighborhood into thinking an arsonist is on the prowl firebombing homes, when in fact we are not certain. Until then, I don't want you or Ms. Sterling to discuss arson with anyone. Is that understood?" Beale looked at both of them and waited. Lou Bravo replied, 'Yes.'

The loss of a home is a devastating experience. The destruction deliberate. Unthinkable. The violation goes well beyond the ruin of the bricks and mortar structure. Arson is an intrusion into a person's spirit and claws away at one of society's core values, the sanctity of the home. Consumed by fire, the devastation not only leaves the victim physically unprotected, but mentally abused.

Blaine Sterling was no stranger to adversity and while she watched her home burn a string of sorrows flooded back to her. The rape and acquittal of her attacker the first year as a park ranger on Fire Island, New York. Shot twice while watching the Christmas Boat Parade in Venice, by Remi Cole, a fired park ranger who thought she caused his termination. The unexplained disappearance of her husband of less than a year, and then notification eight years later he died in a car accident attempting to locate his birth parents brought tears. Now her house intentionally set on fire. Misfortune tests an individual's resolve. The old adage, 'When the going gets tough, the tough get going,' illustrated precisely the resolve that made Blaine Sterling unique. With all she'd endured, she never gave up. She was a fighter.

"It's only a house. No one was injured and that's the important thing. No, Detective, this was not a gang initiation or some teenage prank. My house was targeted. The arsonist knew today was my birthday, knew I was at a party at Lou Bravo's house, and knew my cell phone number." Blaine glowered at the detective and said, "He even had the audacity to send me a picture of the house burning."

"What! The arsonist sent you a picture of your house burning?" Beale shouted in disbelief.

"He also sent a text message, '*Sorry I couldn't make your party. I'm tied up at the moment. Happy Birthday. This is only the beginning.'* It's obvious this fire was planned to intimidate me."

"I need your cell phone, Blaine. We'll have our IT guys look at it and find out who made the call and its location." Beale stuck out his hand.

"I don't have it. I gave it to my friend Marybeth Maiello; she's probably standing behind the police barrier with my daughter."

"Okay, let's go get it. The sooner the IT guys work on the phone, the sooner we can locate this guy and lock him up." Beale, Blaine and Lou Bravo headed towards the crowd.

"There they are," Lou Bravo shouted and pointed to a group of people in cowboy hats standing up against the yellow caution tape.

"Mommy, I'm over here," a young voice called out as a small arm waved frantically. "Please come. I'm scared." Tears flowed down Brooke's face as Blaine pulled her into her arms. The young girl shook uncontrollably.

"I'm Detective Beale, from the Venice Police Department. I need to talk with Marybeth Maiello. Is she here?" Beale held up his shield.

"I'm Marybeth Maiello. What can I do for you, Detective?" A voice answered and a young attractive woman in her early twenties stepped to the front of the group. Her long brown hair hung over her shoulders. She had a slender athletic figure and without the cowboy hat stood about 5' 7", Beale calculated.

"I need Blaine Sterling's cell phone."

"Why?" Marybeth answered, took a step back, reached into her vest pocket and popped out the metal ring that surrounded the charger port.

"Don't move, miss, I need that phone," Beale yelled and grabbed her arm.

"Marybeth, it's okay. Give the Detective the phone. I told him about the message and picture," Blaine said and walked over to Marybeth carrying Brooke in her arms.

Marybeth pulled out the phone, with her right thumb pushed in the charger port cover and handed the device to Detective Beale. Beale opened the file and stared at the message and picture. "This fire was intentional; someone is out to harm you, Ms. Sterling. It's a person who knows you. This individual, or individuals, knew it was your birthday, knew your address and cell phone number. He has a grudge against you, but worst of all, threatened to harm you again. Do you..." In mid-sentence, Hordowski walked up and interrupted.

"Old carrot top says hello. Man does he have a head of red hair. Anyway, he found glass and gasoline residue. His preliminary findings indicate a Molotov cocktail. He'll know more by morning. So I guess the teenage prank theory is out the window."

"You could say that Detective-- take a look at this," Beale said, and handed him the phone.

Hordowski's eyes bulged out, "This is sick. The guy sends you a picture of your house burning, wishes you a happy birthday and threatens to continue the harassment. This person is dangerous. What does he mean, 'I'm tied up at the moment.'" Hordowski handed Beale the phone.

"I don't know, but I'm going find out. There's not anything more for us here. Need to wait for the fire marshal's report. Let's get this phone back to headquarters and see what the IT guys can decode. Do you need a ride some place, Blaine?" Beale asked and put the phone in his pocket.

"That won't be necessary Detective," Lou Bravo, barked out. "She and Brooke can stay at my house tonight. I have plenty of room."

"Are you sure? We can always go to a hotel. I don't want to be a burden." Blaine turned and smiled at Lou Bravo. "Detective Beale, can I go inside and get some of our clothes?"

"Definitely not," Beale replied. "This is an official crime scene, and no one is permitted beyond the yellow caution tape." He and Hordowski turned and walked back to a white Crown Victoria parked along the driveway.

Mrs. Brecht pushed forward and put her arm around Brooke, "Don't worry, sweetie, I have some clothes of yours when you slept over a few weeks ago and I'm sure I have a nightgown that your mother can fit into."

"It's settled then." Lou Bravo took both their hands and the three of them trudged wearily back down the street.

Chapter Six

It's almost impossible to fall asleep in a strange house. The unfamiliar sounds that hum in the dark, a muffled conversation from another part of the house, the sudden creak from down the hall, and of course the all too hard pillow that won't fit a tired head, make for a restless night. To compound matters, Blaine dreaded the call to her insurance company. Would there be enough coverage to repair the house, where would they live while the new construction was under way and most worrisome, would Brooke have to attend a new school? All these unanswered questions rolled around in her head for hours. Finally, exhausted, Blaine fell asleep just before dawn.

"Good morning sleepyheads," Lou Bravo announced from the kitchen as Blaine and Brooke walked in. "I thought we'd go to Patches for breakfast since I have to meet someone there. How does that sound? My treat."

"Awesome, they have the best pancakes in the world," Brooke said and pulled at her mother's arm.

"I don't know about the best pancakes in the world, maybe in Venice, Florida. Sounds delicious, but we need to brush our teeth and I have to put on some make-up."

"Okay, I'll wait for you outside. "Just as Lou Bravo stood the phone on the kitchen counter rang. Lou Bravo's kitchen was massive. His late wife Maria, who passed away nine years ago, loved to cook. Every Sunday she would have friends and family over for a traditional Italian feast. The homemade marinara sauce, fresh pasta, sausages, meatballs, salad greens, tomatoes, cucumbers from the garden, baked breads, and last but not least, Maria's mouthwatering cannolis smothered in confectionery sugar. So the kitchen became the focal point of the house and their life. A state of the art kitchen with an old Mediterranean world accent. Custom dark cherry wood cabinets, a wrought iron chandelier hanging above a large butcher block table that sat fourteen comfortably. All stainless steel appliances, orange flaked Camille granite counter tops, a deep triple country sink, and Italian marble terrazzo tiled floor covered the nine hundred square foot room. Everything sparkled, showroom clean, waiting for another Lou Bravo house party.

"Hello. Yes she is, one minute please." Lou Bravo reached across the counter and handed Blaine the phone.

"Hello. Oh, hi Marybeth. Yes, we're fine. We're going out for breakfast. Yes, that would be great. I'd love to. See you at twelve o'clock, 'bye."

"What did Marybeth want, Mommy?" Brooke chirped and looked up into her mother's bright blue eyes.

"She invited me to have lunch with her at the Upper Crust Restaurant tomorrow. The restaurant heard about the fire and are baking a special strawberry shortcake for me. She also has something to tell me."

"Am I invited, Mommy?" Brooke asked in a mournful tone only a seven-year-old child could make.

"Of course sweetie, but first we need to brush our teeth and I need some make-up." Blaine and Brooke walked to the bathroom, Lou Bravo to the garage.

Chapter Seven

The color banana yellow shouts, *look at me!* A banana yellow trailer screams, *circus in town!*

Lou Bravo backed his El Camino out of the driveway, turned right on Serpentine Lane and slowly moved up the block. In the distance, a banana yellow trailer parked on Blaine Sterling's front lawn glowed. As they approached the property they noticed that all the trucks and firefighting equipment were gone, as were the police and CSI vans and the yards and yards of yellow police tape. All that remained was a banana yellow trailer. A group of men busily placed lattice fencing along the bottom section of the trailer while a worker with a hand truck rolled a propane tank towards the back. "Mommy, what is that yellow box doing on our lawn?"

"I don't know sweetie, maybe it's for the police investigation. There's a small sign on the side of the trailer. Can we stop the car for a minute please?"

Lou Bravo pulled to the curb and stopped. Blaine looked out the window and read, "Banana Trailers, Trailer King of Florida. Lou Bravo, do you know anything about this banana yellow trailer?"

"Yes, but I'll tell you about it during breakfast. I'm starved." He stepped on the accelerator and swiftly pulled away from the curb.

Patches, Lou Bravo's favorite breakfast restaurant, was packed. The morning crowd had descended like starving pythons (or something) and by nine o'clock all the tables were full. A handful of people anxiously waited outside. Lou Bravo squeezed through a crowd standing around the front desk, where Jackie, the owner, informed him that his friend had already sat down and was on his second cup of coffee. The trio zigzagged between tables and pushed through to the last booth along the windows where Tony Lilly sat. Tony was hard on the eyes tall, over six feet, skinny, bald, long neck, hooked nose, but he had a great personality.

"Brooke, I'd like you to meet Mr. Lilly. This is my daughter Brooke," Blaine said as everyone sat down.

"Hi, I remember you; you're the ice cream man from the Venice Boat Parade. The man the police officer was going to give a ticket to because you didn't have a license to sell ice cream in Venice. Thank you for lending us your ice cream truck; I had a great time selling ice cream during my winter vacation."

"That's right. You have a very good memory, Brooke. Pleased to meet you. And thank you for selling so much ice cream. There was only one box of ice cream sandwiches, a few bags of potato chips and a handful of blow pops left. Great job! I have a present for you and your mother, a little something Mrs. Lilly bought in Nassau from a beach vendor. Had I known you and your mother were coming today, I would have brought them. I'll give them to Lou Bravo to drop off at your house."

"Good morning. Is everyone ready to order?" Victoria Koklovia, their server, a large, buxom Russian with a no-nonsense reputation, said. "I'll start with you, Lou Bravo," and took out her order pad. Two orders of blueberry pancakes for the ladies, two orders of eggs for the men and of course an order of extra crispy bacon for Lou Bravo, a large glass of orange juice for Brooke, two coffees and an iced tea completed the order.

"Now, what is that banana yellow trailer doing in my front yard?"

"Well, Blaine, it is like this," Lou Bravo took a gulp of coffee and sat up straight ready for combat. "I know you and Brooke don't want to stay in my house for any length of time. You need your privacy and so do I. Plus, Brooke has to go to school and to move out of the area would be too disruptive. Not to mention, driving her back and forth to school would be very difficult for you to juggle." Lou Bravo took a nervous gulp of coffee. "So I thought, if you remained at your house, but not in your house while repairs were made, Brooke could attend her present school uninterrupted and you could oversee the construction."

Blaine didn't speak. She took a sip of iced tea and waited. For Lou Bravo it seemed an eternity. He could hear the pounding of his heart increase by the minute and feel beads of perspiration form under his armpits. His head started to spin and thoughts of impending doom flashed before him. What was he thinking when he called his friend Joey Banana last night and asked him to drop off one of his trailers at Blaine's house? Joey said he had a brand new, ready to move in trailer. Two bedrooms, two baths, modern kitchen with new appliances, washer, dryer, a small living room, all the conveniences of home compacted into a 23' x 40' banana yellow trailer.

"What a great idea!" Blaine exclaimed just as breakfast arrived. Everyone breathed a sigh of relief and began to eat.

Half-way through the meal, Brooke asked, "Who is a Joey Banana?"

"That's a very good question, Brooke," Lou Bravo responded. "Joey Banana isn't his real name. Everybody just calls him that, it's a nickname. His real name is Joey Jupiter and he owned Jupiter's Food Emporium around the corner from my automotive repair shop in Central Islip, New York. I'd stop by his market every morning for my daily cup of java and over the years we became good friends. One day a robber comes in, points a gun at Joey and demands all the money. Joey is standing in the produce department with a handful of bananas in his hands. Maybe he was frightened or just tired of being robbed, but he threw all the bananas at the robber. The gun fell to the ground, a bullet shoots the robber in the foot, and when he turned to run away, he slipped on a banana and fell to the floor. Joey immediately sat on him and called the police. At two hundred pounds, and eating a banana, Joey had everything covered. The local newspaper nicknamed him *Joey Banana* and he became an overnight hero who fought crime, one banana at a time."

"Tell them about the TV shows he took us to," Tony added, and gobbled down the last forkful of hash browns.

"Saturday Night Live had him on the show reenacting the banana robbery scene that ended with a banana eating contest between Joey Banana and the Coney Island hot dog eating champ. David Letterman sent a limousine to drive him into New York City for his late night show, and Jay Leno, a week later, had a banana gun fight with Joey outside a D'Agostino's food market. It was fantastic, we were signing autographs all over town, we were like Hollywood celebrities. To answer your question, Joey Banana sold his market, made a bundle of money, moved to Sarasota and started a construction trailer rental business and called it Banana Trailers. His trademark banana yellow trailers are all over the state and he is living the good life. A mansion on Long Boat Key, a yellow Bentley, and a forty-two foot yacht docked in his backyard. But with all his money, he never forgot his friends. Still a stand-up guy, right, Tony?"

"That's right. Joey's still a great guy and a damn good poker player. We play cards once a month at his place." Tony laughed, "What I lost to him, I bet, helped pay for his new John McEnroe tennis court overlooking the water."

"What's the inside like?" Brooke asked.

"The place looks like an ad from *Beautiful Homes of the Rich and Famous*. Joey had an interior decorator from Naples design the entire estate. Everything brand new, designer names, expensive and white. The sofa, chairs, tables, lamps, carpets, drapes, and marble floors, white. Too much white for my taste. And art all throughout the house. Paintings on every wall, old stuff, not my style, but 'to each their own.'"

"No, I meant the yellow trailer. What does the inside of trailer look like?" Everyone laughed.

When the laughter died down, Lou Bravo continued, "Top of the line. Everything is brand new, and completely furnished. Two bedrooms, two baths, complete kitchen, living room, washer/dryer, dishes, pots, pans, linens, and it even has cable TV. It's just like a house, but banana yellow."

Everyone laughed and sang out, "Banana yellow, yuck!"

"It's a new business venture Joey is starting. Temporary trailer rentals for Floridians because of a natural disaster, fire or misfortune, who need reasonable living spaces until their home is rebuilt. Currently he has thirty units up in Ocala where last week's windstorm destroyed one neighborhood and he has a contract with the State to have three hundred banana yellow trailers available for emergency use during hurricane season."

"Let's take a look at our new home before I change my mind," Blaine said.

"Before we leave, I have to ask you both about a phone call I received yesterday from the Osborne Group, the company that contracts me to clean all the offices at the Brickyard Plaza in Venice. They got a call from Trace Foundation, the company that locates biological parents, the suite you two cleaned," Tony said.

"Yeah, we know all that stuff. Get to the point, Tony," Lou Bravo barked. "We have to get going."

"Well, they said someone broke into their files and they are cancelling their contract and moving out of the complex immediately." Tony wiped his forehead with his napkin. "Now, Osborne wants to cancel my cleaning contract, wants me to reimburse them the lost revenue and threatened to report me to the Venice Chamber of Commerce."

"That's a bunch of crap, all we did was open one file and take some pictures. We put everything back," Lou Bravo snapped.

"That's right, Tony, that's all we did. Trace wanted five thousand dollars for my husband's file. I don't have that kind of money, so we photographed the pages and left."

"Listen, Tony, I wasn't going to tell you this, but you need to call this Osborne Group and tell them you have information that Trace Foundation planned to break its lease all along. That you have credible evidence they were going to move the office back to Portland, Oregon, as soon as they digitized all the files. Plus, if you have the balls, demand a raise. There aren't one hundred and eighty-five files in Suite 223, but two hundred in their file room."

"What are you talking about? What evidence do I have?" Tony's face turned bright red and his breathing labored, a tell-tale sign of agitation.

"Blaine, you tell him."

25

Brooke began to fidget in her seat and said, "Mommy, can I go out to the car and listen to my MP3 player? All this talking is very boring."

"Okay, sweetie, but stay in the car and lock the doors." Blaine followed her with her eyes as she pushed open the door and disappeared into the parking lot. "Now, Tony." Blaine explained how her newspaper carrier, Star Trek Guy, was a computer genius. That he belonged to a computer club, and that her friend, Marybeth Maiello, also belonged to the club told him about the problem with Trace Foundation. Star Trek Guy hacked into Trace Foundation's computers, and copied an email between the CEO of Trace and someone from the Venice office, stating that the Venice office was to close as soon as the programming of all the files was complete.

"So it had nothing to do with my business. Just an excuse to break their lease, those sleazy bastards."

"That's right, old friend. They don't give a damn about the years of good service you provided. All they care about is the money. Tell Osborne you will send them the evidence and that they should be suing Trace Foundation, not you," Lou Bravo growled. "Plus, tell Osborne you want a raise for all the extra cleaning you performed!"

"Thank you, Lou Bravo, and thank you, Blaine. I'll call them when I get home."

"Okay, let's get out of here. We have a banana yellow house to look at," Lou Bravo said quickly and picked up the bill. In unison the three sang, "Banana yellow, yuck," and walked out the door.

Chapter Eight

The yellow Bentley Continental GT turned onto Serpentine Lane and slowly headed down the road straight for the banana yellow trailer. It's not every day a $200 thousand car rolls down a working-class neighborhood street. As a result, all the neighbors were out in mass snapping pictures of the spectacle taking place in front of Blaine Sterling's house. There on the front lawn, sparkling in the sun, was a brand new banana yellow trailer, a glittering yellow Bentley, and Joey Jupiter, a.k.a. Joey Banana, dressed in a yellow, sharkskin suit, and holding a large bouquet of yellow roses. Waving to the crowd, Joey Banana was in his element. He loved the attention and played to the audience like a seasoned circus ringmaster. Dressed in his signature yellow suit, his thick black hair slicked back into a small ponytail, with a perfectly trimmed thin goatee and a big broad smile, Joey Banana exuded an air of success. It was a sea of yellow and all the residents reveled in the moment. Neighbors, Ken Brecht and Greg Butterworth, were snapping pictures of each other in front of the Bentley when Lou Bravo pulled up in his yellow El Camino. The addition of another yellow vehicle only added to the circus atmosphere. Everyone erupted in a standing ovation and howls of welcome when they saw Blaine and Brooke exit the car.

Joey rushed over, introduced himself and handed Blaine the large bouquet of yellow flowers. "I wanted to personally stop by and express my deepest regrets about what happened to your home. It is unconscionable. And may I extend a warm welcome to you and your daughter into your new house."

"Thank you, Mr. Jupiter. We haven't had a chance to see the inside yet. I just hope it's not yellow," Blaine said and accepted the flowers.

"My dear lady, call me Joey and no, the inside isn't yellow," Joey Banana laughed. "Let me give you the *Official Joey Banana Tour.*"

The four marched across the lawn and into the trailer. "Very nice," Blaine said, "I like the way the kitchen, dining area, and living room all flow together, looks open and airy. I like the leather sofa, matching brown chairs and wicker tables. And no, the inside is not yellow; the antique white walls are refreshing." Blaine stepped into the kitchen, "I love the kitchen, a small breakfast nook, wood cabinets and stainless steel appliances all add a rich appeal. Plus every room has a window, it definitely brightens up the place."

"Look, Mommy, a flat screen television. It's humongous and covers the entire wall. Can I turn it on?"

"Sure you can, Brooke. Here's the remote." Joey said. "You have cable, one hundred plus channels, Showtime and wireless computer connections. How's that sound?"

"Great, but where's my room?"

"Right over there," Joey pointed to a door off to the right of the living room. Brooke's room was pink. Pink walls, pink carpet, pink furniture, pink bedspread, and a pink shell mobile hanging in the center of the room.

"I love it, Mommy. How did they know my favorite color was purple?"

"A little birdie told me Brooke," Joey said, and winked at Lou Bravo. "Take a look at this, ta da!" and pushed back a pocket door. "Your own bathroom, complete with double sink, closet and shower. So what do you think of your banana yellow house now?"

"It's the best, Mr. Jupiter. Thank you," Brooke crooned and dove onto her new, pink bed covered with fluffy pillows and stuffed animals.

"Now let's go see your mother's bedroom," Joey added as they trooped across the trailer to the opposite end of the house.

"I hope the little birdie didn't mention my favorite color was purple," Blaine called out from the back of the room.

"As a matter of fact he did," Joey laughed and pushed open the door.

Blaine's bedroom was twice the size of Brooke's, not pink, but a pale beige with a rose carpet. A queen-sized bed, dresser, two night stands with lamps and a high back chair, all white wicker with a Florida motif completed the room. Her bathroom was identical to Brooke's.

"Thank you, Joey. The trailer will be perfect and thank you, Lou Bravo, for orchestrating the entire arrangement." Blaine took Brooke's hand, walked to the front door and said, "Now gentleman, if you don't mind, we have some shopping to do. 'Bye!"

"That went well, I'm glad she liked the place. I need to get out of here too. I'm picking up a client at the Sarasota/Bradenton Airport in about thirty minutes and I can't be late. Some art dealer from Boston, a stuck up snob, but very rich, so I have to put up with his attitude, for a little while anyway. See you and Tony next month for cards, and don't forget your money. I have a hunch I'll be in a very wealthy mood."

"We'll be there," Lou Bravo reached out and shook Joey's hand. "I'll remind him later. I have to help him move some furniture today. His helper, some dumb ass kid named Hubba Bubba, broke his arm last night at the Van Wezel Concert Hall and can't work for three weeks. He and about two thousand other kids were at a punk rock concert and Hubba Bubba gets this hair brain idea to jump into some mosh pit, whatever the hell that is. Guess what, the punk rockers drop him, and now his arm is in a cast."

"Hubba Bubba, what kind of name is that?" Joey asked and pushed open the trailer door.

"The kid chews bubble gum all the time, that's the name of the gum. He probably had a big wad of gum stuck to his face. The kids catching him, saw the mess and dropped him." Lou Bravo laughed. "Thanks again Joey, see you in a few weeks." The two banana yellow cars pulled away from the curb and drove off to very different destinations.

Chapter Nine

Jet Blue, flight 234, from Boston's Logan International landed at Sarasota/ Bradenton's International Airport on time, 1:35 p.m. in the afternoon. A hard landing unnerved the passengers. The captain apologized for the sudden impact, wished everyone a pleasant visit to Sarasota, and urged them to enjoy the sunny, 82 degree day.

For passenger, Godfrey Molenar III, enjoying the Florida sun was the last thing on his mind. The thought of leaving Boston three hours earlier, with four inches of snow on the ground and more falling, biting cold winds, a wind chill factor of 15 degrees, and now walking along the concourse observing people in shorts and tank tops, did not seem real. Then again, Godfrey Molenar III wasn't real. Dressed in a custom-tailored, black wool, Armani suit, an Ike Behar pink dress shirt, with a Robert Graham burgundy silk tie, and a new pair of Edmonds Strand walnut Oxfords, Molenar's three-thousand dollar attire perfected his deception. Distinguished, polished, aloof, his silver-gray hair perfectly styled, a thin gray mustache, and a faint English accent Godfrey Molenar III epitomized a successful antique dealer. A charade he had honed for the past twenty-three years as a renowned antique buyer for The Edwin Talbot Galleries, a well-established family antique house in Boston. Carrying $10 million in his Claire Chase carry-on Pullman, Godfrey Molenar III, walked outside into the bright Florida sunshine. For the first time in twenty-three years, FBI Agent, Ross Burkhardt, aka Godfrey Molenar III was about to solve the mystery of who stole $500 million in artwork from Boston's Isabella Stewart Gardner Museum. The last piece of the puzzle was about to fall into place, or so he thought.

Along the curb, a yellow Bentley idled, and standing in front of the car in a matching yellow suit was Joey Banana. It

31

was difficult to tell which man appeared more eccentric, but heads turned when the two shook hands. An odd couple for the Florida books, tourists snapped pictures, children giggled, a few adults frowned, but the airport police, stoic as ever, barked out orders to move the vehicle or get ticketed. Molenar placed his carry-on in the trunk and the two got into the car.

"So how was the flight?" Joey asked as they pulled away from the curb.

"Uneventful," Molenar replied. "Just the way I like it."

The Bentley eased into traffic, exited the airport and headed west to U.S. 41.

"What's that in front of us, Mr. Jupiter? That big building straight ahead."

"That's the Ringling Museum. It was the winter home of John and Mable Ringling. He was the owner of the Ringling Bros. and Barnum & Bailey Circus. It's quite a place, his Ca d' Zan Mansion, art museum, circus memorabilia exhibits, theatre, and beautiful grounds overlooking Sarasota Bay. It attracts thousands of visitors each year. If you like, we could tour the place after we finish our business?" Joey turned onto 41 and headed for the Ringling Causeway Bridge and St Armands Circle.

"I don't believe that will be possible, Mr. Jupiter. I have a 4:00 p.m. flight back to Boston that I can't afford to miss."

"Maybe next time." The Bentley stopped at the light before the Causeway. "Take a look at the statue across the highway, *Unconditional Surrender*, the famous V-J Day kiss at Times Square. It's still creating an art controversy. What do you think Mr. Molenar?"

"Iconic, a delightful perceptivity of art, but fails, in my humble opinion, to communicate a sense of space."

"Well, the statue is there to stay, a WWII veteran donated $500 thousand to keep it right on the corner for everyone to see. "

The Bentley raced over the Ringling Bridge, past Bird Key, and down to St. Armands Circle, Sarasota's elite shopping destination. "Stephen King, the author, spends his winters down here in paradise. Beats shoveling snow in Maine, but I don't suppose he does any of the shoveling. He purchased two homes on Casey Key, right on the Gulf, one for himself, and the other for his kids when they visit. Nice lifestyle, if you can afford it, and as a nationally acclaimed author, Stephen King certainly can."

"Who has a house? Steffen King? What type of genre is his writing?" asked Molenar in an avuncular voice, staring out at the water.

"Stephen King, not Steffen King. He writes horror, suspense, science fiction and an occasional general fiction novel. Some of his books made the big screen, *The Shinning*, *Carrie*, *Children of the Corn*, *Pet Cemetery*, ever see any of them?"

"Can't say that I have."

"What about *The Green Mile*, *Shawshank Redemption* or *Stand by Me*? He wrote those stories and about fifty other novels."

"*The Green Mile*, sounds familiar, but I'm not certain."

Bored with the entire conversation, Joey concentrated on his driving and followed the flow of traffic around the Circle. "There," pointing to his right, "The Columbia Restaurant. Last winter I spotted King and his wife, Tabitha, right there at an outdoor table. I parked my car, ran over to their table and asked for an autograph. What a great guy. I framed it. I'll show it to you when we get to the house."

Molenar idly observed the busy shops and crowded restaurants as they circumnavigated the Circle and pushed north along Gulf of Mexico Drive. A squadron of brown pelicans caught his attention, all in formation they glided effortlessly out over the bay barely skimming the aqua blue waters. He smiled and mused how perfect the day would be out on the water. Behemoth waterfront mansions dotted the bayside of the highway in Great Gatsby-ish splendor. Each McMansion bigger or higher than the other. With their manicured lawns, massive array of lush, exotic vegetation, and miles of shuttered iron gates, each property announced that strangers were not welcome.

"By the way, what type of books do you enjoy reading, Mr. Molenar?" Joey asked, dreading a laundry list of titles he never heard of, or possibly could comprehend, that was about to flow so eloquently from his visitor's lips.

"Oh, I'm reading a wonderful book on Salvador Dali, an expansive repertoire of his best known works. It's a very passionate range of his work on the surrealist art form. It's compelling, a real page turner." Molenar remarked with an air of grandiosity.

Joey rolled his eyes, "What a coincidence, the Dali Museum is in St. Petersburg, maybe you could visit the museum before you fly back to Boston. I'm told they house the largest collection of Dali artwork outside of Europe."

"It is a great disappointment, but I am unable to reschedule my flight. I must return to Boston after we conclude our business." Molenar gazed out the window at the aqua blue water and faintly smiled.

Chapter Ten

Three minutes past the Chart House restaurant the Bentley pulled off the highway and braked in front a massive ornate black wrought iron gate with two tremendous golden bananas hanging from both sides of the double gate. The driver's side window lowered, Joey leaned out, punched in the four digit code and waited as the gates slowly pushed open.

"Mr. Jupiter, are those bananas on the gates?"

"Yes. It's a long story, Mr. Molenar, maybe next time," Joey blurted out and raised the window.

"I don't believe there will be a next time, Mr. Jupiter." Molenar quipped and looked straight ahead, taking in the grandeur of the property with an unobstructed view of Sarasota Bay.

"Never, say never, Mr. Molenar. Who knows what unexpected opportunity might suddenly arise?" Joey replied and eased the Bentley around a lush stand of palms along the circular driveway in front of the house. The two story, all white stucco and glass contemporary, glistened in the mid-afternoon sun as the two men exited the car. Large white pavers led from the driveway to the main entry, where two large glass doors opened into a spacious sunlit foyer. Beyond its shiny white marble floor was a large, open, airy living room with nearly a thirty foot ceiling and matching glass windows. "Please make yourself comfortable," pointing to the sunken living room, "I need to use the bathroom," Joey called out as he walked down the hallway to his study.

Molenar stepped down into a sanctuary of elegant custom-designed furnishings. The living room's conversation grouping included three, deep-seated white leather couches, two white upholstered chaises by Le Corbusier, a pair of 1929 gray-and-chrome Wassily chairs and a glass and dark stained oak wood

35

coffee table. A white baby grand piano framed the far wall while artwork by famed Venice photographer, Clyde Butcher, filled the opposite wall with a huge, black and white panoramic photograph titled *Myakka River1- Sarasota, FL*. Over a natural stone fireplace, a 70-inch flat screen television, purposely positioned months ago by the FBI, captured the view of the entire room. "Smile for the camera," Molenar whispered as he stepped towards the wall of windows. Potted palms filled every corner of the room accented by white orchids on almost every table. But the true grandeur of the living area was the exhilarating combination of how the windows embraced the use of indoor-to-outdoor design, making it difficult to tell where the indoors ended and the outdoors began. The sweeping vista was magnificent.

A lush green lawn, dotted with palm and oak trees led down to the bay, and a new wooden post boat dock. Tethered to the dock cleats, a 1960 fully restored, 50 foot, Chris-Craft Constellation cabin cruiser. The sight took Agent's Burkhardt breath away. "Oh my God," he gasped as a feeling of nausea, combined with dizzying vertigo, enveloped his entire body. Weakly he leaned up against the window, pushed his face against the glass and held his breath. Indeed it was the same cabin cruiser that haunted his dreams. The pounding in his head intensified and the memory of that horrific night flashed in front of him again. He fell back into a chair, leaned against the cool leather headrest and slowly massaged his forehead like he did many times in the past to erase the nightmares. But he never could.

"Why did I insist on going out to eat?" Burkhardt whispered and closed his eyes: *It was their honeymoon, one week at the magnificent Nassau Beach Hotel, Nassau, Bahamas. The concierge mentioned how romantic Café Martinique was, that all newlyweds go there to celebrate their marriage and it was only a short ferry ride to the restaurant on Paradise Island. The concierge was correct; the restaurant was an outstanding dining experience. Delicious food, romantic candle-lit tables, great service, along with a quiet old-world elegance made for an amazing dining experience.*

But the ferry ride back changed everything. The ferry had just pulled into the channel. I walked up front to get a match, when out of the dark, a large cabin cruiser smashed into the back of the ferry. The small blue transport was no match for the fifty foot Chris-Craft. The back of the ferry was a mangled mess of splintered wood and broken seats. There was nothing left to the back, and my precious wife of only one day, was gone. The driver of the Chris-Craft was drunk and in a hurry to get to the restaurant. "Why did I insist when we had a whole week?" Burkhardt moaned and painfully opened his eyes.

"Spectacular view don't you think?" Joey bellowed, as he straightened his yellow jacket that hid the belt holster in the small of his back and the Glock 17 he retrieved from his desk drawer. "What do you think of my boat? It's a classic. My wife's father had it completely refurbished after it was in an accident in Nassau. Are you okay? You're as pale as a ghost."

"I'm fine, a slight headache that comes and goes." Burkhardt turned and looked out at the boat. "A 1960 Chris-Craft Constellation, a fifty footer, I believe."

"That's right, do you own one?" Joey asked in a self-satisfied tone.

"No, but I viewed countless pictures of that model Chris-Craft. Were you and your wife on the boat when it crashed?" Burkhardt added and looked up at Joey.

Unnerved by the probative questioning, Joey's demeanor changed and snapped angrily, "No, my wife's Uncle Billy and some friends, but I think it is time we get down to business. Please, follow me to my office."

Burkhardt stood and they both walked down the 70 foot hallway to the study. Just beyond two museum-quality, antique Chinese vases, perched on top mahogany and glass cabinets, Burkhardt surmised belonged to the Ming Dynasty, Joey stopped and pushed open a weathered double-arched walnut door. A small windowless room, filled with shelves of books from floor to ceiling enveloped all four walls of the study. Compared to the rest of the house the room seemed austere, almost out of place. To the left of the door stood an antique, oak, Chippendale writing desk and two high-back, gray herringbone chairs. Their footsteps echoed as they walked across the walnut floor, and over an antique Oriental rug to the desk. Joey sat behind the desk and motioned to Burkhardt to be seated in one of the high-backed chairs. Joey reached under the right side draw, pushed a button, and immediately the book case behind him parted, and there hanging on the wall behind him was Rembrandt's the *Storm on the Sea of Galilee.* The only seascape he ever painted.

Burkhardt jumped to his feet and began to weep uncontrollably. Holding his face in his trembling hands, tears of joy dribbled through his fingertips. "My god, I finally found the masterpiece. I can barely contain my joy. The bright colors, the detail, and descriptive brushwork, it takes my breath away. May I please, Mr. Jupiter, take a closer look?"

"By all means, Mr. Molenar, look all you like. It's your $10 million." Joey laughed as he unzipped the suitcase. "Or should I say, now, my $10 million."

Burkhardt walked behind the desk, stood motionless, inches from the fishing boat battered by violent waves crashing against its bow. He breathed in the fury of the dark, ominous sky, and the fear in the faces of the terrified disciples. At last, Burkhardt rejoiced at the depiction of Christ peacefully seated at the back of the boat ready to avert disaster and calm the storm. His exhilaration climaxed when he reached into his suit pocket, took out a small magnifying glass, and skillfully moved the glass along the rudder. "The signature, Rembrandt. f and the date 1633 looked authentic. I don't see any changes or inconsistencies in the lettering, and the original cracks all appear undisrupted. One last test and that will conclude our business."

"And what test is that, Mr. Molenar?" Joey asked and reached behind his back.

"Modern technology, my dear Mr. Jupiter, enables art appraisers, like myself, to keep one step in front of the bad guys." Reaching into his breast pocket, Burkhardt pulled out a cigarette-sized black box. "A Florescence Spectrometer, state-of-the art X-Ray imaging device that can detect any chemical inconsistencies in the artwork, and analyzes the paint distribution by timeline in minutes. This instrument will tell if the painting was created in 1633 or sometime afterwards. Any changes in the paint from the original artist, in1633, will tell me whether it's real or a fake."

Burkhardt held the spectrometer inches from the painting and starting in the top left hand corner, directly over a dark black cloud, he switched on the device. A faint blue glow illuminated the corner of the painting as he moved the light across the top of the painting. Across the clouds, along the sky, down to the boat and the disciples, the rudder, the rocks and finally, the black waves at the bottom right of the painting. A beep sounded. "It is authentic, and for twenty-three years you have taken very good care of the painting. I congratulate you, sir. My buyer will be extremely grateful."

Burkhardt turned and fired one bullet into Joey's forehead.

Chapter Eleven

A single purple balloon tied to the back of a chair floating whimsically above the heads of patrons looked curiously out of place. The dining room of the Upper Crust Café and Bakery at noon was packed. All the tables were full with diners and customers arriving from church or a late sleep lined up outside patiently waiting to be called. Six crystal chandeliers hung from the ceiling filling the room with a delicate glow. Mirrors of all shapes and sizes adorned the walls and reflected the ambient light upon delicate linen tablecloths that cradled elegant china tea cups, saucers and plates. The Victorian tea room at the cafe is uniquely charming, but the real experience is in the freshly prepared dishes. Nancy, a tall attractive server from Illinois, greeted Blaine and Brooke in her bright and cheery manner and informed them there would be a thirty minute wait. Blaine pointed to the balloon and said, "I believe that's our table," smiled and walked to the back of room.

Marybeth stood and waved. "Over here," she said and pulled out the balloon chair for the guest of honor. Standing next to her was a tall, lanky man in his late twenties or early thirties, geekish looking and wearing black horned rimmed glasses. After all the hugs and kisses Marybeth said, "Blaine, I'd like you to meet Myron Weeder, Star Trek Guy."

"Pleased to meet you, this is my daughter, Brooke." Blaine offered her hand.

"The pleasure is all mine," and shook Blaine's and Brooke's hands.

The server came over and asked Marybeth if they were ready to order. She took the order: three iced teas, one milk, two veggie omelets, a club sandwich and chicken tenders with French fries.

Marybeth leaned in, "Blaine, you remember me telling you that I belonged to a computer club and Star Trek Guy was the president. After your problem with Trace Foundation, Star Trek Guy modified your new cell phone to block all tracking devices when you made a call, plus he installed a microchip to fingerprint the digital trail left by the cyber invader. The night of the fire, I planned to give Star Trek Guy your cell phone to track the call, but you told me to give it to the detective. Before I handed over the phone I removed a small silver microchip from the charger port. That chip was a tracking device programmed to locate incoming calls. I gave it to Myron Friday night and he insisted that we meet."

Before Star Trek Guy spoke, the server brought lunch. The dishes were beautifully presented, each on its own distinctive china plate and creatively garnished with a colorful variety of fresh fruit. The food was meticulously prepared and absolutely delicious. Finicky eater Brooke devoured every morsel, even the fruit. Half-way through the meal, Star Trek Guy asked Blaine, "Do you know a Katie Piper?"

Blaine swallowed, wiped her mouth with her linen napkin, and replied, "Katie Piper, never heard of her. Why?"

"Never had any contact with her at the park? Maybe she was a volunteer or camped at the park. What about Brooke's school; could you have met her there?" Star Trek Guy pushed a picture across the table.

"No, I'm sorry, but I've never seen this girl before. Brooke, have you ever seen this girl?"

Brooke shook her head and said, "No."

Star Trek Guy folded the picture, placed it in his shirt pocket and whispered, "The text message and picture of your burning house came from her phone."

The statement started a cascade of emotions which churned within Blaine's every fiber. It was as if someone poured an ice cold bucket of water over her and rudely woke her from a deep sleep. *Why would a complete stranger want to burn her house down, it doesn't make sense,* Blaine thought.

"Katie Piper is a senior at Venice High School. She is on the girls winning volleyball ball team, has a 3.85 grade point average and will be attending Georgetown University in the fall.

Oh, I almost forgot, she is in the school chorus, and while they were competing in Orlando last week, she lost her cell phone."

"So, who made the call?" Blaine blurted out.

"Patience, curious one," Star Trek Guy answered and took out his smartphone. "That is the million dollar question and here is the answer," and Star Trek Guy held up his phone. On the face of the phone was a map of Florida with hundreds of thin blue lines crisscrossing the state, but only one red line from Venice running north to Raiford, Florida. At the bottom of the screen was the inscription in bold letters, Tower Dumps. "Your phone call originated from Raiford, Florida, and yes, Katie Piper did not make the call. To my knowledge, the young girl never visited Raiford, and with a grade point average of 3.85, never will."

"That still doesn't explain who made the call," Blaine snapped back. Before Star Trek Guy could reply, Nancy and two other servers appeared singing Happy Birthday. The entire restaurant heartedly joined in as Nancy placed a large slice of strawberry shortcake, with a single burning candle, in front of Blaine. Linda, the owner of restaurant, came to the table to convey her best wishes for a Happy Birthday and express how upset she was on hearing about her house fire. She gave Blaine a big hug and told her that lunch was on the house. With the help of Brooke, they blew out the candle and everyone clapped. The rest of the table received smaller portions of strawberry shortcake and were deliciously surprised.

After dessert, Star Trek Guy, handed Blaine a small package wrapped in Star Trek blue paper, with a gun-metal gray wax impression of the Starship Enterprise embossed in the center. "Happy Birthday *Intrepid Voyager.* Inside I believe you will find a new communication device that will help connect you in your travels," he said with a big smile. "The police will eventually discover that the phone used to call you was stolen, and that the call originated from Union Correctional Institution in Raiford, Florida."

Everyone's jaw dropped and a shocked expression glazed over all their faces. It was as if someone had sucked the life from them. No one could catch their breath to speak. The image that a prisoner had Blaine's cell phone number, sent a photograph of her house on fire and made reference to Blaine's birthday party, left everyone speechless.

"What is a correctional institution?" Brooke asked. So innocently did the two words bring the adults at the table back down to reality.

"It's a jail, sweetie, where people who break the law live. It's far away, so don't you worry." Blaine turned her gaze towards Star Trek Guy and whispered so that the entire Café wouldn't hear. "Prison, how could that be possible? I don't know anyone in prison. You must have the wrong information."

"No, the data is accurate. You'll see when the police talk to you in a day or two," Star Trek Guy explained in a very analytical tone.

Blaine tore at the paper and with trembling hands pulled out a brand new smart phone. "I can't accept this. It's too expensive. Please take it back." Blaine pushed the phone across the table.

"Sadly, young neophyte, your cell phone will not make the return voyage back to your earthly possession. The many parts abducted from your mobile device are transported to another galaxy and become police evidence. Your new mobile device is very special, a malware program I constructed will catch a ride on all incoming calls, infect and replicate the network, which in turn encrypts a tracking device onto the software and sends a flow of data to its creator. Now, we can record each digital trail Katie Piper's phone creates."

"What are you talking about, Myron? Marybeth, would you please translate into English what he just said," Blaine gasped in desperation and grabbed Marybeth's hand.

"He installed a program that will record all the calls made and received on Piper's phone."

"Now I see. Someone sent the convict a picture of my house burning. Find the number and we find the individual who fire-bombed my house," Blaine said with an air of confidence.

"You're a fast learner, young traveler. However, the caller may not necessarily be a prisoner. He could be an employee, and for your statistical analysis, I am head computer geek at Best Buy and receive a very generous employee discount. Please keep your birthday present. It is an order from your

President!" Star Trek Guy handed her the phone and stood. "I need to go to work now. At a gift shop down the block, the Green Parrot Gift Store, someone hacked into their computer system and all their receipts say "Green Pickle" with an image of a pickle dripping pickle juice down the side of the paper. Never a dull moment in Venice, or should I say, in the Cosmos. Thanks for the cake. Happy Birthday, Blaine. 'Bye all." Myron, raised his hand and gave the Vulcan salute.

"I need to go also, Blaine. I have to pick up my science fair applications from the Chairman of the Science Department. He's a friend of mine, Steven Le Roux. He called yesterday and said the forms just arrived. You remember, the Science Fair, my school. You volunteered to be a judge? Please, don't give me that blank stare."

"Yes, of course. I'll be there and I can't wait to see your students again. What a great day we had when your class visited the park. Their science projects were outstanding. I'm sure they'll all excel at the fair. By the way, how's Will doing?" Blaine asked in a faraway voice.

"Better. I think letting him present his group's science project in front of the class made a big difference. He is more self-confident and the students treat him better. I hope it will stay that way."

"Mommy, can I go to the science fair with you? I love science, please, Mommy." Brooke pleaded, tugged at her mother's arm and looked up with her beautiful blue eyes.

"Of course, sweetie, but it's more than a month away. We have plenty of time."

"You may have plenty of time, my dear Blaine, but I don't. The work to get my students ready to complete, and then present their projects is already underway. And we still have a long way to go."

Everyone stood. Blaine left a generous tip and they walked outside. "Steve Le Roux is your age, intelligent, handsome and single." Marybeth smiled mischievously and walked quickly to her car.

Chapter Twelve

Morning broke above the ancient oaks at Osprey State Park as three black tractor trailers lined up in front of the ranger station. Their shiny, black Peterbuilt cabs, with the name Bolt Construction and a gold lighting rod embossed on the driver's side door, towered above the office building. The roar from the diesel engines sent a pair of mourning doves flying for cover and dispatched the park ranger outside for an official greeting and registration.

"Good morning. Welcome to Osprey State Park. We've been expecting you," ranger Diana Stinson shouted over the deafening sound of the engines. "Drive down the main road, about a quarter of a mile, and across from the Nature Center, the Assistant Park Manager will direct you to the construction site. Have a nice day."

Slowly the three trucks lumbered down the road periodically shearing off clumps of branches that hung down across the road. At the top of the rise, Blaine Sterling stood in the center of the road flashlight in hand as she waved the first truck to a stop. Dressed in her forest green uniform and polished black boots she conveyed an air of confidence and authority. "Good morning. The entire field behind the yellow construction trailer is where you'll drop all the construction equipment. There are workers back there to help you unload."

Throughout the week a steady flow of heavy equipment, supplies, trucks and workers moved into Osprey State Park. By Friday, a survey team marked out a schematic grid of the park for the sewer lines. The system, originating at the county hook-up on Tamiami Trail, consisted of over one mile of sewer pipe. Lines of orange paint crisscrossed the park from Tamiami Trail, to the ranger station, then to the park offices, across to the science research offices, over to the ranger residences,

47

down to the campsites, the Nature Center and finally ending at the lake restrooms.

Thor Boltier walked over to the construction office, opened the door and walked inside. "You wanted to see me, Uncle Roy?" Thor, a recent May graduate, and standout defensive end from Venice High School, was now playing at the University of South Florida on a full football scholarship. He was on winter break, and as a favor to his father, accepted a job working at his uncle's construction company. At 6'5", 293 pounds, Thor had no problem doing physical work. Not only would he be paid, but the manual labor would help keep him in shape during football's off-season. A win-win situation for Thor since he always needed cash for his gas guzzling Hummer and high maintenance girlfriend, Mercedes Autumn. She like the car, demanded to be driven in style, not for one season, but all year long.

"Yes, have a seat," Boltier said. Unlike his older brother, Charlie, who was a giant of a man, Roy Boltier didn't receive any of the giant genes at birth; Roy was average height, average weight and average looking. The only distinguishing characteristic Roy possessed was his dedication to his work. He was an honest, hardworking businessman, who built-up Bolt Construction Company from a two man operation to the second largest commercial sewer installer in Southwest Florida.

"How's your father? I feel terrible that I haven't spoken to him in a while, but I've been buried in work and haven't had a free minute lately. So how is he, Thor?"

"How does anyone do in prison, Uncle Roy? He hates it. He's a caged animal, locked away, just because he was driving a boat. That's not justice!"

"I agree. It doesn't seem right, Thor, but..."

"And one other thing, Uncle Roy. I don't know about you, but what makes this whole thing so creepy is that now I'm working at the very park where those events took place. Plus, Blaine Sterling, the park ranger who put my father in prison, is walking around talking to me and the crew like nothing ever happened. I don't think she knows who I am!" Thor turned and wiped a tear from the corner of his eye.

Roy leaned forward and in a low serious tone said, "I think you're right, Thor. She doesn't know who we are, but the company won the sewer bid before your father was incarcerated. And yes, it does feel a little creepy, but we have a job to do, and I have a business to run."

For the next thirty minutes Boltier explained that he needed Thor to sleep in the trailer for the month it would take to complete the job. At the last job someone stole ten thousand dollars' worth of supplies and equipment and he didn't want that occurring at this job site. He would pay extra and at the end of the job, if all went well, Thor would receive a very substantial bonus.

"No problem, when do I start!" Thor answered, calculating in his head what a week's paycheck would look like with all the overtime hours.

"Tonight, go back to college, pack some clothes and be back at five. Here's a company cell phone, the foreman and you are the only employees with one. It's connected to my business line and you can reach me 24/7. Here's two hundred dollars to pick-up some food and any other items you may need for the week. Next week I'll give you another hundred for groceries. And, Thor, if you talk to your father anytime soon, tell him I'm thinking of him and plan a call."

Thor jumped in his truck and drove out of the park. This new arrangement couldn't have worked out any better had he planned it himself. No awkward explanations for nighttime visits to the park when he lived there. Now all of his energy will concentrate on executing his father's plan to pay back Blaine Sterling.

Thor took out his cell and punched in his father's number, "Hi, Dad. It's Thor. You're not going to believe this. I just finished talking with Uncle Roy he sends his regards and will call soon. I'm working for him during winter break and guess what. His company is installing the sewers at Osprey State Park, but that's not the best part. Uncle Roy wants me to sleep in the construction trailer and keep an eye on all the equipment. Now I'll be able to dig out the cave, look for that gold Remi Cole told you about, and take care of Blaine Sterling like you instructed without worrying about being seen."

"Great news, son, but don't call me on this line again until she is entombed in that cave. I don't want any calls traced back to you."

"Don't worry. There's no way they can connect me to this call. I went to Publix, paid cash for a throw-away phone, a hundred and twenty minute phone card and a charger. It's not possible to connect me to this call."

"Still don't call," Boltier shouted. The line went dead. The call registered on a computer in Venice.

Chapter Thirteen

Five feet from the lake trail, a thick clump of Saw Palmetto concealed the opening to the cave. On the sixth night, Thor dug through all the rock and dirt left behind by the police and cleared the twelve stairs that lead down to the entrance of the cave. He settled into a very comfortable routine as the weeks passed. By day he labored alongside the construction crew putting in sewers, and at night he implemented his father's plan to pay back Blaine Sterling.

Poised to enter the cave the following night Thor was caught by surprise as he walked past the lake, "Hi, Thor, want to go skinny dipping?"

"How do you know my name?" Thor asked and looked down into Ryder Gorman's sparkling green eyes. Barely reaching five foot, with light brown hair in a pixie cut, a short nose and a perfect tan, this petite cutie was a knock-out. Thor recognized her immediately from her daily beach bike rides past the construction site on her way to the lake. She always wore a brightly colored string bikini, which brought excited cat calls from all the aroused workers and a slightly embarrassed smile as she rode by.

Last Friday, during one of Ryder's trips, the back hoe operator was so distracted he dug up a three-foot section of black top road instead of a three-foot trench to hold the twenty-foot PVC sewer pipe. The foreman cursed him out and threatened to dock his pay for the repairs. He didn't because he was just as distracted as the rest of the crew. Curious about the bikini girl, Thor checked his uncle's work chart last week and located the only family with a teenage daughter, Dr. and Mrs. Kenneth Gorman, daughter Ryder, Stony Brook, New York, campsite #17.

"I asked," She said, as her orange flowered Tommy Bahama beach dress fell to the blanket. "Are you coming?" She shouted and ran into the water.

Thor didn't need any prompting. The sight of Ryder's naked body was more than enough encouragement for any hormonally raging teenage boy. He tore off his clothes and raced down to the water. The initial plunge sent shock waves through his rock hard body. The cold water deflated his erection, but the desire to hold a naked girl brought back the urge. He looked around, but no naked swimmer, only deep reds and bright orange colors danced along the surface of the lake as sunset approached. Sadly, the water was mirror smooth, not a single ripple from the naked siren. "Ryder, where are you?" Thor, in a pitiful muffled scream, called out. No reply. Did he imagine the whole episode? Was he so consumed with his father locked in prison and the cave thing, that he had lost his mind?

Suddenly, something grabbed his leg and moved up along his body and into his arms. The warm naked body of a girl pressed against him. "I'm not crazy," Thor shouted, and pulled her close to him. She reached around his waist and clung on to him. He could feel her breasts press against his chest; his erection grew. Ryder reached down and pulled him in as far as he would go. She wrapped her legs around his throbbing body and melted into his space. Together their bodies locked and began to move as one. Their passion heightened and exploded in a climax of total ecstasy.

They held each other tight and slowly floated back towards the beach blanket where they continued their lovemaking. Passionately, Thor caressed every curve and valley of Ryder's willing body until the excitement reached an unbearable height for the both of them. With one stimulating movement, Ryder pulled him on top of her and fulfilled their lustful desires. Exhausted, they collapsed on the blanket and fell asleep in each other's arms until Ryder's phone rang.

"Hello, I'm at the lake. I must have fallen asleep on the blanket. Yes, I'll be back shortly. 'Bye." Ryder leaned over, kissed Thor on the cheek, slipped on her dress and walked back to her campsite.

The next day, campsite #17 was deserted.

Chapter Fourteen

The hole in Joey Banana's head oozed a thin line of dark red-brown blood that traveled down his forehead, alongside his nose, across his cheek and finally puddled onto his yellow jacket. Burkhardt pushed the chair holding the dead body into a corner of the room. Like some mischievous schoolboy punished for an unspeakable deed, the corpse sat silently facing the wall.

Burkhardt walked back to the desk, leaned against the wooden top and quietly absorbed the majestic beauty of the three hundred and eighty year old painting. For the first time, he realized that he was in the presence of a Master. The only seascape Rembrandt created was a breath away. "All these years, locked behind a bookcase. What a travesty," Burkhardt whispered. A chill ran down his spine. Was it fear or a humbling sensation now that the fate of this masterpiece was in his hands? He wasn't certain.

Burkhardt picked up the desk phone and dialed the FBI, Boston office headquarters and after two rings, "May I please have the Art Loss Register please, executive director Richard Pembroke. This is agent Ross Burkhardt."

"Hello, Agent Burkhardt. What is the status of the operation?"

"Better than expected, sir. Both packages are secured. Mr. Jupiter is tied up at this time. I have the painting, the *Storm on the Sea of Galilee*. It's authentic and in excellent condition. I fly out of Venice Airport tomorrow morning and should arrive back in Boston in time for lunch."

"Good, I've arranged to have a Gulfstream GV at the FBO site in Venice by nine o'clock, which will give you ample time to load the painting, Mr. Jupiter, and let's not forget, our $10 million. Our people will meet you at Logan Airport and escort you and your packages through security. By the way, we picked up Jupiter's father-in-law, Sonny Bugler, the Boston mobster charged with killing thirteen people. Arrested him and his girlfriend in San Diego. We've been hunting that bastard for twenty-three years. He disappeared the same time the artwork from Boston's Isabella Stewart Gardner Museum disappeared. He's singing like a canary, wants to work out a deal. Says he knows where the rest of the artwork is, some farmhouse in Connecticut. We always thought there was a connection and now maybe we'll have the proof. See you tomorrow." The phone went silent.

The phone back on its cradle, Burkhardt walked over to Joey and pushed him over to the Oriental rug in the center of the room. In one fluid movement he dumped the body out of the chair, rolled it up in the rug and slung it over his shoulder. Burkhardt left the house through the living room, walked down to the dock and onto the boat. He placed the body in the forward guest stateroom and closed the door.

Burkhardt knew everything there was to know about the Chris-Craft and the Bugler family; he had years to relive that horrific night his wife was killed. And now, by some twist of fate, he found the boat that killed his wife. But it wasn't fate; it was relentless police work. After Diane's death he threw himself into his work, except for a two year detour to Vietnam. Another relationship was out of the picture. He was married to the job and to the task of exacting justice for his wife's murder.

In Nassau, waiting for the trial of Billy Bugler to begin, Burkhardt read in the local paper Bugler was murdered in a holding cell the day before jury selection began. The article reported that Bugler disrespected another inmate awaiting trial for murder, and was murdered himself. Graphic pictures and details of the murder were plastered on the front page. A witness testified that he saw Bugler beaten unconscious. Wads of toilet paper were stuffed down his throat to muffle his screams and finally he choked to death.

The FBI agent knew differently. In the early '60s the extent of professional courtesy for a grieving fellow police officer and two thousand dollars cash would go far. For widower Burkhardt, there was very little solace knowing that the man who murdered his wife was also viciously murdered. Even after Nassau, Burkhardt was still consumed by grief and thought only of revenge.

Burkhardt compiled a dossier on the Bugler family, found out that Billy Bugler was originally from Boston, moved to Key West, Florida, and became a successful yacht broker. Single, a heavy drinker, every June he cruised down to Nassau for a get-away vacation and a lot of partying. After Billy's death, Bugler's older brother Sonny sold the yacht business, repaired the Chris-Craft and used the Key West house as a winter retreat for the family.

Twenty-three years later, Sonny disappeared. About to be indicted in connection with thirteen mob related murders, received a tip and vanished. He left behind him rumors about his involvement in the theft of some artwork. Donna Bugler, now Mrs. Joey Jupiter, inherited everything. She went to college at USF and majored in Art. After graduation, she opened a jewelry store in Sarasota and met Joey Jupiter. They married, sold the Key West house in 2001 and moved to Long Boat Key. Donna Jupiter was the last piece to Burkhardt's revenge puzzle. Her death would complete the riddle.

Burkhardt returned to the study, removed the picture from the wall, placed it in the leather art case Joey left resting against the desk and closed the bookcase. He picked up the suitcase and the painting, then walked down to the dock and onto the boat. He left both packages in the main salon and walked back to the house to wait.

"Hello, Joey. I'm home!"

Chapter 15

The yellow school bus braked to a stop in front of 204 Serpentine Lane. Flashing lights blinked red, as the caution stop signs popped open on the driver's side of the bus. Finally the front door slapped open and a skinny, blue eyed, blond haired little girl bounced down the steps. Feet firmly planted on the ground, she adjusted her backpack, looked up at the yellow trailer and began to cry. Brooke Sterling's heartbreaking day at school finally came crashing down on this sorrowful second grader.

"Brooke, what's wrong, darling?" Mrs. Brecht called out and cradled her in her arms. "Why are you crying? Did something happen today at school to upset you?" Charlene Brecht, a family friend, neighbor and babysitter for the past seven years, was almost a second mother to Brooke. She and husband Ken had adopted Brooke and her mother after the disappearance of Blaine's husband.

"Yes, the kids were calling me names."

"Let's go inside and talk. I already poured you a glass of milk and baked your favorite homemade chocolate chip cookies." Mr. and Mrs. Brecht were old school. Their philosophy was snack first, then homework, and if there is enough time before dinner, outside to play. "Now, Brooke, tell me everything that happened today at school."

"It was during recess. Lilly and I were on the swings, when Angie came over and said, I lived in a banana, and then the rest of her friends called me *banana girl* and ran around the playground screaming *banana girl*. It was horrible. I told my teacher, Mrs. Cordas, and she told the class that calling people names was very hurtful and will not be tolerated in her classroom."

"That was the perfect thing to do, tell your teacher. I guess Mrs. Cordas put Angie in her place!" Mrs. Brecht said, and offered Brooke another cookie. She refused. "What's wrong?"

"Angie handed me this at the end of the day." She passed a crumpled up piece of paper across the small kitchen table. Mrs. Brecht unfolded the tear soaked piece of white lined paper and read, *See you tomorrow, BANANA GIRL. HA, HA.* Meticulously, she smoothed out the paper, folded it four times and put it into her pocket.

"Kids can be very cruel sometimes. I remember when I was in grammar school, third grade, I believe, and someone was stealing my snack. Every morning all the kids would put their lunch boxes in their cubby and then go to their desks. At ten thirty, we would have our snack, but one Monday, no snack. At first, I thought my mother forgot to pack one, so I ate half my sandwich. When I arrived home, I asked my mother if she gave me a snack, she said she packed a brownie. On Tuesday, same thing, no snack. I told the teacher and she asked the class if anyone had taken my snack accidently?"

"Did anyone confess?" Brooke chirped. "Or see the thief with confectionary sugar on their shirt? I know how messy brownies can be, Mommy's are filled with lots and lots of white powder."

"No, but that night after my mother wrapped up two chocolate chip cookies for my snack, I took my fountain pen and placed two, tiny red ink dots on the top of the package."

"What's a fountain pen, Mrs. Brecht?" Brooke asked, "Do you decorate packages with it?"

"Oh, my child, how things have changed. No, you write with it silly; it's a pen. You fill the pen with ink, from an ink bottle, usually black ink. A little lever on the side of the pen opens and draws ink into the pen, similar to drinking soda through a straw, and then you write."

"That sounds like a lot of work. Why not just use a Sharpie?"

"They didn't make Sharpies when I was a little girl. Anyway, I wanted the red ink to get on the fingers of the thief. Just to be sure, I put another two dots on the wax paper before

I placed my lunch box in my cubby," Mrs. Brecht added with a satisfied smile.

"Did you catch the thief? Who was it? Was it a boy or a girl?" Brooke's impatience exploded, as she consumed the last chocolate chip cookie in one bite.

"At ten thirty I went to my cubby, and my snack was gone. I explained to the teacher what I did. She called the nurse over the intercom, I'll explain what an intercom was another time), and two minutes later the nurse arrived."

"Oh, Mrs. Brecht, don't be silly. I know what an intercom is. We have them at school. Why did your teacher call the nurse, why not the principal?

"The nurse announced that she was there to complete the annual school cleanliness report for the State, and that today she was examining the second and third grade classes. She walked up and down the rows, checking the heads and hands of each student. Five minutes later she thanked everyone for their patience and left."

"Well, who was it? How did you find the thief?" Brooke groaned and put her head on the table, exacerbated from the total exercise.

"The intercom rang, and Rylee Ward was asked to report to the office."

"Rylee Ward? Who was Rylee Ward and why did she take your snack?"

"Rylee was a small, sickly looking girl, hardly ever said a word in class. She never bothered anyone, never played with anyone at recess. Day after day, she just sat on the same picnic bench, by herself and watched the children play."

"So why did she steal your snack? Why not someone else's snack?" Brooke questioned.

"My cubby was next to hers. She always came to school late. She ate it when she arrived and then hurried to her seat. Her father lost his job at the Weston Egg Processing Plant and they didn't have enough money to put food on the table. She was hungry, she told the principal."

"How sad. What happened, was she kicked out of school? Did she have repay you for the snacks?"

61

"We became best of friends. My father gave Rylee's dad a job at his gas station in town. And from that day on, I got to eat my snack at ten thirty in the morning with all the other children. Rylee and I are still friends and we call each other once a month. As a matter of fact, she still lives in Ohio. She and I were the stars on the high school field hockey team that won the State Championship back in... oh never mind the date."

"I remember, Mrs. Brecht, it was 1962," Brooke shouted out, "and your team won 3-2."

"Thank you, dear. Brooke, I have an idea that just might work. Let's go for a little ride, but first I need to make a phone call."

Mrs. Brecht reached into her pocketbook, pulled out her cell phone and called home. "Hi, Ken, I want you to do me a favor. Drive over to Publix and buy, hold on a minute. Brooke honey, how many children do you have in your class?"

"Twenty-one, why?" Brooke answered after she swallowed the last of her milk.

"Ken, please pick up twenty-two ripe bananas. Speak to Melody Pruitt, the store manager. Mention that Brooke has a school project due tomorrow and needs twenty-two ripe bananas. Knowing how professional Melody is, she will most likely walk you over to the produce department and help you select Publix's finest. Please bring them over to Blaine's house in about an hour. I'll explain later. Thanks, hon. 'Bye."

Mrs. Brecht put the top down on the red Sebring, turned on the radio to cheer Brooke up and backed out the driveway. They drove over the Venice Avenue Bridge and onto the Island. They made a U-Turn at Nassau Street and squeezed into a spot in front of Bresler's Ice Cream & Yogurt. "Are we going to have, ice cream?" Brooke called out with excitement.

"Maybe, but first my dear Brooke we're going to buy you a T-shirt."

"A T-shirt? I don't need a T-shirt," Brooke gasped and gave Mrs. Brecht a surprised glance.

"Oh, yes you do. It's all part of the plan, sweetie, *Operation Banana Split*," Mrs. Brecht answered and pulled open the door to The Shirt Stop. A destination stop for exceptional casual wear, The Shirt Stop is sandwiched between an ice cream parlor and a men's clothing store on Venice Avenue. For thirty-four years this establishment has produced high quality custom T-shirts, sweat shirts, shirts and sweaters for tourists and residents of Venice. The owners Richard and Dot left the cold of Michigan, with their dog Molly, trading in their snow shovel for the warm Florida sunshine.

"Hi, Dot, how are you today? I just want to say the black T-shirt with the rhinestone flip-flops looks great on. I've received so many compliments. Maybe I should get a commission for all the new business I'm sending your way?"

"Thank you, Charlene. Maybe after I've banked my first million we'll talk." They both laughed. "How can I help you and who is this pretty young lady?"

"This is my neighbor, Brooke Sterling and I would like to buy her five T-shirts, no make that four. She would like a pink, blue, red and green shirt, and on the front, in the center, a big yellow banana, and in black letters Banana on top and Girl below the banana. The writing should be in fancy, swirly script. On the back, also in black ink, but in block letters the saying: A banana a day keeps the doctor away. Can you do that?" Mrs. Brecht smiled and gave Brooke a wink.

"No problem, I can complete the job in twenty minutes. What size shirt?"

"Small, and could you put a turquoise butterfly on the tip of the banana?" Brooke added with a big smile.

"Okay, little lady, how about some ice cream? There's nothing better than homemade ice cream and a plan." The two locked arms and marched out the door.

Chapter 16

The Blendtec Total Blender 320xl screeched out short bursts of grinding, spinning motor sounds that echoed down the long hallway from the kitchen. This magnificent high-tech, and at $454.00, extremely expensive culinary appliance, was the latest *'must have gadget'* in Mrs. Jupiter's arsenal of cooking hardware. Just back from her weekly sojourn to Southgate Mall in Sarasota, and to her favorite cookware destination, Williams Sonoma, Donna Jupiter could hardly contain her excitement to blend up a healthy, fresh, green smoothie. A bag of fresh produce from Morton's Gourmet Market, the only grocery store she frequented for fresh fruits and vegetables for the last ten years, spilled out over the granite counter. Filled to the top of the 64-ounce pitcher was two cups ice, one banana, one mango, two cups almond milk and two handfuls spinach. The spinning green liquid pushed clear to the cap lid and solidified into a creamy, mouth-watering, milkshake consistency.

"Smoothies are ready, Joey. Come and get one, honey," Donna shouted, and began to cut up a few fresh strawberries and pears to add to the surprise.

"I hate green smoothies," a voice growled from the doorway.

Startled by the coarse remark and unfamiliar voice, Donna, spun around to confront her intruder. Standing in the entrance to the kitchen was a tall, gray-haired, impeccably dressed, elderly gentleman with a gun in his hand.

"Who the hell are you?" Donna yelled.

"I'm Godfrey Molenar III, or should I say FBI Agent Ross Burkhardt." He lifted his gun and aimed it at Mrs. Jupiter's face, "and you're under arrest for the possession and sale of stolen artwork. Please drop the knife."

"You bastard! I told Joey you sounded like a phony. The whole story about your art gallery being charged with fraud--it sounded too good to be true. And it was. Where's my husband?"

"He's on the boat. I'm not going to tell you again. Drop the knife," Burkhardt barked out for the second time, but this time with a menacing glare as he moved forward.

In one fluid motion Donna threw the knife, ran to the back door and raced outside to the yacht. The carving knife sliced Burkhardt's right bicep causing the gun to drop, and blood to explode all over his white shirt and Armani suit. The pain was excruciating. He grabbed a hand towel off the counter, wrapped the wound, picked up his gun and ran down to the boat.

"Looking for these, bitch?" Burkhardt shouted, and dangled the keys to the boat in front of her face. "Turn around while I put these cuffs on." He unlocked the cabin door and shoved her inside. "Have a seat on the couch, and don't try anything stupid. I need to go to the head and look at this knife wound."

"Where's my husband?" Donna screamed, but Burkhardt disappeared into the forward head. "I want to know where my husband is. You said he was on the boat and I want to see him."

Burkhardt peeled off his jacket and blood-soaked shirt. The cut wasn't as bad as he thought. The wound only grazed the upper curvature of his bicep, so maybe with a tight wrap he could stop the bleeding and forgo a trip to the hospital. Hanging on a hook was a flannel work shirt, most likely Joey's, a little tight, but Burkhardt had no other option. He opened the door, walked back to the main cabin and Donna Jupiter.

"He's dead. I shot him. Don't make the same mistake your husband made." Burkhardt pointed his Glock 23 at her face, "and make me shoot you also. Understand?"

"I don't believe you. I want to see him," Donna cried out.

Burkhardt yanked her off the couch, dragged her down to the forward stateroom and opened the door. There on the lower bunk bed was the body wrapped in the rug. Burkhardt lifted the corner of the fabric and Joey's bloodied face popped out.

Donna Jupiter let out a mournful shriek and fell to her knees alongside the bunk. Hands stretched across her husband's body Donna screamed, "You murdered him, shot him in the head. If I have the chance, I'll shoot you in the head you monster."

"Alright, get up. It's time to go." Burkhardt pulled her back over to the couch and locked one of the handcuffs to the metal railing leading down to the forward stateroom. He stepped up to the helm, started the twin Crusader 454xl engines, untied the dock lines and eased the Constellation out into Sarasota Bay. Once in the channel, he turned south along the Intracoastal towards Sarasota Bayfront Park. The weather looked a little soupy towards Sarasota. A light rain covered the bridge's windshield and a slight chop framed whitecaps out on Bay. Burkhardt checked the Loran, punched in the coordinates for Marker 10, Marina Jack, switched on the Raytheon Auto Pilot and pushed the controls to cruising speed. It was times like this when he appreciated modern instrumentation.

"Oh, by the way, Mrs. Jupiter, the Feds picked up your father and his girlfriend in San Diego yesterday. Twenty-three years your old man was on the lam. The FBI found eighty thousand dollars in his apartment. He was living the good life, until someone turned him in for the reward. Party's over. More than likely he'll spend the rest of his life behind bars," Burkhardt called out as he walked back to the main salon.

"Thanks for the news bulletin, Mr. FBI man, but how are you going to explain to your superiors how you murdered my husband in cold blood?" Donna Jupiter snapped angrily. "Maybe you'll find yourself behind bars, next to my father. How do you like that news story, Mr. Molenar, or whatever your name is?"

"FBI Agent Ross M. Burkhardt, and speaking of stories, we have about fifteen minutes until we reach the John Ringling Causeway when I'll pilot the yacht over to mooring field and drop anchor. So how did dear old dad get to keep the *Storm on the Sea of Galilee* painting?"

"What's the M stand for?" Donna Jupiter asked sarcastically.

"Major, after my father's favorite hunting dog."

"How appropriate, named after a dog. It really should stand for *Moron!* Too bad you don't know jack about tracking the stolen paintings from the Isabella Stewart Gardner Museum, Mr. FBI man. You think my father stole the paintings. What a bunch of dumb assholes." Donna leaned back in the couch and for the next ten minutes detailed how the stolen painting ended up in her house. On March 18, 1990, after leaving a St. Patrick's Day party drunk, her Uncle Billy was desperate to take a piss. He walked into the Palace Road alleyway alongside the museum to relieve himself when he noticed two policeman putting things into a hatchback. After they left, he ran over to the car, stole one of the paintings and ran home. Two days later, the Boston Globe headline read, $200 Million Gardner Museum Art Theft. He realized he had a very expensive piece of art. He tried to sell it to an art dealer in Philadelphia, but that fell through. A few years later, he approached a Connecticut millionaire, but he backed out at the last minute so he just put the painting away. After he was murdered in Nassau, the Key West home was used as a family vacation retreat. Twenty-three years later, right before the house was sold, a secret wine vault was discovered, and inside a tiny passageway was the *Storm on the Sea of Galilee* and a letter. Sonny Bugler never knew his brother had the painting.

"That's some story, but I'm a little old for fairy tales, don't you think, Mrs. Jupiter?" Burkhardt scoffed, and looked out at the rain as the sun began to drop below the horizon.

"I don't care what you think, mister. That's the truth," Donna spit out and glowered at him. "By the way, how did you know we were in the market to sell the painting?"

"Remember, last year when you purchased the FIOS promotion and bundled your television, phone and internet service? That was the FBI who did the installation. From that day, we monitored everything that went on in your house 24/7. The coup de grace was the free 70-inch flat screen television in your living room that you miraculously won at the Venice Chalk Festival. We overheard a conversation you had with your girlfriend, Sam, about attending the chalk festival and that you needed to take a picture of the three-D artwork on Miami Avenue for a jewelry project you were working on for a client.

We paid a shop owner a thousand dollars to put out a table for a free TV raffle. You came by, signed up for the give-away, and the next day I called and proclaimed you the winner. After the television was installed we had visual monitoring of the house. You know what they say, *a picture is worth a thousand words.* Well, my dear Mrs. Jupiter, we have over a thousand hours of video of you and your husband, and an assortment of other individuals whom you had business dealings with. I'd love to continue our little chat, but we're approaching the Ringling Bridge. It's a little tricky so I need to take control of the navigation."

"You bastard, I hope you smash the yacht into a pylon, and drown."

Burkhardt took the wheel, guided the yacht smoothly under the bridge and south towards Bayfront Park mooring field.

Dry rot is the bane of all wood boat owners, especially a weekend warrior who owns a fifty-five year old Chris-Craft. Water, mold and fungus all beat the death knell for wood not properly maintained. Good fortune for Donna Jupiter handcuffed to the railing in the main salon. A cosmetic repair of sandpaper, wood cement, a fresh coat of mahogany Minwax varnish, and the railing looked as good as new. It wasn't and with one hard jerk, the two lower stainless steel screws popped out and the imprisoned arm slipped free. Slowly, she slid off the couch and crawled along teak floor into the aft deck salon. She pushed open the starboard door, unhooked the rail fender and lowered herself into the dark water below.

Bobbing to the surface, Donna floated in the water letting the current pull her away from the yacht towards the shore. She watched the Chris-Craft slow to a stop in the lagoon mooring field and drop anchor. The engines turned silent and the port and starboard running lights went dark. Only the main cabin lights glowed, reflecting thin beams of light across the choppy water. She followed his every move as he switched off the lights on the bridge and moved down to the main salon, only the interior lights from the salon reflected on to the water as darkness closed in. *He knows I have to get to shore and call for help*, Donna Jupiter repeated in her mind, as she turned and began to swim.

"I know you're out there, Mrs. Jupiter. Remember, I know where you live. If you tell the police, I'll find you, and when I do, I'll put a bullet in your head, just like your husband." Burkhardt walked down to the galley, turned on the gas stove, set the timer for thirty minutes, picked up the painting, the $10 million, and exited the Constellation.

The whine from the dinghy's outboard motor broke the silence of the mooring field as the small wooden craft headed towards shore and O'Leary's Tiki Bar.

Chapter 17

The fax machine behind Detective Beale's desk came to life and pounded out four documents onto its bottom tray. Beale reached over and on the cover sheet, in large bold print read: CYBER COMMAND AGENCY / CONFIDENTIAL.

"Hordowski, this is the report we've been waiting for, the one on Blaine Sterling's phone records. Come over and take a look." Cyber Command Agency, headquartered in Sarasota, is an elite team of law enforcement cyber specialists, programmers and computer experts assembled to combat cyber-crimes. The agency collects and evaluates digital forensic evidence, and provides a technology based response assisting law enforcement in solving computer-based crimes.

"Here it is. The night of her birthday party, Blaine Sterling received only one call. It was five after eight, from 941-485-1012. Katie Piper, a senior at Venice High School, called from Raiford, Florida."

"Raiford?" Hordowski asked. "What's a high school kid doing at Raiford?"

"Good question," Beale said slowly, pointing to Raiford on the map above the fax machine. "Miss Piper is an honor student, on a championship volleyball team and will attend Georgetown University in the fall. It is my professional opinion that this young lady would never make a phone call from Raiford, Florida." Beale tapped on the map.

"Bullshit, there has to be more in the report. What is it, Beale?" Hordowski groaned and leaned back in his chair.

"You're correct, Detective, there is more. Katie Piper reported that she lost her cell phone before Christmas, in Orlando, while competing in the All State Sing Festival with the Venice Choir." Still tapping on the map, "Plus, Raiford, Florida, has the Union Correctional Institution." Beale turned the page.

"CCA unscrambled the mobile datasets tracking device, fingerprinted the cell location and concluded that the call originated from the main tower dump at the prison."

"That doesn't make sense. How could someone in prison burn down a house?" Hordowski opened his folder and took out a handful of grainy, 8 x 10 black & white photographs. "We have security camera pictures from Blaine Sterling's neighbor across the street. The pictures are cloudy, but there is a definite silhouette of a large person holding, what appears to be something burning, maybe a Molotov cocktail, and the outline of the back of a vehicle, maybe a van or SUV, right before the house goes up in flames."

"No, the caller didn't fire bomb Blaine Sterling's house! Remember the message. He said he was tied up at the moment. The arsonist was someone the caller knew, a person that would obey orders from a man locked up in prison, maybe for a lifetime. We are looking for a person so loyal or so afraid, prison is not a deterrent." Beale looked down at the file. "Charlie Boltier is in Union Correctional."

"That's right!" Hordowski shouted. "Boltier, the guy who drove the boat at the Venice Boat Parade, when Remi Cole shot Sterling and killed a lady from Michigan watching the parade. Does the report say how long Boltier is in prison?"

"Let's see. There's a shopping list of offenses," Beale moved his finger down the page, "but accessory to murder is the most damaging, thirty to life."

"I'd say loyalty. Boltier could be locked up for life. This guy is not afraid of him. He's following orders out of respect or love. Yeah, I'd say love or respect, family member, relative, old school buddy, someone who owes a favor, a lover?"

"Run a check on Mr. Boltier's family, business associates and friends. I'll call Ms. Sterling. We should drive out to Osprey State Park and ask her who she knows at Union Correctional."

Chapter 18

The early morning phone call from Star Trek guy emptied the breath from Blaine Sterling's frame. "The arsonist who firebombed your house is in Osprey State Park. Your life is in danger." Horrified, Sterling jerked the Club Car to the side of the trail, practically catapulting Park Manager John Forrester from the seat. She jammed on the brakes and froze.

The Annual All Trails Hike was to take place in two days. The park was alive with last minute preparations. Park staff and volunteers were setting up signs, a registration booth, guide tables, refreshment stations and pet water areas all along the twelve miles of trails throughout the park. *The Hike*, as it is affectionately called, has evolved into a premier physical fitness hiking event complete with costumes, music and good old merriment. But most of all, *The Hike* had been popularized as a family friendly outing for all levels of hikers. Pets were welcome, and an ever increasing number of costumed hikers each year added to the festive atmosphere of the event.

Although the park recorded eleven inches of rain the past two days, given the porous, sandy soil, a favorite habitat for the scrub-jay to bury its acorns, Sterling and Forrester certified that all six trails were in first-class condition. As she was returning to the Nature Center, Blaine's cell phone broke the morning silence.

"Blaine, what's wrong?" Forrester asked after he pulled himself back onto the seat. "You look like you've seen a ghost." Blaine put her cell on speaker phone.

"The individual at Union Correctional received a call this morning, which I traced. I couldn't get the identity of the caller, but I was able to trace the serial code numbers of the caller's phone and found that the phone was purchased at Publix on West Venice Avenue in Venice. It is a *No Name* phone and the person paid cash for the device, so no permanent address to access. However, young neophyte, I did trace the GPS call track, and it originated from Osprey State Park." Star Trek guy waited.

"So what you're saying is, the arsonist, either camps, visits, volunteers or works here at the park?" Blaine asked and looked over at Forrester.

"Yes, youthful traveler, and I foresee another physical encounter with this outlander. I behest that you communicate with the detective investigating the arsonist attack. Converse forthwith."

"Detective Beale, from the Venice Police called. He is coming to the park today. He said he had information on house fire, and…"

Before Blaine could finish her sentence Forrester leaned over and said, "Why does he think this person will attempt to hurt you again? Ask him that."

"Star Trek guy, John Forrester is here with me, and he wants to know, and so do I, why you believe this man will make another attempt to harm me?" Blaine leaned back in her seat.

"Because he went to the trouble to purchase a non-traceable phone. He has something else planned. I must go. I have customers waiting. Stay safe, young neophyte." The phone went silent.

"Star Trek guy, what kind of name is that? Who is that person?" Forrester shook his head. "Why does he talk like that, young neophyte, youthful traveler, outlander; no one on this planet talks like that. And how does he know anything about the arsonist?"

"Where do I begin? It's such a convoluted tale." Blaine, turned off the engine and for the next twenty minutes chronicled the story of Myron Weeder, a.k.a. Star Trek Guy. Myron was a computer genius, worked at Best Buy in Sarasota, delivered newspapers at night and was president of a computer club, her friend, Marybeth Maiello belonged to. Myron helped locate Blaine's late husband, who died in an auto accident attempting to contact his birth parents. A Trekkie, he's obsessed with everything Star Trek, masquerades as Spock, and oftentimes stayed out there in the Universe too long. He believes the arsonist is in the park and will make another attempt on my life.

"Right now, I need to get back to the office and meet Detective Beale. I'll drop you off at the Nature Center if you'd like?"

"That would be fine; Blaine, please keep me informed. If there is anything I can do, well you know." Forrester reached over and touched Blaine's shoulder, "Anything, just ask."

Blaine exited the Blue Trail at the Nature Center, dropped Forrester off and drove west on the main road to the office. As she turned onto the shell road, she spotted a white Crown Victoria parked alongside her building.

Chapter 19

Texting, ice cream, and walking can be hazardous to one's health. Brooke politely held open the door to the Venice Avenue Creamery while a family of four with triple-scoop ice cream cones in hand, trooped outside into the sunlight. Disaster struck as the last girl reached the doorstep. Smartphone in one hand, and a vanilla, chocolate and strawberry cone in the other, she was too preoccupied texting to notice a slight dip in the walkway. Creating the perfect storm for mayhem, in one awkward motion, the cone, smartphone and teenager tumbled forward into her waiting parents, whom in turn dislodged their cones, creating an ice cream disaster. Twelve scoops of vanilla, chocolate and strawberry ice cream, flying in the air like cannon balls fired at close range, sent pedestrians running in all directions. Loud screams of panic could be heard all the way down the block. Not one scoop of ice cream was left intact on the homemade waffle cones. Messy ice cream covered the family, the sidewalk and their rental car parked in front of the Creamery. Screams of indignation from the father echoed into the ice cream shop as Jimmy, the ice cream server, ran outside to assist. Towels in hand, he had everyone cleaned off and in their car in no time. He offered them free ice cream, but the parents were so upset with their daughter that they politely declined and drove off. During the excitement Evan, the second ice cream server, hosed the entire sidewalk off until it looked like new.

"Who said Venice isn't an exciting place to visit? And it's not even five o'clock yet. I can just imagine what that family will tell all their friends up north about their visit to the Venice Avenue Creamery and how much fun they had not eating ice cream!" Mrs. Brecht gave Brooke a wink and they both walked inside the ice cream parlor. "So, my dear, what's your pleasure?"

"I think I'll have a Super Hero Birthday cone." Brooke answered. "With chocolate sprinkles."

"What on earth is a Super Hero Birthday cone? Today's not your birthday?" Mrs. Brecht questioned and approached the counter.

"It's a blast! All the kids order them." Jimmy, explained with a big smile and a glint in his eye. "And what about you, madam?"

"I'll have one scoop of coffee ice cream in a cup, please. And, Jimmy, I was very impressed with your actions outside. You were thorough, attentive and that was a very magnanimous offer of free ice cream."

"What's magnanimous mean, Mrs. Brecht?" asked Brooke.

"Very generous. It was very generous of Jimmy to offer to buy the family another ice cream."

"The owners, Randy and Karen Etzkorn, insist on good service and delicious ice cream at the Venice Avenue Creamery all the time, young lady." Jimmy reached over and handed Mrs. Brecht her cup. At the same time, Evan, the other counterman, handed Brooke her Super Hero Birthday cone with sprinkles. "Enjoy, ladies," Jimmy sang out in a cheery voice.

"I still can't get over the new name, *Venice Avenue Creamery*. For forty-six years you were Bresler's Ice Cream & Yogurt. You'll always be Bresler's to me." Mrs. Brecht handed Jimmy the money, and she and Brooke walked over to a table by the window.

Mrs. Brecht took a spoonful of coffee ice cream, closed her eyes and smiled. "They may have a new name, but the ice cream still has the same old homemade taste. Now, young lady, let's talk about your problem."

Mrs. Brecht put down her spoon and detailed *Operation Banana Split,* a deliciously novel plan to stop the teasing and improve health benefits one banana at a time. Each day Brooke would wear a different color banana shirt and bring a banana snack for the class and the teacher. Mr. Brecht would bring bananas for Tuesday, banana bread on Wednesday, fruit cocktail with bananas Thursday and Friday, the big surprise, banana split ice cream in yellow bowls for everyone.

"Also, I know you have been working on your Shelter project in Social Studies for Mrs. Cordas. It's due tomorrow. I think your yellow trailer with pictures of the inside, including your own bedroom, the kitchen and let's not forget the 60" flat screen television, will prove to the class that your yellow banana shelter is a wonderful home. I'm convinced, that you will make some new friends, when they hear about your 60" television."

"Does mommy know about our plan?" Brooke asked and took the last bite of her cone.

"I'm going to tell her as soon as we get back. She needs to call your teacher and explain what we are planning. It's important that you give your report tomorrow. Now let's go get your shirts."

They waved good-bye to Jimmy who was busy scooping out a perfect ball of pistachio-mint ice cream for a little red-headed girl whose face was glued to the ice cream window. Mesmerized by the ice cream man's creamery magic, her expression was priceless. Jimmy flashed one of his big mid-western smiles, nodded, and dug into the container for a second scoop.

"We're back," Mrs. Brecht called out as she and Brooke stepped inside the Shirt Stop. "Are the T-shirts ready?"

"Perfect timing," Dot called back holding up a pink banana Tee. "What do you think?"

"It's beautiful, and the butterfly on the banana is so cool. Can I try it on?" Brooke asked and ran up to the counter. "A perfect fit, now the kids will see bananas are cool, and it is cool to live in a banana yellow house. I'm definitely going to wear it to school tomorrow."

"Good idea, Brooke, and why don't you keep it on to show your mother," Mrs. Brecht added. "It will assist in explaining our little banana project for school."

"That will be forty-one dollars, plus tax," Dot said politely. Mrs. Brecht reached into her pocketbook and handed her a credit card. "By the way, Brooke, did you know that one million people every day wear decorative T-shirts? That was a trivia question last week on Jeopardy."

"Wow, that's a lot of t-shirts, but today it's a million-one," Brooke sang out in a cheery voice. Everyone laughed. Mrs. Brecht collected her purchases, and she and Brooke walked out to the car.

The drive home was filled with playfulness and laughter. Not even a sudden downpour along 41, which forced Mrs. Brecht to the side of the highway to raise the top, could dampen their spirits. Mrs. Brecht began the banter stating that a popular actress; she couldn't recall her name, a senior moment, believed people should start all their meals with dessert. That way the person enjoys the sweet, luscious, morsel throughout the entire meal, instead of hurrying through the food to get to the dessert. In the end, the diner may eat less conceivably losing weight. "She called it, *The Dessert Diet.*" They both laughed.

Brooke continued the tomfoolery with an array of knock-knock jokes that kept the two of them laughing all the way home. The last one, as they pulled into the driveway, was ridiculously hilarious:

"Knock, knock."

"Who's there?"

"I scream."

"I scream who?"

"I scream, you scream, we both scream for ice cream."

Once inside the yellow trailer, they spied Blaine starring quizzically at the twenty-two, fresh, yellow, bananas in the center of the kitchen table while Mr. Brecht explained, "I don't know. All Charlene told me was to pick up twenty-two bananas from Publix, ask Melody Pruitt, the manager, to help select ones ripe enough to last four days and bring them here. I explained to Melody, the bananas were for Brooke's class project."

"Class project, Brooke's project is due tomorrow. It is a Social Studies project on shelter. She's talking about the fire that destroyed her house, the charitable gift of the trailer and ending her speech with the 60" television that every Joey Banana trailer is furnished with."

"Isn't the trailer yellow?" Ken quipped.

"Hello, we're back," Brooke called out and raced into the kitchen. "Like my pink T-shirt? Mrs. Brecht bought it!"

"Banana Girl? I don't understand?" Blaine asked and shot Mrs. Brecht a questioning glance.

"I can explain," Mrs. Brecht replied, and sat down across from Blaine and the fired-up Brooke. For the next half hour, over two cups of Chamomile tea, Mrs. Brecht detailed how Brooke came home from school crying, that a girl in her class, Angie, teased her about living in a banana house, and called her *Banana Girl*. She described the plan to treat the class to a little banana magic. Starting tomorrow, Blaine would bring to class twenty-two banana snacks, and ending Friday with a yummy banana split ice cream delight, served up in twenty-two yellow bowls to educate the class about the wonders of the banana.

"Oh, sweetie, I'm sorry you were teased today, but the children in your class don't know how wonderful this house is. When you give your report tomorrow, and hand out the bananas for snacks, I'm positive that the teasing will end. Plus, when the kids see how cool your banana shirt looks, they'll all want one."

"So, Brooke, *Operation Banana* starts tomorrow. Good luck. I can't wait to hear how your day went. I'll be preparing everything for Banana Split Friday." said Mrs. Brecht, as she and her husband exited the trailer.

"Thank you, Charlene. I'll e-mail Brooke's teacher tonight, inform her of the teasing and get permission for *Operation Banana*." Everyone laughed.

"Mom, did you know one million people each day wear a fancy T-shirt!"

Chapter 20

Blaine parked the Club Car across from the pole barn and walked back to the office. Detectives Beale and Hordowski were looking at the bulletin board in the foyer when she arrived. Greetings exchanged, they walked back to her office. Beale was first to speak.

"Ms. Sterling, you look nervous."

"I just received a call from a friend who informed me that the arsonist is in the park, and that he made a call this morning to Union Correctional Prison!" Blaine stated in a constrained voice.

Startled at the revelation, Beale took out his notepad and wrote; friend called, drew a question mark, arsonist in park and sketched a flame. "Who called you, Ms. Sterling, and where did this person get that information?"

"All I'm telling you is that my friend traced a call someone received at Union Correctional, and that the call originated from this park."

Beale wrote down computer hacker, drew a computer and underlined hacker.

"That confirms our news on the person or persons that may be involved in the firebombing of your home. The call to your cell phone, the night of your birthday party, originated from Union Correctional. We believe an inmate at the prison made that call. We contacted the director and they did a complete sweep of Cell Block D, but no phone." Beale opened the folder he carried into the office and showed it to Blaine.

"Why only Cell Block D? Why not the entire prison?" Blaine snapped angrily, and looked down at the open folder. "Oh my god, I know that man. It's Charlie Boltier. I had him arrested for trespassing when he was four-wheeling in the undeveloped part of the park. He caused thousands of dollars' worth of damage with those three vehicles. Today, it's still an environmental disaster back there."

"Blaine, I remember. I was there. Charlie Boltier is in Union Correctional Institution, Cell Block D." Beale pointed to his picture. "Administration checked their records and found that Boltier withdrew three hundred dollars from his prison account before Christmas. We're convinced he made that call. But firebombed your house?"

Hordowski opened his folder, "I may have the answer, Ms. Sterling. We have over one hundred photographs taken from security cameras across the street from your home the night of the firebombing. Two pictures in particular may help us find the arsonist. Please take a look." Hordowski slid the pictures across the desk and waited.

"These must have been taken by Mr. Gallagher's security cameras. His entire house is ringed with them. The place looks like an advertisement for Radio Shack. Gallagher believes there is a conspiracy of dog owners from our community and surrounding neighborhoods, targeting his house as a 'doggie poop destination.' He photographs every dog owner, dog, doggie mess, and posts the infraction online at DoggiePoop.com. Last month, one dog walker accused Mr. Gallagher of putting dog poop on his doorstep, setting it on fire and ringing the doorbell. The two got into a shouting match that ended with the police being called." Blaine remarked with a faint laugh.

"Yes, it's all detailed in this report. The dog owner, Sebastian Billardello, charged Mr. Gallagher with harassment and in return Mr. Gallagher filed an order of restraint against Billardello. End of story." Hordowski looked up at Blaine and smiled.

"That's not the entire story, Detective. The next thing the community knew, the two of them were on the Judge Judi Show, with dogs, pictures of doggie poop on fire, police reports and the video tape of the 'doggie confrontation'."

"That's also in the report, Ms. Sterling. Quite a television circus. Judge Judi humiliated both of them in front of 5 million viewers. However, in the end she adjudicated a happy ending." Hordowski removed a picture from the New York Post that showed Mr. Gallagher and Mr. Billardello shaking hands and

Judge Judi holding the four-legged culprit, JC, a playful, chocolate & cream Dachshund. Below the picture the caption read, *Pooper Scooper Not Indicted, Doggie Peace Found in Judge Judi's Courtroom.* End of story."

"Not exactly, Detective. Although great publicity for Judge Judi after the show, our neighborhood was besieged by newspaper, television and tabloid reporters for weeks. They flocked to our neighborhood in droves to see Mr. Gallagher and, of course, JC. It was a media maelstrom. Everyone wanted an exclusive with Mr. Gallagher and Mr. Billardello." Blaine reached behind her desk and lifted off a picture from her bookcase. "My daughter even became a pawn in the media hype. Here is one of many pictures of her with Mr. Gallagher and his dogs, Chief and Cleo, two black and white Havanese, and Sebastian and Virginia Billardello with their dog, JC. That's right, Mr. Gallagher now has two dogs, and he and Mr. Billardello are best friends." Blaine placed the picture back on the shelf. "Now they only argue about baseball. I pray the New York Yankees and the Boston Red Socks aren't in the Division Payoffs this year. I don't think the community could handle another media blitz."

"Back to the pictures, Ms. Sterling. As you can see, in the first picture, a person in front of your house is holding an accelerant, we suspect is a homemade Molotov cocktail. The fire marshal reported glass fragments from a pop bottle were found at the origin of the fire. We believe that the picture, plus the glass fragments support the Molotov cocktail theory. The next picture shows the individual standing alongside a vehicle, a truck or large SUV. The arsonist is tall, estimating the height of the vehicle, we determined that the person to be at least 6 foot tall."

Blaine took a closer look. "I can't identify this person. I can't even tell if it's a man or woman."

"We believe, the arsonist has a strong connection to Charlie Boltier, either family, close friend, indebted employee or lover." Beale interjected and proceeded to take over the conversation.

"Bolt Construction is owned by the younger brother of Charlie Boltier, Roy Boltier, and Charlie happens to be incarcerated at Union Correctional, Raiford, Florida." Beale's words hung in the air, thick and heavy, like a shroud smothering the very breath from Blaine Sterling's body.

Gathering her strength, Blaine stood, looked at both men and said, "I can't believe it. The company putting in the park's sewer system is owned by the same family that's terrorizing me. Why haven't you arrested him?"

"It is not that simple, Blaine," Detective Beale stated emphatically. "We've reviewed personal and business online transactions, tracked all landline and cell phone calls, and nothing connecting him to you or to his brother in prison turned up."

"He only called the prison three times in three years, all on April 3rd, his brother's birthday," Hordowski interjected.

"Of course not!" Blaine replied. "I was told, that the phone used to call Charlie Boltier was a *No Name* cell phone. That phone can't be traced. This guy's no dummy. He's out to hurt me and my family. He seems to have some twisted notion that I am responsible for his incarceration. He's just as sick as Remi Cole and you know what Cole tried to do!"

Beale reached for his notepad, jotted down *No Name* phone, drew a picture of a cell phone and underlined phone twice. "Blaine, how does your friend know a *No Name* phone was used?" Beale looked over at Hordowski, then the two looked back at Blaine Sterling and waited for a reply.

"I told you he's some kind of computer guru."

Beale turned the page in his notepad, wrote computer guru, computer store, Venice, Sarasota, drew a big question mark and circled Sarasota. "How did your friend know the phone call came from the park?" Beale asked as he drew a tower.

"I don't know. He said something about a cell phone tower next to the park or something. What does that have to do with anything? What about Roy Boltier? What are you going to do about him?" Blaine exclaimed and glowered back at the two detectives.

Beale wrote in his notepad 'check calls and drew a tower.'

"That's against the law, Ms. Sterling. Your friend could be arrested." Hordowski blurted out.

"Against the law? You're joking Detective, don't you read the newspapers? What about the NSA and charges of illegal domestic surveillance of the American public. At this very moment, the Senate Intelligence Committee is investigating NSA's surveillance tactics of mass collection of wiretaps without warrants, unrestrained gathering of telephone records and accumulation of Internet correspondence routed through NSA each day. Why don't you first see what the government does about NSA, Detective Hordowski. Then we'll worry about my friend. Right now what are you going to do about my problem?"

Beale closed his folder, stood up and said, "I think it is time we pay Mr. Roy Boltier a visit."

Chapter 21

The eleven inches of rain that swamped Osprey State Park during a two day rainstorm turned every corner the park into muck, mud and brown-green ooze. Hiking trails throughout the park resembled Old West wagon routes, rutted, grooved and puddled from start to finish. Bolt Construction was brought to a standstill. Every piece of heavy construction equipment was mired wheel deep in mud and water. Unable to maneuver or excavate the three-foot-deep trenches, and then connect the twenty-foot sewer pipes, each Bobcat, backhoe and dump truck sat idle waiting for the sun to dry up the ground.

The only consolation from the drenching rains was that Roy Boltier was shuttered in the construction office for two days and completed the backlog of construction bids, billing statements and payroll. Boltier was in the process of signing the final ADP check when the office door burst open, and in a flurry of rain and wind, appeared construction foreman Erwin Zaretsky. Soaking wet he stepped into the office, turned and slammed the door shut. Zaretsky was a tall, muscular man, with big, weathered hands attached to thick arms and broad shoulders. A face lined from sun and age chronicled his twenty hard years of labor for Bolt Construction.

"Zaretsky, you must be clairvoyant. I just signed your paycheck and here you are." Boltier smiled, reached across his desk and handed him the check.

"Thank you, Mr. Boltier. I don't know about being clairvoyant. I got your message on my phone to go to office and here I am." Although Zaretsky was ten years his senior, he always addressed his boss by his surname. Respect was the cornerstone of Erwin Zaretsky's way of life, a trait instilled in him at any early age by his Russian parents and passed down to his two teenage children today.

89

"Zaretsky, I need you take a look at this last sewer blueprint. The section of red lines, circled in yellow, is what remains to complete the Osprey project. My calculations show, maybe two days, what do you think?"

Zaretsky reached into his shirt pocket and took out a pair of reading glasses. An occupational hazard that arrives with old age, failing eyesight, but for ninety-nine cents at the local dollar store, a burden he could endure. Zaretsky bent over, glanced down at the patchwork of lines and dots that carpeted the blueprint before him. The picture reminded him of a New York City subway map. A byway of blue, green, orange, purple and red lines intersecting and crisscrossing each other from Chelsea to Greenwich Village, to So Ho down to TriBeCa, and then back to the East Village. A trip he took daily when he worked in New York City a long time ago.

"Let's see, it's 500 yards from the Nature Center to the main restrooms. That's seventy-five sewer pipe connections. I think one full day of work should do it. The weather forecast calls for clearing in afternoon, which should be plenty of time to dry out the area. We can start tomorrow morning and finish around five o'clock." Zaretsky put his glasses back in his shirt pocket, turned and faced Boltier.

"That's good to hear, Zaretsky. One day will help my bottom line, but there's just one little problem. We can't work tomorrow. Last week I had a meeting with John Forrester and Blaine Sterling, the park managers. They informed me that tomorrow will be their All Trails Hike and they expect over one hundred participants hiking the 12-mile route Saturday. That means no work Saturday, but I need you to organize the final work crew for Monday, and have Greg McDaniel start up all the construction machines today. I want every engine in top running condition Monday. I can't afford to have the crew show up Monday morning and all the motors are waterlogged. He's the best damn mechanic in Florida. If anyone can get an engine running after standing out in the rain for two days, it is Greg McDaniel."

"Yes, sir, I will have Greg work on those engines now that the rain has stopped," Zaretsky replied, and glanced out the

90

window at a white car splashing through the water towards the office. "Are you expecting anyone, Mr. Boltier?"

"No, why do you ask?"

"Because two men are getting out of a white car and walking up to the office. If I had to guess, they're cops," Zaretsky added, as the door flew opened and two men entered.

Beale stepped forward, took out his identification and said, "I'm Detective Beale, and this is Detective Hordowski. We're investigating the firebombing of Blaine Sterling's home. Are you Roy Boltier?"

"Excuse me, Mr. Boltier, I'll be leaving now. I will call McDaniel and have him check all the motors. Good-bye, sir, and to you, gentlemen."

Boltier put down his papers and replied, "Yes, how can I help you?"

The detectives sat down directly in front of Boltier and Beale immediately sensed a nervousness in Roy Boltier's demeanor. A steady clicking of Boltier's pen top signaled an uncomfortable tick that Beale recorded in his notepad. He drew a pen and wrote *lying*.

"As I said, we are looking into a number of leads pertaining to the firebombing of Blaine Sterling's home. We have reason to believe, the night of the fire, that a phone message and photograph of Sterling's burning house came from Union Correctional Prison. Sterling's phone records substantiate that timeline. Your brother Charlie is at Union and we believe he made that call. Have you spoken to your brother recently?" Beale turned to a new page in his notepad. Boltier started clicking again.

"No, I haven't spoken with Charlie since his incarceration. What has it been, three years, maybe more? No, wait, that's incorrect. I called him for his birthday, April 3rd. I wished him a happy birthday, exchanged a few pleasantries and hung up. We really didn't have anything to talk about. Boltier put the pen down, shuffled some papers on his desk and placed them in the out basket. "I read about the fire in the newspaper, disturbing event, a person's home burning down like that. But I'm a little confused, Detective. How could Charlie burn down Sterling's house if he was in prison?"

"We suspect he had an accomplice. Where were you the night of the fire, Mr. Boltier?" Beale asked. The clicking started.

"Me? Don't be ridiculous! Why would I burn down Blaine Sterling's home? I don't even know where she lives," Boltier snapped angrily. "What possible motive would I have?" The clicking increased.

"Did Charlie ask you to firebomb her house? Retribution for putting him behind bars?" Hordowski asked.

"That's preposterous. I'm going to risk losing my business, my family, because my brother asked me to burn down some park ranger's house? Detective, I love my brother, but in case you haven't noticed, we travel in different circles. He's into motorcycles, dirt bikes, boats, fishing, hunting, heavy drinking and wild parties. None of that interests me. So no, my brother did not ask me to firebomb that lady's home." The clicking continued. "By the way, Detective, what was the date of the fire?" Boltier snapped.

"January 6th at eight in the evening," Beale replied. The clicking stopped.

Suddenly, Boltier's expression transformed from hunted to hunter. A power he knew well when an athlete realized that he had the upper hand over his competition. A track star in high school and college, Boltier now enjoyed the same exhilaration.

"January 6th you said," Boltier repeated and swiveled around in his chair, grabbed a red, white, and blue Lego framed picture from the bookcase behind his desk and handed it to Detective Beale. "For your information, on January 6, I was vacationing with my family at LEGOLAND in Winter Haven. For the past year, my daughters Zella and Matilda pleaded with me to visit the amusement park. Finally, I surrendered and purchased a two-day family pass."

Beale looked at the souvenir picture and handed it to Hordowski. Their expressions were grim. Before them was a 5"x10" color photo of Boltier, his wife and two daughters standing under a large Lego giraffe in front of the LEGOLAND Imagination Zone entrance. There in the bottom right hand corner was the date, *January 6.*

Boltier picked up the pen, but this time instead of clicking, he pointed to the picture in Hordowski's hand and said, "As you can see, Detectives, the date on the picture reads January 6." Boltier smiled and placed the pen on the desk. "Clearly, I could not have possibly firebombed Ms. Sterling's house! I was in Winter Haven, over one hundred miles from Venice. We had reservations for January 6th at the Hampton Inn Winter Haven, and checked out the following morning after their complimentary breakfast. I'm certain the hotel will confirm that we checked out on January 7."

Hordowski returned the photograph to Boltier, removed four black and white pictures from a manila folder he had on his lap and arranged them in a row on the desk. "Mr. Boltier, would you please look at these photos and tell me if you recognize the individual standing by the vehicle?"

Boltier inched his chair forward, picked up his pen and glanced neutrally at the pictures. The clicking started. "No, I can't say that I do. The photographs are very dark and grainy. It's impossible to see any detail. Whoever took these photographs needs to buy a better camera. Sorry, I can't even discern if the individual is a male or large female."

"Could it be Charlie's son, Thor? He's a big guy. We contacted Charlie's ex-wife. She's living in Tucson, Arizona, in a mansion in the foothills overlooking the city. All she knew was that Thor was a freshman at FSU, lived in a fraternity house off campus and only calls her when he needs money. She said he took the divorce hard and blamed her. Mr. Boltier, please take a closer look."

"Sorry, I can't make out a thing."

"The photos were taken the night of the firebombing from a neighbor's security camera across the street from Blaine Sterling's home." Beale pushed the last picture directly in front of Boltier and said, "Mr. Boltier, take another look at this picture. Maybe you recognize the vehicle in this snapshot?"

"It looks like some sort of truck or large SUV. Possibly, a Ford Expedition, GMC truck or maybe a Hummer," Boltier acknowledged and pushed the picture back across the table. The clicking quickened.

"We called the college. They're on Winter Break. Thor's fraternity house was open, but no one has seen him since the break. Doesn't Thor drive a Hummer?"

Beale flipped to a new page in his notebook, sketched a truck, and wrote Hummer with a big question mark. "Mr. Boltier, one last question and then we'll let you get back to your work. A call was made to your brother the other day from the park. Do you have any knowledge of a call?" Beale looked at Boltier and waited. The clicking repeated.

"How can you be certain that the call to my brother was from the park?" Boltier scowled.

"We monitor all outgoing and incoming calls from Union Correctional," Hordowski interjected. "A cell tower adjacent to the park triangulated the GPS coordinates and bingo, we have the location, cell phone number and time of call. I repeat, do you know why anyone from the park would call Charlie Boltier?"

"I'm sorry, Detective. I can't help you. I didn't call my brother and I don't why anyone from my company would call Charlie." The clicking quickened.

Beale circled the sketch of the cell phone and wrote: Boltier knows who made the call and put the notepad back in his pocket. "Thank you for your time, Mr. Boltier. You've been very helpful. We'll be in touch if any other leads materialize."

No sooner had Beale and Hordowski left the office, Boltier slammed his pen down, picked up the construction phone and called his nephew, "The police just left. We need to talk. Come to the office when you get this message."

Chapter 22

Shadows danced along the earthen walls, down twelve stone stairs and into the bowels of a cold, dry cave. Thirty-four kerosene lanterns, strategically placed throughout the subterranean maze, provided the only glint of light in the total darkness. Footprints from an ancient time and, more recently, from Remi Cole, the disgraced ranger, were visible in the pebbled sand of a dried–up riverbed and led deep into the cave. Hulking chunks of rock, the size of a small car, were broken off from the ceiling, littered the floor and made walking laborious at times. Slowly, the main passageway curved and opened into a maze of stalactites and stalagmites. Giant columns of limestone were lined up in rows like preserved soldiers left on parade. One after another they filled both sides of the path, leaving only a small walkway down the center of the room that was lit by the glow of the kerosene lanterns.

Twenty minutes later, the tunnel opened into a colossal, cathedral-size gallery marked by lanterns at the four corners of the room. The height of the room was too high to calculate as the ceiling disappeared into darkness. Large blocks of stone filled the beginning half of the gallery floor, leaving only a single stone path through boulders to a two tiered stone platform that occupied the entire west side of the theater. In the center of the platform stood a clay sculpture of a giant, headless creature. Standing on two hind legs, with two front legs kicking forward at an invisible enemy, the imposing beast was well over twenty feet tall. Alongside the beast was a perfectly preserved, twelve-point deer skull, that must have fallen from its crowning point years long past. When complete, the stag stood almost thirty feet tall, defiant and a dangerous foe to early hunters in search of game. Primeval puncture marks over the body of the animal, along with broken spear points, and arrow heads at the base of the statue, suggested that generations ago, some type of hunting ceremony took place on the platform. Arranged in a circle around the giant deer were twelve stone blocks, eleven cut the same size, and color; however, the block facing the charging beast was larger and painted white. Every block cradled a colorful palm frond facemask.

Finally, primitive drawings of the hunt covered the entire back wall. Changes in color, style and topography suggested that time, and different artists, chronicled the various hunts.

Tucked away in a tiny corner off the back wall was an alcove not readily seen, nor easily accessed. Not as grandiose as the hunting platform, the room was small and Spartan at first glimpse. Unlike the main room, alive with numerous, colorful wall drawings, the antechamber possessed only one primitive drawing that enveloped the back wall, a scene of twelve crestless blue-gray birds circling the sun. Lastly, in the center of the room, covered in dust, stood a small wooden table. Carvings of birds, animals, and people were etched deep into the wood, filling the entire surface of the ancient piece of furniture. In the middle, remnants from a different time, twelve bird nests with dappled blue-gray eggs, rested in a perfect circle. Waiting for the hands of time to call, these sentinels stood silent, unable to work their magic.

Thor walked to the table, removed the thick metal chain that hung from his shoulder, unlocked the padlock attached to the bottom links and wrapped the chain around the furthest leg from the entranceway. He locked the padlock, pulled up on the chain until it reached the top of the table, and confident the contrivance was secure, he shouted. "Hello, anyone there?" His call echoed throughout the passageways, and deep into the darkness, but there was no reply. Thor laughed. He knew no one would answer. It was a rhetorical question. The silence was deafening, but that would change by tomorrow.

The heavy rains that bogged down Bolt Construction cancelling work for two days enabled Thor to complete the excavation and search the entire cave. Every waking moment for the past forty-eight hours, he scoured the cave from top to bottom, but the treasure his father spoke of was nonexistent.

He followed towering rock walls until they collapsed into choking passageways that squeezed into dead ends. Time and again, he climbed over, around and under huge chunks of rock that blocked manageable access off the main chamber. He explored tunnels and pathways that eventually snaked back to the main chamber or terminated before a huge mountain of limestone.

On the final day, Thor discovered a narrow, sandy path that lead to a natural stone bridge deep inside the cave. Carved out by ancient waters thousands of years ago, and approximately forty feet above the cavern floor, the bridge eventually crossed above a hollow that looked down upon a large, dried-up lake. Lowering his lantern by rope, the beam of light reflected an orange glitter off the myriad of sand crystals embedded in the soil along the sides of the hole. "Sand. There must have been water back here at one time," Thor mumbled to himself. About fifteen feet below the valley floor, light reflected off an object protruding from the outer ridge of the hole. Lowering the lantern to the rope's end, a beam of light caught the outline of a curved tusk sticking out about four feet from the base of the wall. "What the hell, a woolly mammoth down here," Thor shouted. "That definitely looks like a tusk from a woolly mammoth. I'm sure." Unable to descend, Thor gazed down recalling his visit to the Venice Museum and Archives, and listening to the director, James Hagler, talk about how in 1926, the partial skeleton of a woolly mammoth was discovered by workmen digging a drainage canal in Venice. The photograph of the Venice mammoth tusks Hagler displayed, looked identical the one jutting out from the side of the cave. Thor took out the company's cell and snapped three pictures. "Mr. James Hagler, wait until you see these pictures. My discovery will put the Venice Museum in the history books. My find will be known as the archeological discovery of the century. People will call me the young Howard Carter of Venice, Florida. Scientific journals will detail my worthy accomplishments and money will flow in. I'll be rich. My name will be synonymous with archeology, on the lips of all the noted paleontologists worldwide." Thor pulled up the rope, and started back along the bridge.

Halfway across, he stopped and realized that it would be impossible for him to publicize this momentous, archeological discovery. If known, he clearly would be implicated in the abduction of Blaine Sterling and ultimately end up in jail alongside his father. The greatest discovery of the 21st century would have to remain his secret. What a mammoth disappointment for the young spelunker and mankind.

His company cell rang. Startled, Thor immediately pulled the phone from his back pocket and looked down at the number, but in the process lost his footing and jerked forward. Reaching out to cushion his fall, the phone slipped from his hand and tumbled over the edge into the abyss. "I don't believe it," Thor screamed and stared down into the darkness.

Regaining his balance, Thor slowly inched his way across the bridge onto solid ground and headed out of the cave. Navigating the maze of passageways, Thor climbed over huge blocks of stone, pushed between formations of stalactites and stalagmites, crawled under rock inclusions that protruded from the cave wall, and with each stop, extinguished a kerosene lantern.

Finally, Thor reached the main gallery, sat down on the platform in front of the headless statue, picked up his backpack, and took out his burner cell phone. "No gold! No silver! No treasure!" The irate words echoed deep within the belly of the cavern and in the empty pit of his despondent heart. "That lying bastard, Remi Cole. He just played my father," Thor cried out. "Planted the idea about a big treasure, buried deep within the cave, a bonus for kidnapping Sterling. Get rid of the girl who sent you to prison and get rich in the process. What a load of crap."

Thor punched in his father's number, and spoke, "The trap is set, waiting for Saturday's rabbit."

"Be patient." The phone went silent.

Chapter 23

The tropical beat from a steel drum band floated across the water. The melodic sounds from O' Leary's Tiki Bar and Grill, pierced the heavy rains and guided the dinghy towards the beach. Burkhardt cut the 5hp engine and for the last ten feet silently glided through the darkness to shore. He tied the dinghy to an empty anchor along the water's edge, picked up the painting, and the money, then walked over to the tiki bar.

Rain has a way of keeping people inside. Heavy rain, thunder and lightning, frighten normal human beings. The saying, "Only mad dogs and Englishmen go out in hot weather," resonated in Burkhardt's mind just as a lightning strike exploded over the water less than fifty yards away. He shouted, "But, only madmen and criminals go out in thunderstorms," only to be drowned out from a second thunder clap.

There under the thatched roof tiki bar, was a young female bartender and a lone male patron seated on a barstool drinking beer. Smoke rings circled his head and floated up into the thatched roof. Burkhardt recognized the man. Months ago he arranged to meet him at O'Learys, on this day, at five o'clock, rain or shine. He was *Gunny*, Vietnam Veteran, Gunnery Sergeant John Mousser, 227th Assault Helicopter Battalion, port side machinegun marksman, friend and co-conspirator. Gunny was a hulk of a man, more fat than muscle, now that his days, and one evening a month, were spent sitting at a desk looking down on the Intracoastal Waterway, waiting to open the KMI Bridge for an occasional sailboat. His large football-shaped head, broad shoulders, short thick neck and huge arms made an intimidating impression.

"Gunny, good to see you. What's it been, thirty, forty years?" Burkhart reached out his hand. "I see you're still smoking. Those cigarettes will kill you one day, mark my words."

"Good to see you Commander. Yeah, it's been a long time since we were flying out of Nui Dat together. That was another world back then, and yes I'm still puffing away on these cancer sticks. Can't kick the habit. How about a beer for old times?" Gunny lit another cigarette.

"Sounds great, Gunny." Burkhardt sidled up on a stool.

"Joanie, two more beers, sweetheart," Gunny called out and downed the last drop from his glass. "She's my new rainy day friend, from Ohio, just like me. She recognized my red Ohio State hat, see the big O on the front. We're both fans. I think she likes me. What do you think, Commander?"

"I think you're dreaming, Gunny, you're old enough to be her father. I think all she sees in you are dollar signs." Joanie placed two cold beers down on the bar, smiled and walked back to the register.

"There, did you see that Commander? She smiled at me. I think we have a connection. It's that old Buckeye State connection, similar values." Gunny lifted his glass, saluted Burkhardt, and they both drank. "Yeah, we did some crazy things over there, I'm surprised we're still around to talk about it." Gunny took out his wallet, removed an old, wrinkled photograph and slid it across the bar.

Burkhardt picked up the picture, a slight smile cracked the stoic façade and a faraway look glazed over his eyes. The photograph showed Major Ross Burkhardt, in uniform, standing in front of a Chinook helicopter, holding a black and white goat in his arms. A large purple and orange banner over the airport hangar read, Home of the Billy Goat Battalion. The identical stoic look from the past that chronicled Burkhardt's pensive mood brought an irritating dryness in his throat. A long, slow gulp of beer remedied the situation.

"I don't believe it. You still have this picture, I remember the day you snapped it. It was the first day of my initiation into the Billy Goat Battalion. Here I was, a major in the U. S. Army 227 Assault Aviation Battalion, and for three weeks I had to feed, groom and parade *Billy*, the Battalion mascot, out on the tarmac, to bid farewell to every departing helicopter. I'd stand at attention with Billy, salute the pilots, and wish them a safe mission. Then return to my office and wait for another departing mission. I can't remember. Who brought *Billy* out when we went on a mission?"

"A private from the motor pool, a tall skinny guy, bad acne, from Texas, Bud Dipple, but they called him *dipstick* all the time."

"Oh yeah, Dipple, I remember, wasn't he killed?" Burkhardt handed Gunny back the picture.

"Dumb bastard, forgot to lock the motor hoist safety catch and an eight hundred pound engine crushed him to death. Splat, what a *dipstick.*" Gunny lit another cigarette, inhaled and blew out three perfect smoke rings all in a row.

"What about that madman from An Khe, the master sergeant, what was his name?" Burkhardt picked up his beer and took another long slow drink. "Bull something or other?"

"Bulldog, Master Sergeant Zachary 'Bulldog' Grebinik. That ugly bastard looked like a fucking bulldog. His droopy, fat face, all wrinkly and swollen, shook every time he barked out orders. Plus, his short, squat body was only about five feet off the ground. No wonder everyone called him Bulldog."

"Yes, Bulldog. That fat bastard had a face begging to be punched." Burkhardt laughed, as he finished his beer.

"You did Commander," Gunny laughed, downed his beer and lit another cigarette.

"He had it coming. That fat slob tried to blackmail us. We had a nice little operation going and that son-of-a-bitch wanted to muscle in, demanding sixty percent of the profit, or he'd alert the C. O. Who the hell did he think he was?" Burkhardt waved for two more beers.

"Yeah, it's too bad he had that walk-in freezer accident," Gunny laughed. "Strange how the lock jammed like that. Poor bastard, fat as he was, froze to death."

"Couldn't have happened to a nicer guy. I cried all the way to the bank," Burkhardt scoffed. "The new Master Sergeant fell right into place. He collected a shit load of Military Payment Certificates, plus Vietnamese Piaster bills from village shop owners and we gave him cash. The shop owners couldn't buy imported goods with MPC money, so they paid three times the value in MPC and Piasters to get American currency. The Sergeant took his cut. We got double in MPC and Vietnamese money, then exchanged them for money orders and mailed them to our banks in the States. It was a no brainer. Everyone made money."

Burkhardt looked at his watch. The rain stopped, so he took out a twenty dollar bill and ordered another round. "That little enterprise paid for forty hours of flight instruction, my private pilot's license and a 1976 Beechcraft F33 Bonanza. This year I traded up and purchased a 2014 Cessna Turbo Skylane. A pilot's dream plane Gunny, comfortable four seater, floats in the air, with a cruising speed of 145 knots, state of the art avionics, all for a mere $530 thousand. A beautiful flying machine, Gunny, nothing like that hulk of metal we bounced around in over in Nam."

"Yeah, I made out okay. Bought a two bedroom, two bath condo in the KMI building in downtown Venice with a heated pool and elevator. It's only five blocks from Venice Beach, a short walk to restaurants, shops and the Venice Theatre. Best of all, only a three- minute walk to my job at the KMI Bridge. I also bought a Bertram 38 yacht, completely set up for fishing. I have her docked at the Crow's Nest Marina, occasionally take a fishing charter out for offshore game fish, an easy two thousand dollars in my pocket each charter. That will be your ride back to shore tomorrow morning, Commander. Maybe when this whole operation is done we can do a little fishing? Great way to enjoy life, and maybe reel in a 300 lb. marlin?"

"I don't think so. I have other plans when this project is completed. I'll be out of the country." Burkhardt checked his watch and turned towards the mooring field.

"Have it your way, Commander, just thought I'd offer. Nothing like a big old marlin hanging over a man's fireplace to boost one's testosterone level."

"So what's the name of your boat? *Living in Paradise?*" Burkhardt smirked and looked out into the night.

"Not even close Commander, it's *Billy Goat*," Gunny laughed.

Burkhardt slammed his hand down on the bar and they both laughed. "Well, thanks for the stroll down memory lane,

Gunny, but now tell me about our current project. What have you completed?"

Before Gunny could utter a word, a violent explosion rocked the mooring site out on the bay. Night disappeared into a fireball of red and orange flames that not only engulfed the Chris-Craft, but a small sailboat moored a few feet away. Angry flames clawed at the air, lighting the night sky in a pyrotechnic extravaganza reminiscent of a Venice Beach Fourth of July spectacle. Everything went silent. The music stopped and conversations abruptly ended. People froze, unable to comprehend the terrifying scene unfolding before their eyes. Gunny gasped, spun around on his stool and stared out at the water. Burkhardt smiled, checked his watch and finished his beer. Suddenly, a second explosion sent rockets of angry flames high into the air, followed this time, by large chunks of burning wood that rained down into the water. A menacing hissing sound echoed across the water, accompanied by a nauseating odor of burning wood and flesh.

"I believe that's our curtain call, Gunny. Time to leave. You can give me the details of the operation in the car."

Chapter 24

Fatigue seductively robs the body of all its physical strength, while the pain of exhaustion silently depletes all physical movement. Donna Jupiter could see the twinkling lights across the harbor from Marina Jack's restaurant and patio bar. She could also hear lilting music from a small band playing on the outside deck and carefree laughter from couples dancing next to the dock. But Donna Jupiter could no longer swim. What little strength remained no longer enabled her to raise her arms and propel her tired body forward to safety. Helpless, she clung to the Constellation's white boat fender. She was now at the mercy of the tide and prayed that she would eventually drift to shore in the dark before her strength gave out. She knew she had to be patient and let the current do its work.

Suddenly, a thunderous explosion broke the relative quiet of the harbor and an angry ball of fire lit the sky from the mooring field. Screaming erupted from the restaurant as a second explosion echoed across the bay. People panicked and ran in all directions not knowing if another explosion would engulf the harbor. Donna knew the explosion destroyed her yacht, along with her husband's body. Alone and exhausted, she cried. "Oh my God, sand," as her toes scraped the sandy bottom. Slowly she stood, and gazed up at the statuette dolphin pool in front of her. Carefully, she pulled herself up over the harbor's cement embankment, stepped to the closest bench along the walkway and sat down. Donna Jupiter leaned forward, buried her face in her lap and cried. For the first time, the full impact from the killing of her husband, her kidnapping and near drowning, consumed her. He was gone, murdered, and now his body was lost forever in the explosion. Donna's mind flooded with hundreds of unanswered questions.

"Are you alright, lady?" A quiet voice asked. Standing on the walkway was a skinny, teenage girl no older than fifteen, dressed in black. She had short, spiked, orange hair, along with two silver lip and eyebrow rings that pierced her pasty white skin. The girl appeared confused about the crying woman in front of her. Thick, black eye shadow circled her troubled, blue eyes that darted from side to side, but not focusing on any one thing. Holding a Whitey Panda skateboard under one arm, she reached out with her free hand, touched Donna on the shoulder and repeated, "Are you alright, lady?"

Dazed, Donna looked up, and still disoriented, replied, "I fell off my boat."

"Did you fall off the boat that just exploded at the mooring site?" The girl looked down and noticed the silver handcuff dangling from Donna's wrist.

"What happened over there?" Subtly, Donna covered the loose handcuff with her wet sleeve, but she sensed the girl had already spotted the metal restraint. The expression on the teenager's face gave it away. Donna smiled and nonchalantly asked, "Did you see the explosion?"

"Yes, me and my friends were skateboarding over at the children's pool. We go there almost every night to hang out and skateboard. The pool is awesome sick for railing the skateboards. Benches, curbs, low walls, half pikes, it's a stoked place to roll. The best part is after dark the place is deserted and nobody hassles us. The rain was a downer, couldn't do all the tricks. My boyfriend had a bad fall, cut his kneecap, so we just hung out. After the explosion all the skaters bailed. Didn't want the Donut shop boys arresting us for being in the park after dark. So are you gonna be cool?" Donna rolled her eyes and thought, *what ever happened to the English language, doesn't anyone teach grammar anymore*?

The girl took a step backwards and was about to turn when Donna asked, "Did you see anyone escape from the boat?"

"No, but a half an hour before a dinghy pulled up on the beach in front of O'Leary's. Why?" The girl took another half step backwards.

"Did you see who was in the dinghy?"

"A man, couldn't see his face, he was tall, had gray hair and was wearing a yellow rain slicker."

"He was the man who put these on me!" Donna cried, and held up her arm. "May I use your phone?"

"Oh shit, that's sick." The girl reached into her pocket and handed Donna her cell.

"Hello, Luna's. This is Brandy. How may I help you?"

"Hi, Brandy, this is Donna Jupiter. What, Sam has you working the phones now?"

"Oh no, I was just walking back to the kitchen when the phone rang. No one was stationed at the desk so I answered the call. Want to speak to Sam? She's here now. 'Bye." Brandy handed the phone to the owner and whispered, "It's Donna Jupiter, sounds a little stressed."

"Hi, Donna, what's up? Why didn't you call me on my cell?" Sam said, and comfortably positioned the phone under her curly blonde hair.

In the sixteen years Sam owned the Luna Restaurant on the Island in Venice, Donna had not once called her on the business line, let alone at night and during the busy diner hour. The call was out of character, and for Sam, understanding people's character was her forte. Every day, she interacted with customers and was very astute at accommodating their culinary requests. A shrewd and successful businesswoman from Connecticut, Sam had an uneasy feeling that her friend was in trouble.

"Sam, I need your help. My yacht exploded. Please pick me up at the entrance to Marina Jack. Bring some dry clothes. I'm soaking wet."

"Donna, what happened...?"

Before Sam could complete her sentence, Donna broke in and whispered, "I can't talk now, Sam. I'll explain everything when you pick me up." She hung up and handed the girl back her phone. "Thank you. By the way, what is your name?"

"My real name, or what the skaters call me?"

"Both," Donna replied before she realized what the consequences would be. A little voice inside her head reminded her of something Joey would always say, 'Donna, my sweet, be careful what you wish for. It just might come true.' Was tonight the time she would regret what she wished for? If this girl's name was anything like her conversation, Donna cringed at the thought.

"My birth name is Penelope Chavers, but my friends call me *Twilight Skater Bitch*. Because I'm so pale, people think I look like a vampire. I just have light skin and try to stay out of the sun."

"What does your mother think of your skater name?" Donna asked and slowly stood up.

"My mother is dead, killed by a drunk driver five years ago. I live with my father, Sam Chavers, on a boat at the marina. H-dock, slip #36, he's the harbormaster and I bet he's over at the fire freaking out like crazy." Penelope dropped the skateboard, stepped on it and rolled away into the darkness.

"I'm sorry. Thank you for your help, Penelope," Donna called out and started toward Marina Jack.

Chapter 25

Pulsating lights, red, blue, red, orange, and white streamed into Bayfront Park, as a cherry red Chrysler 300 turned onto Tamiami Trail and drove south. Piercing, warning blasts from the first wave of responders trumpeted across the harbor and into downtown Sarasota. A convoy of fire engines, crime scene vehicles, emergency rescue trucks, EMS vans and marked and unmarked police cars, sped past the Art Deco entrance arch, across the park lawn around the Olympic Wannabees sculpture and towards the water. A row of fire engines lined the harbor bulkhead, as hundreds of pounds of water cascaded down onto the burning yacht.

Slowly the cherry red Chrysler eased into the left lane, merged with the flow of traffic just past the outdoor sculptures along the Sarasota Bayfront, and began to distance itself from the mooring field fire.

First on the scene was Sarasota County Fire Department Public Information Coordinator, Captain Susan Pearson. Recognizing the severity of the situation, she immediately called dispatch and ordered that the fire/rescue boat docked at Mote Marine Laboratory be dispatched to the mooring field at Bayfront Park. Halfway into her message a civilian ran along the walkway frantically waving papers in the air and screaming, "Who's in charge? I need to talk to the person in charge. It's a matter of life or death."

Pearson stepped forward and blocked his path, "I am, sir, Fire Captain Susan Pearson. How can I help?"

Gasping for air, the man coughed out, "Oh, thank God. I'm Sam Chavers, the harbormaster for Marina Jack and the Bayfront Mooring Field. The yacht that's on fire, has the couple on board been rescued?"

Rescued! A sinking feeling of concern grabbed hold of Pearson and clawed at her very core. Trained to evaluate and control emergency situations, Pearson, a ten-year veteran of the Sarasota Fire Department, was no stranger to command decision situations. Immediately, she instituted ADR protocol. The three steps taught to all cadets at the academy to control a potentially dangerous situation were ADR, the acronym for assess, defuse, and restore. The primary guideline that codified every firefighter's stratagem of action.

Two months earlier, a similar situation occurred during the Halloween Haunted Trails event at Osprey State Park. While patrolling the haunted adult trail, three teenage girls, dressed as vampires, complete with blood dripping from their mouths, ran up to Pearson screaming hysterically that their friend couldn't breathe. With arms hooked, the girl in the center slumped forward, her white hair practically touching the ground; she appeared dead. "It just happened. We were walking along the path, laughing and fooling around, when all of a sudden, a chain saw zombie jumped out of the bushes scaring us half to death. We ran. Except Tanner, she just stopped, grabbed her neck and collapsed. Please help her."

Pearson pushed a clump of white hair aside, and immediately realized Tanner was not getting enough carbon dioxide into her body; she was hyperventilating. Pearson reached into her fanny pack medical kit, pulled out a brown paper bag and pushed it up to Tanner's face.

"Tanner, listen to me. I'm Captain Susan Pearson. I'm a firefighter and I want you to breathe slowly into this paper bag. This bag will help you breathe normally. Take your time. You will be fine in a few minutes. You had a bad fright. Just breathe slowly. That's right, good girl." A few minutes later, Tanner's panic attack subsided, her breathing returned to normal and she and her two vampire friends were itching to finish the fun.

Unfortunately for the three little vampires, Halloween was over.

Assistant Park Manager, Blaine Sterling, checking on all the trick-or-treaters, drove up in her Club Car and determined that Tanner be examined by the Nokomis Fire Department paramedics at the medical station setup at the Nature Center. Captain Pearson called the parents, reassured them Tanner was fine had them pick up their daughter. No other incident occurred that fright night at Osprey State Park. Pearson shook her head and shouted, "What couple?"

"Mr. and Mrs. Joey Jupiter reserved mooring number 7 for this weekend. Here, I have the paperwork Mr. Jupiter sent from Boston last month. *Knot At Home*, a 1960, fifty foot Chris-Craft Constellation cabin cruiser, a copy of the vessel registration, insurance coverage, cashier's check for security deposit, signed mooring agreement and date of arrival. Here take a look," Chavers shouted waving the papers in the air.

Captain Pearson looked down at the document and spoke into her phone, "Dispatch, I need you to notify Sarasota Police they need to get their dive team down here ASAP. We may have two bodies to recover. Also, I need the Coast Guard to put in the booms to contain any oil or gas spills, and protect the integrity of the crime scene."

Plumes of dark black smoke rose high above the tree line as Gunny accelerated, and sped past the Marie Selby Botanical Gardens and south towards Venice. "Look at that fire, Gunny. Those flames have to be forty feet high." Burkhardt exclaimed and stared out at the harbor. "That poor bastard anchored on the starboard side, sure hope he has his insurance premiums paid up."

Across from the children's pool, a battalion of firefighters concentrated on controlling the spread of the fire. A continuous spray of water directed on the burning yacht, separated from its mooring, enabled the firefighters to direct the burning hulk away from the surrounding boats. The fire boat approached from the west, positioned itself aft of the burning yacht and attacked the blaze with blasts of salt water pumped from the harbor. With each volley from the shoreline and fire vessel, the angry red flames that clawed at the night sky gradually lessened until only a plume of black smoke rose from the charred hulk floating out on the bay.

Police moved swiftly to secure the Bayfront and control the flow of traffic brought to a standstill along the harbor in front of Marina Jack. Painfully traffic congestion slowly improved as cars inched past the fire zone, crawled north beyond the John Ringling Bridge, and finally moved back-up free beyond the Sarasota Bradenton International Airport. However, the drive south along Tamiami Trail towards Osprey, Nokomis and Venice was another story. Vehicles crossing the Ringling Causeway Bridge were in full view of the pyrotechnic extravaganza unfolding on Sarasota Bay. Drivers jumped out of their cars, snapped videos of the burning vessel, their passengers, themselves, other cars, and then posted the phenomenon on YouTube. The Sarasota Bay fire went viral, over 5,000 hits the first hour, a 100,000 by the end of the night. As a result, a parade of bumper-to-bumper vehicles lined the bridge all the way back to St. Armands Circle, and southbound traffic was at a standstill from the *Unconditional Surrender* statue in front of the Fishing Fleet docks to O' Leary Tiki Bar.

"We made it out just in time Commander. Look at that parking lot behind us. Those poor bastards. It will be hours before any of those cars get home."

"It's all in the timing, Gunny. Timing is everything, one wrong move and disaster. Just like all the people behind us. They're in the wrong place at the wrong time. Now, what about our timeline! First, did you arrange for accommodations?"

"No problem Commander. Last week, I phoned Mark Floryjanski, a Venice real estate agent, told him that I was interested in renting a furnished, one bedroom apartment, on the Island of Venice. I stressed that privacy was paramount and that I only needed a three month lease." Gunny lit a cigarette, lowered the driver's side window and took a long, slow drag.

"Those damn things are going to kill you some day," Burkhardt barked out with an added tone of indignation blended into the remark.

"We all have to go sometime, Commander," laughed Gunny, as he took another drag on the cigarette.

"It may be sooner than you think Gunny, sooner than you think," Burkhardt mumbled to himself.

"So the next day, I stop by Floryjanski's office on Venice Avenue and using the bogus identification you sent me, I introduce myself as Billy Joe Conway, a cattle rancher from San Antonio, Texas here in little ol' Venice for a well-deserved vacation after rustling up a million-dollar cattle deal back in Texas. It was just like a big ass Hollywood movie. I strut in, dressed in a ten gallon hat, cowboy boots, jeans, denim shirt and leather vest, Mr. Texas cattle ranch owner. I pull out a big wad of bills, count out $6 thousand and pay in full the three-month lease. The only thing missing was a big ol' horse hitched to the parking meter out front." Gunny took a last drag from his cigarette, flicked it out the window, and smiled.

"So we're bullshitting about Texas, and cattle ranching, when out of the blue he asked me if I knew of any PGA golf courses in San Antonio. Said, he and his wife, Mary Jo, were planning a vacation to San Antonio during her school's winter break in February. She's a high school art teacher who wanted to visit and paint the Alamo and the River Walk. He was only interested in golf. I tell him....."

Before Gunny could finish his sentence, Burkhardt shouted, "Gunny, I don't give a shit about your theatrics. Where's the apartment?"

Gunny reached into the center console, sorted through a collection of papers, mints, and change and handed Burkhardt an envelope. "You don't have to get pissed. I just thought you'd like to hear how the fake I.D you supplied worked?"

"Okay, whatever." Burkhardt opened the envelope, took out a key and scanned the rental agreement. Furnished one bedroom, one bath, kitchen and living room, $2,000 a month, utilities included, paid in full. Casa Luna Apartments, 200 St. Augustine Court. "Where's St. Augustine Court?"

"It's on the Island, just as you asked, and the great part Commander, it's across the street from where I live. My place is in the historic Kentucky Military Institute Building, once the sleeping quarters and classrooms for the KMI cadets. Now it's a shopping mall on the ground floor with condominiums on second and third floors. I'm on the second floor."

"Good for you," Burkhardt snapped, and put the envelope in his pocket.

"Also Commander, you have a great Italian restaurant attached to where you're staying, Luna's. If you like Italian,

Luna Ristorante is out of this world, mouthwatering, homemade recipes that fall off the plate. My favorite is their Mombo Combo; lasagna, cannelloni, eggplant rollentini, stuffed shells and cheese ravioli, smothered in a fresh marinara sauce. Enough food for two people. If you're hungry, we could eat there after you unpack. All the clothes and equipment you requested are on the sofa in the living room."

"I don't think so, Gunny. I'm tired and have to get ready for my flight tomorrow. That reminds me, did you call the taxi for my pick-up tomorrow morning?"

"Yes, and here we are, Commander. Your apartment is on the ground floor, number 22. The entrance is behind the last two outdoor tables along the patio." Gunny pulled the car to the curb, turned off the engine and popped the trunk. Burkhardt walked back around, took out the *Storm on the Sea of Galilee*, the $10 million and closed the trunk. Gunny stuck his head out the window and shouted, "If you want breakfast tomorrow, Le Petit Bistrot, across the street has the best crepes in all of Venice. I recommend the French Breakfast, two crepes stuffed with strawberry jam, C'est magnifique."

"Thanks for the recommendation. I'll keep it in mind. See you tomorrow at the rendezvous location."

Luna's patio was filled with people eating and drinking, but no one took notice of the gray haired gentleman in a black suit, carrying a black leather art portfolio and suitcase walk into apartment 22.

Chapter 26

Sometimes the most obvious is the least observed. No one noticed the petite, middle aged woman, with dripping wet, shoulder-length brown hair, cautiously snake her way through the crowd of people gathered along the walkway. No one realized that the puddles in front of the La Barge Dock weren't from a spilled cocktail prior to boarding the party boat, rather salt water from a woman's dress when she stopped to adjust her red, Salvador Ferragamo leather belt. Not one person thought it odd or out of place, for a woman scurrying along the grass, not to be wearing shoes. After all it was Florida, people dress casually when they live, work and play in paradise. Not even the young parking valet, running through the parking lot in search of a metallic gray BMW Z3 convertible, observed the silver handcuff that dangled from the left wrist of the woman on the bench next to the entrance arch. To the casual eye, the piece could have been a new style of jewelry about to hit the market. Not a single soul noticed Donna Jupiter. All eyes were skyward towards the red flames that engulfed Sarasota's night sky.

Exhausted, cold and heartsick, Donna leaned back against the green metal bench, and gazed at the bumper-to-bumper traffic jamming up Tamiami Trail. Blame it on fatigue, maybe fear, possibly sorrow or probably the brightly colored Circus Days Ice Cream truck, but Donna Jupiter's thoughts weren't about traffic. Her pensive memories drifted back to the moment she first met her best friend, Sam.

One hot, sunny Florida day, at the Save the Venice Circus Arena Fundraiser, how could she forget? "You in line for the trapeze?" A voice asked. "It's number ten on my bucket list." Donna Jupiter turned, behind her stood a firecracker of a woman, dressed in a purple tank top and a pair of designer jeans. Her short curly blonde hair complimented her warm bright brown eyes and big welcoming smile. She exuded an endless amount of energy, contagious by proximity and association.

"Yes, I am," Donna replied and offered her hand. "Hi, I'm Donna Jupiter. By the way, what was number nine?"

"I'm Sam, pleased to meet you. Kayaking on the Myakka River, what a blast. Do you kayak?"

"I'll have to try it someday, but right now, I'm struggling to muster up enough courage to climb this rope ladder, fly out over a crowd of complete strangers, and then drop 40 feet into a net." Donna added and started to climb. "Plus, I can't believe I paid twenty dollars to maybe break my neck."

"Just remember, it's for a good cause, to help save the circus arena. Good luck." Sam genuflected and shot Donna a bodacious smile.

The circus had come to town, if only for one day. The bright sunny skies trumpeted the excitement of the joyous occasion. Passionate speeches from city officials, important dignitaries, and past circus performers spoke of the long, rich history of the circus connection to Venice. Every speaker emphasized the importance of a restored circus arena as a viable performance center, convention hall, museum, and of course, a circus venue that would boost the city's economy and unquestionably make Venice an arts and cultural destination in southwest Florida.

Then a magical celebration unfolded as circus clowns of all sizes and shapes paraded around the fairgrounds entertaining young and old alike. Their funny painted faces and outrageous costumes brought to life once again the merriment from a bygone era. Circus jugglers mesmerized crowds of people by launching bowling pins into the air, while balancing on unicycles, blindfolded. Two jugglers, dressed as pirates, hurled fiery torches over the head of a terrified volunteer, as spectators gasped in amazement.

However, the highlight of the entire Save the Venice Circus Arena fundraiser event, was the trapeze performance of aerialist Ganon Tito and students from his Trapeze School. Ganon, a former Ringling Bros. and Barnum and Bailey Circus performer, entertained the crowd with exhilarating grace and precision. Flying through the air high above the audience, his double twists, triple somersaults one knee hangs and dozens of passing leaps, hypnotized the audience with a lifetime of memories.

On that magical circus day, a bond of friendship was discovered. Two unlikely candidates, one an artist, the other a restaurateur, soared in the air and partnered one enduring bond.

"Donna, it's Sam," a voice behind the blinding headlights of a blue, Chevy Avalanche SUV called out. "Donna, wake-up, it's Sam. I'm here."

Still in a daze and unnerved by the light, Donna stood and staggered towards the voice. A bit wobbly on her feet, she stopped, held on to the end of the bench and shouted, "Is that you, Sam? I can't walk. Please help me."

Sam jumped from the truck, ran to the bench and guided her friend back to the truck. "Dry yourself off and put these dry clothes on. You'll feel a lot better as soon as you warm up. I brought a nice hot cup of soup, minestrone, your favorite." Sam waited for a break in traffic, then eased the truck into the right hand lane and joined the bumper-to-bumper parade. No one spoke, but Sam kept a watchful eye on her friend and the stop-and-go traffic moving painfully towards Venice.

A few minutes later, warm and dry and soothed by the minestrone, Donna Jupiter began to talk. She outlined how she came into possession of the *Storm on the Sea of Galilee* painting, stolen from the Isabella Stewart Gardner Museum in Boston. Detailed the circumstances how she and Joey were offered $10 million dollars for the painting from a Boston Antique dealer, which was actually FBI agent Ross Burkhardt. Also offered a timeline of when Burkhart shot her husband, stole the painting and the money, and then kidnapped her. Finally, with tears rolling down her cheeks, she sobbed out how she escaped from the yacht, the wrenching description of her husband's body on the yacht, and then witnessing the yacht exploding with her dead husband on board. But the most chilling revelation, said in only a whisper, was the threat

Burkhardt shouted before he blew up the yacht. "He threatened to kill me if I went to the police."

"Donna, I am so sorry. I am numb with grief. Your loss is beyond words. This monster has to be stopped. You must go to the police. Don't you have a detective friend in the Venice Police Department?"

"I can't. Burkhardt said he'd kill me if I notified the authorities. Plus, I was in possession of a stolen painting. I just don't know, maybe I could be sent to jail? I need time to think." Donna turned away, gazed out the window and cried.

"I don't think you should go home tonight," Sam added. "That maniac could be lurking about your property, waiting for the opportunity to put a bullet in your head. I have to get back to Luna's tonight. You can stay in one of my apartments next to the restaurant. I only have one renter now, he's in apartment 22 on the first floor. You can have the upstairs apartment. You'll be safe there."

Donna turned, held up her left arm, and with a slight smile, "What about this silver, bangle bracelet? I can't be walking around St. Armands Circle, or shopping at Southgate Mall, or having lunch at your restaurant, with handcuffs dangling from my wrist?"

"I have a locksmith friend who should extricate you from your bonds, fair maiden. Tomorrow morning we'll visit his shop. I must warn you, he is strange, but a damn good locksmith." Sam winked and gave Donna one of her get ready to be scared out of your life smile.

"Weird, what kind of weird?"

"Like vampire weird," Sam added sarcastically.

At that exact moment, a silver Ford Expedition cut in front of Sam missing her front bumper by inches. Sam jammed on the brakes, causing the two of them to jerk forward practically smacking their heads into the windshield. Sam pounded on the horn and screamed, "What is that guy thinking? We're only moving, at the most, ten miles an hour, and that moron cuts me off to squeeze into the right-hand lane. What, he thinks this lane will miraculously speed up?"

"What a jerk," Donna added. "Why don't you smash into him and teach that moron a lesson. Some people believe because they're driving a humongous SUV, they're entitled to drive anywhere or anyway they like. Remember your accident on the Jacaranda roundabout? That's the reason your husband insisted you buy the Avalanche, after some lady driving a humongous Expedition entered the roundabout and smashed into your Honda Civic. She didn't care that you were already in the roundabout. She was in a hurry."

"How could I forget? I was in Venice Hospital for a week with a broken leg, two cracked ribs and a ruptured spleen. It took the fire department thirty minutes, using the Jaws of Life, to cut me out of the car. I'm lucky to be alive today. Plus, I don't think getting into a fender-bender right now would be a good idea, especially after what you've been through."

"The lady that smashed into your car, wasn't she driving a silver Expedition?" Donna added in a bitter tone. "The bitch was late for a happy hour at the Allegro Bistro. You needed to drop off payroll for your other restaurant at Jacaranda Plaza and happened to be in her way. Yes, I'm sure it was an Expedition."

"You're right, a silver Expedition," Sam replied and slowed down to distance her car from the silver Expedition.

"Sam, it could be the same guy, or should I say, the same lady. Yeah, I think the driver has long hair. Just smash into her, you'll feel a hell of a lot better. And it will add closure to the roundabout accident and the just now being cut-off episode."

"That's not a good idea, Donna. Anyway, it's a guy and he's turning into Best Buy. Probably to pick up a forward collision avoidance system for his Expedition so not to smash into to other cars. Sorry to ruin your fun, but I believe you've had enough excitement for one day?"

"We could only hope. More than likely, he'll be picking up a new smartphone, so he can text and drive at the same time." Donna leaned back against the plush leather seat, and closed her eyes.

Thirty minutes later Sam pulled up in front of Luna's Restaurant. "Give me a minute to get the key and then we'll get you settled." Sam jumped down from the truck and walked inside.

The upstairs apartment was spacious and contained every convenience a wintering snowbird guest demanded. Custom designed furniture, modern kitchen with every imaginable appliance, two bedrooms designed with a beach-chic flare, and an antique claw foot bathtub big enough to accommodate three, that Sam immediately started to fill. "What you need is a nice hot bath and a good night's sleep. I'll send up some dinner and see you in the morning. There are some clothes in the closet, a little something I picked up at Sun Bug, while shopping last week in Venice. I believe we're the same size?" She added with a laugh. "I left my cell phone on the night stand next to the bed, just in case you need to call the police for any reason. See you in the morning." They hugged, and Sam left.

The bath was therapeutic, not only did the hot water wash away the caked on salt and dirt from the Bay, but the circulating bubbles massaged the aches and pains that hurt inside and out. Exhausted, Donna walked into the bedroom, crawled under the covers, and fell asleep. The knock on the door went unanswered.

Chapter 27

Angie Stomp was absent from school. A single, yellow banana sat on her desk, uneaten. Everyone else in the class, including Mrs. Cordas, finished their banana Brooke handed out for snack. Everyone, except Angie, who was never absent. Rain or shine, sick or not, Angie rode the bus to school. And every day, without fail, she would tease a little girl, or little boy. Big, mean and loud, Angie was the class bully.

Last month during recess, Angie pushed Ann Harris, a petite first grader, off the playground swing. Ann tumbled forward, put out her hands to break the fall, and in the process broke her right wrist. Angie's parents were called to school, and for the first time in the history of Venice Center Elementary School, a second grade student was suspended.

"Today, of all days for Angie to be absent," Brooke thought, as she cradled her yellow mobile home project, and waited for her turn to present her report. The entire *Banana Girl Project*, which Mrs. Brecht devised, was targeted to teach Angie Stomp a lesson about bullying. Brooke's colorful banana T-shirts, the healthy banana for snack, along with her banana yellow mobile home shelter project, were designed to illustrate how name calling was wrong and should not be tolerated. Mrs. Brecht's scheme was to have Brooke make light of the bullying on the playground about bananas, and demonstrate that bananas are cool, healthy and make great T-shirts. Plus, living in a temporary banana yellow mobile home is an acceptable form of shelter, and a perfect example for the social studies project Mrs. Cordas assigned.

Only two students remained to share their reports, Melvin Zoomas, the class brainiac and Brooke. Melvin was always last. Last to line up for lunch, last to be dismissed, last to have his hearing checked or last to be selected for dodge ball. Except today, Brooke's mom arranged with Mrs. Cordas to have Brooke present her report last. They felt that the impact would be most lasting if the reports ended with Brooke's.

"Melvin, would you please come up and share your report on Egyptian pyramids," Mrs. Cordas requested and put a check mark alongside his name on her grading sheet she held in her hand.

Startled by the sudden modification of sequence, Melvin, pushed his thick, black rimmed glasses up against his face, raised his hand and called out, "What about Brooke? She didn't go yet."

"Yes, I know, Melvin, but today Brooke will go last," Mrs. Cordas replied tersely, gave Brooke a fleeting glance and winked.

Model pyramid in hand, a thick folder of papers under his arm, Melvin Zoomas, not last, triumphantly marched to the front of the room, to share his report on the ancient Egyptians and the construction of the pyramids. His model pyramid, made out of hundreds of sugar cubes, showed numerous passageways and the burial chambers of the pharaoh and queen. His demonstration how the stone chamber door was sealed, so grave robbers couldn't steal the contents within the tomb, was mesmerizing. He explained how the stone doors were held up by a cylinder of sand, and when the pyramid was completed, a stone block was dropped down the shaft, breaking the wooden plugs that held the sand that supported the entrance door. When broken, the sand ran out the bottom of the cylinder lowering the stone door down to the floor of the chamber. Melvin dropped a sugar cube down the shaft. Sand flowed out a hole at the bottom as the sugar cube slid down and blocked the entrance to the burial chamber.

Every one clapped and cheered at the end of the pyramid demonstration. A big smile lit up Melvin's face and he beamed with joy. Not only was his report a huge success, but for the first time, he wasn't last. Maybe his luck had changed. Maybe after today he would never be called, "Last Melvin."

Poor Melvin, his good fortune had not changed, and his moment of glory was but only a fleeting memory. Suddenly, the classroom door opened and Nurse Betty and Angie Stomp stood in the entranceway. The clapping stopped. All eyes were on the doorway. The silence was painfully deafening.

Mrs. Cordas saved the day. "Thank you, Melvin, your report was very exciting. Please take your seat now." Melvin quickly gathered up his project and scurried to his seat in the back of the room.

"Good morning, class, I'm sorry for the interruption, but as you, can see Angie has had an accident and I thought I'd escort her to class today." Angie stood quietly next to the nurse and didn't move. With two crutches hooked under both arms, her body tilted forward, Angie looked straight ahead. She appeared pained, and the awkward stance made her features look tired and vulnerable. Her right leg had a cast up to her calf.

"Angie broke her ankle yesterday. It was a serious break and she will have a cast on her right leg for the next six weeks. It will be difficult for her walk, so she will need a buddy to help her get around the school. Someone to open the door for her, hold her books, help her sit down, but most importantly, she will need a friend to protect her from being knocked down. Who would like to be Angie's buddy?" No one raised their hand.

"How did Angie break her ankle, Nurse Betty?" Sydney Belcher called out with a mischievous smile on his face, and both hands in his pockets.

"I think I'll let Angie explain, but first I want her to take a seat. She can't be standing for long periods of time." Carefully, Nurse Betty guided her back to her seat, and placed the crutches up against the wall next to her desk. "Comfortable?"

"Yes," replied Angie and grimaced when she inched back in the seat.

"I'll be leaving now, class. Mrs. Cordas, I'll meet with you later to review Angie's injury report, but children, please remember not to bump or knock against Angie's cast, or Angie for that matter. And please, Mrs. Cordas, assign a buddy for Angie. She will need someone to help guide her from class to class for the next six weeks while her ankle is healing." Nurse Betty left.

"So, Angie, please tell the class how you broke your ankle?" Mrs. Cordas asked.

"Yesterday, after school I was swimming in my pool, when my dog Buddy, picked up my headphones for my MP3 player and ran off with them. I jumped out of the pool and tried to kick him as he ran past me. I missed, slipped on the pool deck, and fell backwards onto the tile pavers." Angie's voice trailed off, and in a faraway tone, almost inaudible continued, "I heard a loud snap, like a branch breaking, and then felt terrible pain."

"Nice yellow cast, Angie, can I sign it?" Sydney called out from the back of the room along with his signature mischievous grin.

"Maybe later, Sydney, but right now Brooke needs to present her shelter report." Mrs. Cordas picked up her grading sheet, put a check mark next to Brooke's name and circled yellow mobile home. She smiled as Brooke slowly strode to the front of the room, wearing her black Banana Girl shirt for Angie to see, and holding her banana yellow mobile home project with both hands.

For the next five minutes Brooke talked about the fire that destroyed her home, the police search for the fire bomber, and the importance of mobile homes across the United States. Brooke ended her speech with the joyous announcement that she will be moving out of the yellow mobile home and into her repaired home in a few days. Everyone clapped. Finally, Brooke brought out the model yellow mobile home and methodically described each room, highlighting all of the included amenities. When Brooke pointed to the drawing of a 60" television in the living room and stated that all Joey Banana's yellow mobile homes have them, the class went bananas. An uproar of crazy screaming children, demanding a yellow mobile home, echoed throughout the classroom and down the hallway.

It took Mrs. Cordas a few minutes to quiet everyone down before Brooke could answer any questions. Unquestionably, ninety-eight percent of all questions were about the 60" television, and what was the telephone number for Joey Banana Trailers?

"Thank you, Brooke, your report was excellent. Also, thank you for providing a delicious banana for snack, which I see

Angie is eating now. Brooke, would you kindly turn around so the class can read what is written on the back of your T-shirt."

Brooke turned around. "Angie, would you please read what is printed on Brooke's shirt," Mrs. Cordas instructed.

Angie swallowed the last of her banana, and read, "A banana a day keeps the doctor away."

"Thank you, Angie," Mrs. Cordas said. "Does anyone know what that means? A banana a day keeps the doctor away?"

Ivy Cricket was the first to raise her hand. Ivy never volunteered. Ivy rarely talked in class, and did so, only when called upon by the teacher. For Ivy to raise her hand and initiate conversation was momentous. Every student froze and stared in disbelief at what had just transpired.

Pointing to the first seat, in the first row, in front of the teacher's desk, Mrs. Cordas triumphantly said, "Ivy, please tell the class what the saying on Brooke's shirt means."

"It means if you eat a banana you will be healthy, and won't have to go to the doctor. A banana is loaded with potassium, a vitamin that helps lower blood pressure, reduces strokes, prevents heart disease, helps eyesight, and keeps bones strong. Bananas rock."

"Very good, Ivy, bananas are important for a healthy diet and everyone should appreciate their benefits. I guess you could say, *bananas rock*! They certainly form a strong foundation for healthy living. By the way, Ivy, how do you know so much about bananas?"

"My mother is a doctor, and we eat a banana every morning with breakfast," Ivy chuckled with an impish glint her eye.

The rest of the day passed quickly, and without incident. Everyone signed Angie's yellow cast in black magic marker, after Mrs. Cordas cautioned that any mean spirited remarks would be erased and the perpetrator would lose recess time. Every saying was positive, and the entire class enjoyed a playful recess, except Angie who had to sit on the bench and watch.

When the class returned from reccss, Mrs. Cordas posted the rotating schedule, in reverse alphabetical order, to be Angie's classroom buddy. Melvin Zoomas almost fell out of his seat when the schedule was read. Immediately, he high-fived the air, smiled, and gave Mrs. Cordas a big thumbs-up. What a day he thought, "*The class bully broke her ankle, Ivy Cricket spoke, and Melvin Zoomas is finally first.*"

Brooke was about to step onto her bus when something pulled back on her arm. Brooke turned and saw Angie standing right behind her. Surprised, because Angie rode a different bus, Brooke's initial reaction was to defend herself. "No wait, she just wanted to give you something," a voice shouted. Melvin, Angie's bus buddy, stepped forward and handed Brooke a folded piece of paper. "It's a note from Angie, she wanted you to have it before you went home today."

Melvin helped Angie turn around and they walked back to their bus.

Brooke sat in her seat, unfolded the note, and read.

Dear Brooke,
I am sorry for making fun of you, and calling you banana girl. I won't do it again. Can we be friends? I would like to come over to your house and watch television. With my cast I can't go outside and play.
Your friend,
Angie

The school bus stopped in front of the yellow mobile home, the door opened, and out tumbled Brooke playfully singing all the way up the steps. In the doorway, Mrs. Brecht waited breathlessly for the day's classroom report. The big smile on Brooke's face added an immense sigh of relief to the babysitter's heart, and the extra skip in her step answered the question before it was asked. "So Brooke, how was your day?" asked Mrs. Brecht, as they walked into the kitchen.

"It was great. Everything went just as you planned." Brooke chirped and handed Mrs. Brecht the note.

"Oh, Brooke, I am so pleased, and now you have a new friend. Your mother called a little while ago. She will be so relieved. Let's call her now."

126

Chapter 28

The caller said, "Be patient," and hung up. Thor lowered the flame on the last lantern ever so slightly. Carefully, in faint light, he climbed the stone steps, repeatedly brushing up against the dirt wall for orientation and added support. Finally, squeezing through the rock entrance, Thor, blinded by sunlight stumbled, forward face first to the ground, barely missing the painful thorns of a Saw Palmetto Palm. Regaining his composure, he picked himself up, walked over to a bench along the pathway and sat down.

Thor was immediately drawn to the lake, everyone was. The crystal, clear blue- green water looked so peaceful and inviting, it was impossible not to marvel at its beauty. Lush green water plants surrounded the border of the lake, while the sandy white beach invited afternoon swimmers to enjoy a refreshing dip. *"A water paradise in the center of the park,"* Thor mused. A splash at the far end of the lake caught Thor's attention as he watched the ripples slowly move across the water. His father's advice for patience and a story he heard as a boy, flashed through his mind as the last ripple of water touched the bank.

It was late afternoon and the sun beat down mercilessly. Behind the bulrushes, motionless, two yellow/green eyes watched. Not a twitch, as a dragonfly buzzed overhead and landed on a cattail leaf. A splash broke the silence and sent vibrations rippling out in circles. A gush of water brushed over his nose while the splashing continued. Hidden behind pond reeds, the hunter patiently waited.

Days passed, and again the late afternoon heat was unbearable. The sun baked the earth a scorched, parched brown. A splash pierced the silence of the pond and pushed ripples of water to the edge of the reeds. A stream of water

127

brushed over his head, and back into the reeds, while the splashing continued. Stealthily, the hunter drifted closer to the front of the pond reeds and patiently waited.

On the third week, without a cloud in the sky all day, the late afternoon sun burned the hottest. The temperature reached a blistering 96 degrees. A splash cut the silence of the pond, and sent vibrations across the water. The stream of water brushed over his entire body. This day the hunter was waiting on the forward edge of the pond reeds. He submerged and glided silently towards the splash. In one powerful movement the splashing stopped, and silence again returned to the pond.

A chill ran down Thor's spine. He shook his head and instantly fixated on a small white sign next to the steps that lead down to the lake, *Beware of Alligators.* "Enough daydreaming," he added out loud, "I have to see Uncle Roy." He stood and followed the path behind the Nature Center to the yellow construction trailer.

"Hi, Uncle Roy, you wanted to see me," Thor announced and pushed open the trailer door.

"Yes, please take a seat." Boltier pointed to the folding chair in front of his desk. "The police were here a few hours ago and wanted to know who was calling Union Correctional?"

"What, how do they know that?" Thor blurted out.

"They seem to know a lot. Traced a stolen phone to the penitentiary, which they believe your father bought with money you gave him before Christmas. They traced a call from a *No Name* cell phone bought at Publix to Union Correctional. And yesterday, a call from the park, on the same cell phone, to the prison."

"That's bullshit. They can't do that, no way," Thor screamed.

"Plus they have pictures of the guy who firebombed Sterling's house and his vehicle. The pictures are surveillance camera pictures, not clear at all, but I get the impression they think you're the firebomber, and the pictured vehicle, they believe is a Hummer. You own a Hummer."

"A million people own Hummers. How can they pin this on me?"

Boltier reached into his desk, took out an envelope and handed it to Thor. "I want you to take this and go back to college. I don't know if you made the calls or not. I don't want to know. You did a great job and I'm grateful, but I can't afford having the cops around."

"Do they know I'm working here?" Thor stood up, put the envelope in his pocket and looked at his uncle.

"As far as anyone is concerned, you never worked here. You were not on the payroll, not on the books, no you were never here, period." They shook hands and Thor opened the door. "Say hello to your father for me."

Thor closed the yellow door, but he wasn't leaving for college, not just yet.

Chapter 29

The FBI's Gulfstream 450 luxury jet, N4718C, taxied onto runway 23, and sat second in the queue for take-off from Logan's International Airport. Air traffic control confirmed their flight plan into Venice Municipal Airport, Florida, filed weeks ago from FBI headquarters in Boston. Pilot-in-command Hal Hollister made a last minute check of the flight deck, while co-pilot, Kent Burns, loaded the GPS overlay approach to KVNC (Venice Airport) into the navigator. Captain Hollister, a ten-year veteran pilot with the FBI, knew the takeoff drill by heart: *hurry-up and wait*. Burns, on the other hand, was new to the company and was going through his three-page procedural checklist. Recently back from a three-year tour in Afghanistan flying Harrier Jets off aircraft carriers, this was his second assignment in a Gulfstream 450 and his first flight with Captain Hollister.

At 6:10 a.m. in the morning, air traffic control radioed, "Gulfstream N4718C clear for take-off on Runway 23." The twin turbo Rolls-Royce engines came to life, lift-off was smooth and uneventful, just the way Hollister liked it. Twenty minutes later, they leveled out at 35,000 feet and with a cruise speed of 450 knots, passed over New York City. Clear skies all the way to Tampa were forecast, however south of Tampa, the weather changed dramatically. A cold front was stalled over Venice, Florida, and reports of widespread fog were predicted. Burns switched on the auto-pilot, and he and Hollister sat back to enjoy the three-hour run to Venice.

"So, Captain, do you know FBI Agent Burkhardt?" Burns asked, and gulped down the last of his coffee. "What exactly are we picking up in Venice? The rebound manifest states two passengers, painting and currency."

"I sure do. While you were on vacation last month in sunny Mexico, I flew Agent Burkhardt to Germany, ice cold, snowy Germany. I shiver just thinking about that flight."

"Germany? What was the FBI doing in Germany?"

"Burkhardt was investigating a connection with the Boston's Isabella Stewart Gardner Museum robbery (which he is in charge of) and the discovery of 1,500 works of art confiscated by the Nazis during World War II that German authorities recently found in Berlin."

"Connection, what connection? We're talking about a sixty-year difference and two different continents." Burns scoffed, and checked the SVT symbols, all controls were bright and in synch with the flight plan. All systems looked good to go.

"In his investigation, Burkhardt heard suggestions that some of the museum's stolen artwork was sold to an art dealer in Europe. He was sent to examine the German collection and determine if Cornelius Gurlitt, the eighty-year-old son of a Nazi art dealer, had any works from the Gardner Museum."

At 6:52 a.m. the aircraft entered Delaware airspace. Burns contacted Delaware air traffic controllers, was informed to move to 45,000 altitude, and that they were on schedule to approach Charlotte at approximately 7:34 a.m. in the morning.

"So did Burkhardt find any of the paintings from the Gardner Museum?"

"No, but he said Gurlitt's apartment was an unbelievable treasure-trove of artwork. Paintings from Rodin, Picasso, Matisse, Chagall, and other famous artists covered every wall, table and floor space in his tiny four room apartment." Hollister radioed Charlotte for a weather update. Forecast was the same, clear to Tampa; at Venice fog set in and visibility was poor.

"Sounds like that trip was a waste of time," added Burns.

"Not really, Burkhardt is a pilot. He's been flying for years, even has his own plane, a 2014 Cessna Turbo Skylane." Hollister answered with a big smile. "That's a $530,000 flying machine, son."

"Wow, that's some kind of plane. Where did he come up with that kind of money on an agent's salary?"

"Don't know, and I didn't ask, but what I do know is that he flew the Gulfstream back from Germany like a pro. Handled the controls flawlessly, was familiar with the integrated avionics suite, needed some assistance with the cursor control system and the enhanced vision system, but he flew for six hours straight. Gave me a big rest."

"Maybe I'll ask him to fly us back to Boston. I could use a couple hours nap time before we land. How does that sound, Captain?" Burns leaned back in his chair, closed his eyes and pretended to sleep.

"I wouldn't mess with him if I were you. Rumor has it he killed a man in the Bahamas. Beat him to death." Hollister reached over, took the young co-pilot's arm. "This man has a very short fuse."

"Beat a man to death, why did he do that?"

"The guy killed his wife. He was drunk and smashed his yacht into the ferry Burkhardt and his wife were in. She died instantly and he never got over her death. They were on their honeymoon. The guy was convicted of murder, sent to prison, and one night he was found beaten to death. Bahamian officials reported that it was a jailhouse fight, but word inside the Bureau was Burkhardt did it." Hollister looked down at the avionics panel display suite as they passed over Charlotte, North Carolina and headed south towards Jacksonville. "Right on schedule, should reach Jacksonville around eight o'clock."

"Thanks for the heads-up. I'll be on my best behavior, mi Capitan, wouldn't want any fireworks exploding in this new plane." Burns looked down at his checklist. "So now, what's so important about this pick-up in Venice? Why the big show with this new Gulfstream 450?"

The plane was the latest edition to the stable of corporate jets the FBI operated globally, the $39 million 2015 Gulfstream 450 was put in service to make a strong public statement: *FBI solves Boston's Isabella Stewart Gardner Museum Heist.*

The aircraft embraced every aspect of luxury and comfort, plus an added FBI seat adaptation for secure prisoner transfers. The spacious thirteen passenger cabin contained sculptured leather seats, with a four person conference group arrangement and a three person divan. A fully equipped forward galley, state-of-the-art communications, with internet accessibility and entertainment connectivity provisions rounded out the features.

The four aft seats were equipped with security modifications that electronically activated the two metal arm restraints, hidden under the side leather panels which could be remotely engaged to restrain a convict during an arrest flight. Flight N4718C was just such a flight, and the infamous passenger was none other than Mr. Joseph Jupiter, a.k.a. Joey Banana. This Gulfstream 450 was going to present the backdrop for the culmination of a twenty-three-year worldwide investigation and recovery of the $500 million in stolen artworks from the Isabella Stewart Gardner Museum. A national press conference, including the FBI Director, a delegation from the museum, and representatives from Boston's FBI, Boston's mayor, and every national reporting agency were scheduled to meet the returning flight at Logan International Airport.

"Code One priority, you'll figure it out when we land at Logan. That's all I can tell you."

After a cup of coffee, black, no sugar, one pit-stop to the head, the Gulfstream flew over Jacksonville, where Hollister received final flight instructions from Tampa International and initiated the descent into Venice. Ten miles out from Venice Airport, with visibility less than a quarter mile, Hollister switched off the auto-pilot and took control of the aircraft. The enhanced vision system displayed a picture of runway 4, while the voice simulator delineated the approach landing space to touchdown. Hollister followed the prompts, 500 feet, 400, 300, 200, 100, landing complete. The Gulfstream taxied towards the main terminal and was flagged to a secluded area north of the terminal where the two pilots completed the shutdown checklist.

Hollister took out his phone, "It's 9:35 a.m. The eagle has landed, waiting for package to arrive."

Chapter 30

Sea fog pushed up from the Gulf, crawled past the sands and blanketed the island of Venice with a cold, damp mist. Everything in its path was hidden under a shroud of gray. An eerie stillness filled the air. The only discernable sound was a hypnotic drip from the fountain in front of Luna's Restaurant as each droplet splashed against the puddled rocks and echoed across the courtyard.

Burkhardt stood on the sidewalk in front of Casa Luna Apartments. Dressed in his black Armani suit, pink shirt, burgundy tie and walnut Oxfords, he held in his left hand a dark brown Claire Chase carry-on suitcase, filled with shredded newspaper and one-million dollars in cash. Resting against his right leg was the empty black leather art portfolio case. Burkhardt checked his watch it was eight thirty-five. "Where is that taxi?" He mumbled, "It should be here by now."

Burkhardt stared into the haze, no taxi, only the pale outline of a fountain and the haunting sound of water falling against pebbled rocks. He thought he heard another sound, a soft metallic ping against stone. Slowly, Burkhardt cocked his head, closed his eyes and listened. Water splashing against rocks was the prominent noise, but in the background, he thought he recognized the faraway sound of a single tap of metal. He steadied himself against the handle of his suitcase and shivered. That soft, rusty metallic sound was part of a tormenting memory, one that chased him from the mist of Vietnam, and reared its ugly head deep within his conscience.

Burkhardt had just flown a squad of fourteen Green Berets to a small village deep within the jungle north of Saigon. Headquarters received information that a farming village housed a large cache of weapons and explosives for the Viet Cong, and in two days, the enemy was planning a major offensive in the South. An elite Special Operations Team was deployed to search and destroy that large supply of lethal hardware. For his own safety the Berets gave Burkhardt an M-16 rifle and took him with them to the village. He was instructed to remain by the town fountain and wait.

The eerie silence of the morning was shattered by loud screams, American commands, and then the endless sound of gunfire beyond the haze of the village. Burkhardt jumped to his feet, picked up the M-16, and stared into the mist. Waiting for what seemed a lifetime, he scanned the perimeter of the courtyard, moving the M-16 back and forth, anticipating an onslaught of Viet Cong from behind the gray mist. Suddenly, he heard a metallic sound from behind the fountain and instinctively fired round after round towards the sound. Burkhardt took a deep breath, held the rifle close to his chest, and guardedly inched his way to the back of the fountain. Frozen he looked down at the blood puddled around the lifeless body of a young girl. No older than six, her bullet riddled body lay curled up against the back of the fountain. A small metal pail, half full of water, sat on a stone next to her tiny hand. Burkhardt studied the child with detached indifference, *collateral damage he tried to tell himself*, and turned away.

Five minutes later, the Special Operations Team was airborne and headed back to Saigon, while the village with its cache of arms and ammunition were in flames.

"Taxi, sir, did you call for a taxi?" A voice called out from inside the yellow cab standing at the curb. Burkhardt looked down, composed himself and climbed into the back seat. The cab pushed through the fog and headed for the Venice Municipal Airport. Burkhardt took out his phone.

Chapter 31

B*illy Goat* slowly pushed back from slip #18 at 7:10 in the morning. With stern and bow lines neatly coiled on deck, the twin 454 hp MerCruisers effortlessly pulled the Bertram 38 into the channel. Gunny eased the port throttle forward, the yacht came about, drifted forward and came to a complete stop facing the breakwater. He lit a cigarette, the third that morning. A nagging cough that showed up a week ago broke the silence of the water. *Maybe I should pick up some cough medicine*, he thought and flicked the cigarette into the water. Looking back over his shoulder through the wet gray mist, Gunny spotted the silhouette of The Crabby pushing water towards the Crow's Nest gas dock. The washed out blue and white, 43-foot hulk of a crab boat, loaded down with empty traps stacked shoulder high on the deck, lumbered to a halt against the wood pylons. Captain Dill "Stoney" Monday, was a legend along the southern gulf coast. A fifth generation crabber, Stoney started crabbing at thirteen on his father's boat, the "Missy May," more than fifty years ago. If Stoney wasn't crabbing, he was fishing, and if he wasn't fishing, he was making repairs on his crab boat. "It's in the blood," Stoney would always say when asked about why he worked the water. "I learned to mend a net when I was ten. Began commercial fishing at fourteen, and I now make a living catching stone crabs. Wouldn't do nothin' else."

Stoney was a gifted storyteller, and as always with fishing, there inevitably were stories. Last week, Gunny was down at the North Jetty Fish Camp, the local hang-out for Stoney and his fishing buddies. Someone asked Stoney if he had ever fished for grouper. Well, that was the invitation Stoney always loved to hear. Ask a question and Stoney could weave a yarn, as fancy and magical as a Walt Disney movie on a Saturday night.

"Ain't nothin' I haven't fished for," Stoney declared, and slapped his signature camouflage cap against his leg. Without a hat, his thick gray hair and bushy gray moustache revealed pale blue eyes that lit up every time he started a story. "Around 1998, me and Deputy Dan were fishing the Middle Grounds, just west of Anna Maria Island. We were fishing for grouper. We'd bait three thousand hooks, string out our lines in the early morning and start pulling in the afternoon. So we needed a lot of bait for them hooks. One night we were pulling up our line, no grouper, only a bull shark, about eleven feet long, and three hundred pounds of pure meanness. We couldn't lift him onto the boat, too heavy and too dangerous. Deputy Dan shot him in the head twice with a twenty-two rifle that only stunned the beast. We then looped a line around its tail and head, stretched the rope tight and tied it off to a cleat. I jumped in the water with only a big ole fish saw and sawed that shark in half. It took me thirty minutes to cut that monster in half. My arm near fell off, but we had a day's worth of fresh shark bait. That was the best fishing trip all season. We hauled in $5,000 worth of grouper and I got a great fish story to add to my repertoire."

Gunny pushed on the throttle and eased the Bertram along the channel past the North Fish Camp. He wondered if Stoney would be regaling all the regulars and tourists with another *fish story* in the afternoon. Unfortunately for Gunnery Sergeant John Mousser, he would have to miss the camaraderie at that very special place. Today, he was on a mission: to pick up Major Ross Burkhardt.

Two fishing boats emerged from the dark and docked at the Fish Camp to pick up bait and coffee. Sunrise was an hour away as the *Billy Goat* plowed through the Venice Harbor breakwater and entered the Gulf of Mexico. The Bertram cut northward through a blanket of fog that immediately enveloped the entire vessel in a sea of gray. Water droplets covered the windows. Gunny flipped on the windshield wipers, but it was still impossible to see past the bow of the boat. "Thank god for this navigation package," he mumbled, "I can't see a damn thing," and punched in the coordinates into the GPS/ Auto Plotter. He powered up the Bertram to cruising speed and sat back in the captain's chair with eyes glued to the radar screen.

The sound of bells, whistles and an occasional motor going by echoed through the misty fog. Infrequent dots on the radar screen indicated a boat passed within 1/8 of a mile of the *Billy Goat*, a ghost ship pushing through the mist. Gunny scanned the waters almost expecting to see a pirate flag and skeletons hanging from the riggings of a passing boat. No such luck, only an empty gray canvas painted with raindrops and an eerie haze blanketed the morning.

An hour later, sunrise burnt through the fog as the *Billy Goat* motored past Longboat Key and its necklace of sandy white shoreline. Bright blue skies, white billowy, cumulus nimbus clouds and aqua green waters greeted mariners with a kiss of good weather. A welcomed relief from the suffocating fog earlier in the morning. Mousser pushed open the port window, breathed in the fresh sea air and scanned the horizon. A school of dolphins raced along the port side, jumping and flipping over the boat's wake, and then disappearing under the wave froth, only to suddenly pop up ten feet beyond the boat. Their acrobatics resembled the dolphin show performed at Sea World in Orlando, only this time in the open sea and free.

Gunny's phone rang, pulling him back to reality, and chasing the dolphins back into the deeps. "Hello."

"Gunny, this is Burkhardt. Where are you?"

"I'm passing Longboat Key, right on schedule and should reach rendezvous position, hold on a minute." Gunny looked down at the chart plotter. "Yeah, should be anchored outside our planned rendezvous location, at 9:55 a.m. Commander."

"I'm running late. I'll call you before I board the plane," Burkhardt snapped angrily into the phone.

"No problem, Commander. I'll be there. By the way, you should have seen the school of dolphins swimming along the *Billy Goat*. The way those beauties were leaping through the water you'd think they were auditioning for a position at Sea World."

"Listen, Gunny, I don't give a damn about acrobatic dolphins, or Sea World. All I care about is you plucking me out of the Gulf before hypothermia sets in. Right now the water temperature is about fifty-five degrees. I can't remain in the water for more than twenty minutes. So what I want you to do is concentrate on spotting the jet, and me treading water, not dolphins. Understand!" Burkhardt barked and hung up.

Gunny glanced at the instrument console again, checked the autopilot, lit a cigarette and gazed out the window searching for dolphins.

Chapter 32

Things that go bump in the night make for a terrible night's sleep. "Good morning, Donna, I'm downstairs in the kitchen preparing a tasty little treat for breakfast, your favorite, Spanish omelets. Hurry and get dressed. Everything will be ready in five minutes." Sam plated the omelets and delicately arranged slices of cantaloupe, grapes and strawberries on the opposite side of the dish. The small, round table in the bar was set for two. Five minutes later Donna walked into the bar area and waved to Sam.

"Hi, how did you sleep last night?" Sam asked, and welcomed Donna over to the table.

"Frightfully, is there another tenant upstairs?" Donna moaned and rubbed her half-opened eyes, red and puffy from lack of sleep.

"No, just you, why do you ask?"

Donna took a quick sip of orange juice, and said, "There were sounds of furniture being moved all night long, tables or chairs scraping back and forth across the wooden floor for hours. It wasn't until about four in the morning that everything quieted and I finally fell asleep."

"Oh, Donna, I'm so sorry, but I guess I forgot to mention that these two buildings are haunted! That is, if you believe in ghosts?" Sam added. "Kim Cool, a noted Florida author from Venice, in her book, *Ghost Stories of Venice*, writes about the haunting of Luna's Restaurant. She chronicled places, people and times that unexplained paranormal activity occurred." Sam cut into her omelet.

"Well, I know what I heard, and it sounded like furniture moving around the room." Donna took a bite. "This omelet is delicious. The chorizo gives it a spicy kick and the eggs are so light. I feel a little better today thanks to you. You're the best friend anyone could possibly want."

"Not bad if I don't say so myself, and the melon is so sweet. I picked up the fruit Saturday morning from the Venice Farmer's Market. They have the freshest produce around." Sam took a forkful of melon and smiled. "As I was saying, the restaurant has a haunted history. The two buildings, over the years housed, a garden tea room, beauty parlor, drugstore and two restaurants before mine. Actually, the area in front of the bar was where the set-up table stood for all the sandwiches, scones, cakes, and imported teas when this building was the Garden Tea Room. If you look closely you can see one of the brass bolts that anchored the ill-fated, wrought iron table to the floor. Rumor has it that a server, dressed in an exquisite period costume, while lighting a table candle, set her clothing on fire. Her burns were so severe that she passed away a week later in the apartment where you are staying. Maybe you heard the server setting tables for the four o'clock tea?"

"Maybe." Donna took another forkful of omelet and a sip of orange juice. "I saw a taxi pull up to the front of the building earlier this morning couldn't make-out who got into the cab because the fog blanketed the entire square, but I noticed that the person was carrying two cases."

"That was probably Mr. Conway, a big cattle rancher and art connoisseur from San Antonio, Texas. He rented the downstairs apartment for three months. Mister, mega bucks! He's here for the Dali Art Festival held at the Venice Art Center for one week, then moves to Naples and eventually travels around the state to celebrate the *Year of the Artist.* Every state in the union is participating in the celebration and each state is celebrating a different artist." Sam finished the last of her omelet, pushed her plate forward, and with a contented smile said, "That's it for me. I'm stuffed."

"So where was Mr. Mega Bucks going at eight-thirty in the morning?" Donna asked, and took one last bite of melon.

"I don't know. He said his Learjet was hangared at the Venice Airport. Maybe he needed to check something?" Sam leaned in, "Or maybe, he had a private meeting at the art center. I read the reason the Dali exhibit is in Venice was that the Executive Director of the Venice Art Center, Mary Morris, and a member of the National Art Planning Council convinced the Advisory Board that the Venice Art Center would be the perfect starting venue for the State of Florida. And voilà, *Year of the Artist*, starts in Venice. The Festival begins Monday night, with a celebratory party at Centennial Park, speeches, food and music. All free, and open to the public. How does that sound?"

Donna leaned back in her chair. "I don't know. I really don't feel up to being around strangers."

"Bandana is playing Monday night. It's your favorite rock and roll band of all times. Did you know the lead singer, Butch Gerace, was with Sam the Sham and the Pharaohs? They had that big hit in the Sixties, *Woolly Bully*. Let's go together? It will cheer you up, especially when 'Butch' sings *Woolly Bully*." Sam rocked her body back and forth to an imaginary song and was about to say something when her cell phone rang.

Donna reached into her pocket and handed Sam back her phone. "Hello, yes. I'll be there. Thank you, good-bye." Sam clicked off and slid the phone into her pocketbook. "That was Keep'em Clean Pet Mobile, my pet groomer, with a reminder that she'll be at the house at ten o'clock. My little Peekie is getting her monthly spa treatment, a complete doggie whirlpool wash, total body conditioner rub, fluff and air dry treatment, doggie haircut, and finally, the deluxe pedicure and the cutie nail polish package. A total 15-step multigroom spa vacation for my sweet little Pekingese."

"I could use one of those fifteen step treatments right about now. Maybe Pet Mobile can squeeze me in after Peekie?" Donna laughed. For the first time in two days, Donna smiled and seemed to be getting back to her same old witty self.

"Very funny, I don't think they groom two legged animals, but I'll ask if it keeps you smiling." Sam glanced at her watch, stood and said, "Time to go, it's 9:15 a.m., and Everest Lockley, the locksmith, is now open for business."

Sam and Donna walked out to Sam's truck. "Oh, by the way, I need to warn you about the locksmith!"

Chapter 33

Forewarned is forearmed, or at least, can help a person reduce the embarrassment of the shock. Sam pulled up to the light on Tamiami Trail before the Venice Avenue Bridge and waited for the green arrow. The fog was beginning to lift and the day started to transform into another beautiful day in paradise.

"As I was saying, it's no big deal, but I need to tell you about Everest Lockley, the locksmith, before we reach his shop." The arrow turned green, Sam turned left and proceeded to drive across the bridge.

"Sam, please, haven't I been through enough? My husband has been murdered, I was kidnapped, my yacht destroyed, a mad FBI agent threatened to kill me and last night a ghost kept me awake moving furniture around the room. I don't know if I can take another traumatic episode. What, is this guy some kind of vampire?" Donna turned away and stared out the window.

"Well, not exactly. He's not a real vampire, not even a make-believe vampire, but he looks like a vampire, at first glance. Well, maybe at every glance." The Avalanche reached the top of the bridge and started down the incline towards Tamiami Trail when Sam shouted, "Donna, look over on my side of the bridge. What's going on at Patches Restaurant?"

The entire restaurant was ringed with police cars, police vans, crime scene trucks, police personnel and a Channel Six News van. A group of armed officers were placing a man in a lime green raincoat into the back of a squad car, while a news reporter interviewed what appeared to be a lion, tin man and scarecrow.

"That's Lou Bravo's yellow El Camino parked in front of the restaurant and if I had to guess, he's the character dressed as a Lion. No doubt, his friend, Tony Lilly, is the Tin Man, and

Tony's helper, Hubba Bubba, is the Scarecrow. They're friends of Joey, or should I say, were friends of Joey."

"What's with the costumes? If I'm not mistaken, Halloween is over." Sam jammed on the brakes and came to a complete stop behind a line of cars all rubbernecking to get a glimpse of what was happening at Patches. "What are they, a bunch of weirdos?" A police officer waved the back-up of cars forward and Sam slowly inched over into the right lane.

"They're not weirdos. They just do crazy things sometimes, oftentimes, okay a lot of times. Do you remember last year when that psycho ranger Remi Cole shot Blaine at the Venice Boat Parade? Well, Lou Bravo and Brooke visited her in the hospital, Lou Bravo dressed as a circus clown and Brooke as a pussy cat. You can imagine what a commotion they caused. Plus, Lou Bravo drove up in an ice cream truck, decorated with circus animals and balloons, but that's another story." Donna turned around and watched the trio walk into the restaurant. "After we get these damn handcuffs off, maybe you could drop me off at Patches Restaurant. I need to talk to Lou Bravo."

"So, Donna, about Everest Lockley."

Chapter 34

Routine gives a person direction, while direction rewards an individual with a purpose in life. Everest Lockley, a Venice locksmith, has followed the identical routine Monday thru Friday for the past forty-two years. Roll out of bed at seven in the morning, get dressed in the company's blue work uniform, feed Padlock, a collie mix that turned up on his doorstep ten years ago and made Security Locksmith Company his home ever since, eat breakfast, and then read the Venice Journal Star from cover to cover. Finally, at nine fifteen, Everest Lockley would unlock the front door and officially open the Security Locksmith Company.

The same mundane, lock-step procedure worked for Everest Lockley. He felt secure with the repetitive, recurring routine of his everyday life. He welcomed the comfort in the sameness and the knowledge of how each day would unfold. It gave him the protection that he so desperately needed.

The brutal death of his mother and father during a home invasion ten years ago turned Everest's life into a living nightmare. Unable to cope, he sunk into alcoholism to relieve the pain, but matters only got worse and Everest's life spiraled out of control. He was arrested numerous times for disorderly conduct, creating a public nuisance and drunk driving. Finally, one night, after he drove his car across his neighbor's front yard and into a retention pond, Everest was institutionalized. Three years later, and with extensive psychiatric therapy, Everest completed his sentence and moved back to Venice, Florida. He reopened Security Locksmith Company and worked tirelessly to build up the business. To some, Everest Lockley only exchanged life inside a correctional facility for a prison without bars. Everest didn't feel that way. He felt comfort in his routine, secure that each day, business would be the same and that he would be safe. Everest Lockley wasn't rich by any stretch of the imagination. Actually, he barely eked out a living, but at the end of the day he paid his bills, and had a few dollars left over to stuff in a jar for a rainy day. But Everest Lockley was figuratively a rich man. His reputation as a skilled locksmith and honest businessman was known throughout Sarasota County. Respect and a sense of pride enriched his life daily.

Five minutes later, Sam turned off Tamiami Trail and onto a narrow, cracked shell road that ended at parking area in front of a weathered, two story cinderblock building. Blue paint, faded from years of sun and heat flaked off the walls in large chips and revealed crusted circles of white from a previous paint job. The front door, in the center of the building, was propped open with a rock. To the right of the door was a single pane window covered with an old, sun-bleached sheet, and to the left, a small sign hung in the window that read Security Locksmith Company. All three windows on the second floor were barred and dirty. From a business perspective, the first impression was not welcoming.

"Don't be alarmed by his appearance. He's very tall, that's why everyone calls him Everest, like the mountain. I don't know his given first name, but he's 6'8" and skinny, scary skinny, maybe weighs 130 pounds soaking wet, and he's very white, white as a sheet. I don't think he ever goes outside in the sun."

"Well, if he looks anything like this building, I'm in for the fright of my life," Donna said jokingly. "You said he did all the lock work for your restaurant addition. How could he do the work and not be outside in the sun?"

"All of the work was done late at night, after the restaurant was closed. He said it would be more convenient, the place would be empty and he could work without distractions. Plus my business could continue uninterrupted during the day," Sam said. "His face may be the biggest shock. His eyes are a pale gray that seem to look right through you, but his teeth, perfect, except for the two bicuspids. They are a little pointed, but he's not a vampire." Sam turned off the ignition.

"Sam, this man could look like Santa Claus. All I want are these handcuffs removed. Let's go inside before it turns dark and Count Lockley has to fly around Venice looking for prospective customers." They both laughed and walked inside.

The inside of Security Locksmith was just as depressing as the outside. For a place of business, open to the public, and not to have a single light on, immediately sent up a red flag. The office floor was littered with boxes, piled one on top of another, some overflowing with papers, others taped closed, but all numbered. At first glance, one received the impression Security Locksmith was preparing to relocate, but the dust covering each box told a different story. Behind the counter, rows and rows of keys hung on the wall. Old safes of different sizes and shapes lined the aisles leaving only a small area for the locksmith to greet customers. Sam's initial description of Mr. Everest Lockley was correct, he looked like a vampire.

"Good morning, Sam, how are you and your friend today? I notice she is wearing an unusual piece of jewelry on her arm?" Everest remarked and smiled, revealing two pointy teeth.

"Good morning, Everest, it's good to see you. By the way, how's Padlock? When you were working at the restaurant you said he swallowed a chicken bone. Is he okay?"

"He's fine. He must have chewed it down into small pieces because the next day it passed. He's out back napping. So I guess you need those handcuffs removed?" Again, Everest smiled revealing those two pointy teeth.

"Yes, we do. This is my friend, Donna. She had a yachting mishap yesterday and needs the handcuffs removed. Can you help?" implored Sam.

"No problem. You're not the first customer to drive up in handcuffs. Last spring break, two college girls pulled up in a fancy red convertible with this guy handcuffed to the steering wheel, naked as a jay bird. He was a beach pick-up who thought he was in for a night of fun with these two beauties, but the girls had other plans. Twenty bucks later, off they go headed for the beach. They didn't ask for directions, and I didn't want to know."

Everest walked down to the end of the counter, reached into an old Mason jar and pulled out a gray and white rabbit's foot key chain. Dangling from the end of the beaded chain was a silver blunt-nosed key that he inserted into the handcuff lock. With one turn, the cuffs fell to the counter. Sam placed a twenty-dollar bill on the counter and smiled.

"That's a relief." Donna said and rubbed her wrist. "Keep the change. You never can tell when they will come in handy?" Donna added sarcastically, and pushed the handcuffs towards Everest.

"So, Mrs. Jupiter, how much fire insurance did you have on *Knot At Home*?" Everest asked.

Donna gasped, and the saucy smile on her face evaporated. "How do you know my name and the name of my yacht?" Donna glowered at him and waited.

"Front page news, Mrs. Jupiter, here take a look at the Venice Journal Star," Everest held up the paper and smiled a toothy grin. "Here's your picture, your husband, and the burning yacht. Quite a story. The police think it was an accident, a gas explosion or something. They found your husband's body, still looking for yours, but I guess that won't happen? Will it, Mrs. Jupiter?" Donna looked down at the paper, and cried.

"Listen, Everest, her husband was murdered and she would have died in that explosion if she hadn't pried loose the handcuffs from a rotted-out handrail. The murderer is still out there and is looking for her right now. So you need to be quiet about all this, understand!" Sam picked up the paper. "The last thing you need is this killer to walk into your shop and put a hole in your forehead. Is it alright if we take the paper?"

"Of course, I've already finished it," Everest uttered in shock. "You can count on me, Sam. I won't say a thing, but Bryce Faceman, from Channel 6 News reported, last night from Sarasota Bayfront Park that he had information the yacht was deliberately set on fire and that Mrs. Jupiter was not on board." Everest didn't smile.

"What does all this mean? That man is such an egotistical pain in the ass. All he cares about is having the camera filming him, not the story. I guess that's why he's called *The Face*. Viewers only see a self-absorbed buffoon." Donna blurted out.

"Don't kill the messenger. I'm just telling you what I saw last night on the news. I'm sure Faceman will be center stage tonight playing up the murder theory."

"Sam, remember that newscast Faceman did on the two kidnapped boys, the exposé he bragged was going to give him a Pulitzer for investigative reporting? My friend, Blaine Sterling, supplied him with all the information, dates, location, descriptions, everything. He had no idea that a child trafficking ring was operating in Englewood and Sarasota. That guy was clueless."

"I remember, it all started because her news carrier, Earl Neigh, blasted his radio late at night. She couldn't sleep and the newspaper didn't silence the loud music, so she decided to dose out some loud music medicine of her own. She and her daughter sold ice cream in front of his Englewood house and woke him up during the day." Sam replied with a smile. "What a devilishly delicious idea. I can see the truck, twenty screaming kids and Neigh, with a pillow over his head."

"Blaine was the one who observed what was going on at Earl Neigh's block. She notified the police and Faceman. The result, two boys were rescued, a child trafficking organization was shut down, and Earl Neigh drove his car into the Intracoastal. Poetic justice, if I don't say so myself."

"Donna, we have to go. I have to get home and meet the dog groomer. I'll drop you off at Patches if Lou Bravo is still there, if not, I'll take you back to the apartment. `Bye, Everest and thanks."

Chapter 35

Which way to Oz? The police cars, fire trucks and news van were gone, but the yellow El Camino was still parked in front of Patches restaurant. Donna pulled open the door, and was greeted by a thunderous chorus of He's A Jolly Good Fellow from all the people inside. Every customer was standing, cheering, clapping, and shouting accolades to three oddball characters sitting in the booth at the back corner. Dressed as a lion, a tin man, and a scarecrow, it could only be Lou Bravo, Tony Lilly and Hubba Bubba in the flesh.

Donna squeezed over to the counter and asked Roseann, co-owner of the restaurant, "What's happening?"

"Some guy in a lime green raincoat tried to rob the restaurant. The maniac grabbed a butter knife off a table, pointed it at my face and threatened to kill me if I didn't give him money. He said he had a gun in his pocket and would shoot me if I didn't cooperate. All of a sudden, the front door flew open and a lion jumped on the guy's back and wrestled him to the floor. Next thing I knew, a tin man and scarecrow piled on top of the man and sat on him until the police arrived." Still shaking, Roseann pointed to the back. "I owe my life to that lion. God bless Lou Bravo."

"He's just the lion I need to see," Donna smiled and again pushed her way through the crowd towards the corner booth. "I don't think this is Kansas, Toto. Mind if I have a seat, boys?" Donna slid into the booth next to Lou Bravo as the waitress brought over a large tray of food.

A tall buxom woman with a heavy Russian accent and a no nonsense expression, stood over the table and barked out, "Let's see, Lion, you have the scrambled egg special and an order of extra crispy bacon. Tin Man, you and Scarecrow have the blueberry pancakes, one with bacon, the other with sausage and coffee all around. Anything else? How about you, Missy, would you like to order?"

"No, thank you. I've already eaten," Donna replied.

"Roseann said the food is on the house, but don't forget a tip, that's not on the house. Enjoy your meal." Victoria turned and walked back to the kitchen.

"What a charmer," Donna uttered sarcastically. "Can't wait to return and order lunch. What's with the costumes? Halloween is over."

"Costumes, forget about the costumes, Donna. What are you doing here? The paper said you were dead. Your yacht exploded, and you and Joey were killed." Lou Bravo added in a confused tone.

Thirty minutes later, a ten dollar tip and three cleaned plates, Donna painstakingly detailed how she inherited the *Storm on the Sea of Galilee* painting from her Uncle Billy. Deftly, she time lined the events where art auction expert Godfrey Molenar, a.k.a. FBI agent Ross Burkhardt, a.k.a. murderer, arranged for the $10 million purchase of the painting. Finally, her kidnapping, escape and a cryptic message from Joey. Donna leaned in and said in a whisper, "He said if anything went wrong with the art deal, see Lou Bravo."

"Donna, I'm so sorry. My heart is broken. Joey was like a brother and now hearing that he was murdered, this guy is going to pay for what he did. Believe me, he'll pay."

"Tell her about our card game last month," Tony blurted out.

Lou Bravo took out his phone, scrolled down to photos, hit open and handed it to Donna. "The card game was a bust. All night Joey seemed agitated and finally he confided that he was concerned about some deal he was working on. We asked, but he wouldn't say what it was, just that it was huge. He pointed out that the transaction would take place in the study, and emphasized that for verification, surveillance cameras would document the arrangement."

"This is just a picture of books," Donna muttered and gave Lou Bravo and Tony a skeptical glance.

"That's right, but Joey wanted us to tell you that a camera and recording device was behind a book, the one with a picture of an eye on the binding. Why? Donna, please take a closer look at the picture."

"Oh my God! The camera is aimed at the false wall where the painting was hidden. Everything was recorded, the transaction, Burkhardt murdering Joey. It's all on the tape." Donna pushed the phone over to Lou Bravo, and sobbed, "I can't go home. What if Burkhardt is at the house waiting to kill me? Right now I'm staying at the Casa Luna Apartments. I know I can't look at the tape alone. Please help me."

Lou Bravo reached over, put his big lion arms around her sobbing frame and hugged her tight. "I will, Donna, but first we have to follow the yellow brick road to Osprey State Park and help Blaine Sterling. You remember Blaine, my neighbor, park ranger, you hosted a big fund raiser to save the Scrub-jays at your house last summer."

"Yes, I remember her, a compassionate woman, dedicated to preserving the environment and not taking guff from anyone." Donna smiled. "I liked her right away. If I'm not mistaken, I believe Joey put up one of his yellow trailers on her property."

"That's right, do you remember the night her house was fire bombed and someone sent her a threatening e-mail? Well, she received another threatening message and believes that the same arsonist will try to harm her today at the park."

"But why today? And why are the three of you dressed like you're auditioning for a part in the *Wizard of Oz*?" Donna said with a quizzical smile.

"Very funny. Today is the All-Trails Hike at the Park, hundreds of people will be hiking over every section of the park all morning long and many of the hikers will be wearing unusual costumes. Hikers bring their children and more than half walk with their dogs. *The Hike* is Mardi Gras, Halloween and New Year's Eve all rolled into one festival. Today would be the perfect time for the arsonist to join *The Hike* unnoticed and wait for an opportune moment to attack Blaine."

"These costumes will help us blend in," Tony added. "Last year, I saw a man dressed as a pirate, with a green parrot perched on his shoulder the entire hike. I wanted to be a pirate, but Lou Bravo said we had to use our costumes from the Halloween Dance at the Venice Community Center, that we didn't have time to shop for new outfits." Tony reached over and took Donna's hand.

"The police believe the arsonist is the son of the man who sent Blaine the e-mail. The father is in prison," Lou Bravo added. "The old man drove the boat on the night Remi Cole, the fired park ranger, shot Blaine. The father has some convoluted idea that Blaine was responsible for his incarceration. The police have a description of the kid, a giant of a man named Thor. That's apropos. They have leads, but haven't arrested him yet. Let's hope they get the bastard before I do."

The four left Patches Restaurant hand-in-hand. The only thing missing was Toto and the red slippers for the ride back to Casa Luna Apartments.

Chapter 36

Sunrise broke through the scrubby Flatwoods along the Eastern section of the park. The night's rain long ended, muffled hues of gray, blue and pink pushed across Lake Osprey and captured a pair of bobcats drinking at the water's edge. Laughter from the Nature Center broke the silence and the elusive cats melted back into the undergrowth. On the grassy bank across the lake, a family of rabbits took one last nibble of green before scampering off into the woods and the safety of their burrows. Along the Yellow Trail perched high in a scrub oak tree, a Florida Scrub-Jay sentinel squawked, warning its family that a group of hikers were approaching. The first of many visitors hiking throughout the day.

At the opposite end of the park, Blaine Sterling downshifted into second gear and slowly maneuvered her red and white Mini Cooper up to the ranger station. A pair of white fuzzy dice hung from her mirror, a birthday present from Brooke that rocked back and forth when the car stopped. Blaine smiled and tapped the dice twice with her index finger for good luck. Fuzzy dice a playful game she and Brooke started shortly after the fire. For Blaine, any diversion to erase the trauma of that night and help reassure a little girl that life would soon return to normal, was worth undertaking. Brooke needed to know that she was safe. Fuzzy dice, how simple, how comforting.

Today would be the first step in that journey. *The Hike* would be the first time Brooke ventured back to the park since the fire, and for Blaine it would be Brooke's homecoming. She was coming with her Brownie Troop and hiking for a good cause. All of the girls received sponsors, and together the troop was going to donate all the proceeds to the Venice Cat Coalition, a local cat rescue organization. Theresa Foley, the director of the Coalition, attended their Brownie meeting last month and spoke about the importance of having a pet. Ms. Foley brought four playful kittens and two adult tabby cats that the Coalition rescued from an abandoned home in South Venice. She mentioned that her organization saved more than five hundred cats last year, many were very sick and starving, and sadly she feared that the numbers were increasing each year. Ms. Foley described how all of the recued cats were taken to a veterinarian, examined, inoculated, a security chip implanted and finally spayed or neutered. She said the kittens had to weigh at least two pounds before they could have surgery. The operation was demanding and the kittens had to be strong enough to endure the procedure. The adult cats were released back to their outdoor homes and the kittens were put up for adoption. At the end of Ms. Foley's presentation, the girls had an opportunity to hold and cuddle with the adorable felines. It was difficult for the girls to say good-bye, but they all decided that it would be a marvelous idea to raise money for the cats, and the All Trails Hike would be the perfect venue. So did Assistant Park Manager, mother and number one sponsor, Blaine Sterling.

"Good morning, Assistant Park Manager Sterling." Ranger Diana Stimson announced as she stepped outside the ranger station to greet Blaine. The salutation ended the daydream and jolted Blaine back to the real world.

"Good morning Diana, how was your vacation at the Dude Ranch last week? Oh my God, what happened to your arm?" Blaine remarked sticking her head out the window and staring at the cast on Diana's arm.

"Well, the first day was perfect. We saddled up early in the morning and rode deep into the woods for about three hours. It was like stepping back in time, back to the Old West. We rode across meadows, crossed streams, over an old wooden bridge, and only heard the quiet sound of nature. The main lodge was gorgeous, a traditional western style log cabin with magnificent views of the lake and horse pastures. The food was delicious, and plenty of it, an evening campfire and real cowboys to help all the greenhorns."

"Sounds like a dream vacation to me," Blaine added. "So why the cast?"

"The second day, after a hearty cowboy breakfast in the dining hall, we set off on an all-day, guided pack ride into the back country. Our destination, after a three-hour ride, was the Snake River to pan for gold. The trail boss, while crossing the first stream, informed the group that one guest last month found a golden nugget worth two thousand dollars. Talk about an incentive, the realization that someone actually found gold, captured all six riders' attention.

"One hour into the ride disaster struck. My horse, third in line to cross a second stream, suddenly leapt into the air, bucked me off and galloped downstream. Flat on my back in about two feet of water, a wild pig chased by a mountain lion exploded out of the bushes. They raced across the stream, inches from me, and disappeared into the wood in a matter of seconds. Painfully, I had to return to the ranch with one of the cowboys. No gold, a broken wrist and the end of an adventure for me. The next two days were spent in pain, lounging around the pool and too much eating in the dining room."

"What a shame. You were so excited about the trip," Blaine chirped.

"I have an appointment to see the doctor next week and I hope she says this thing will come off." Diana held up her left arm revealing a bright yellow cast up to her elbow. "It now itches like mad. Half my day is spent shoving a ruler down the cast and scratching like crazy. I don't know if I can wait until Wednesday!"

"Four more days, how bad could it possibly be?" Blaine added sympathetically.

"Easy for you to say, you're not the one itching all day long! Jim Breidster, the President of the Friends of Osprey State Park, said he'd cut it off for me. All I have to do is walk over to the shop Monday morning when all the volunteers are organizing the work schedule. He'll take out a bow saw and one, two, three, no more itch." Diana remarked with a sheepish grin.

"You're kidding, right?" Blaine asked.

"I'm tempted. Anyway, before I forget, the Park Manager said he'll meet up with you at lunch. A hiker twisted his ankle at Big Lake. He and Ranger Dan took the new club car, the one with the rescue bed, to pick him up."

"Diana, please call me when my daughter's Brownie troop arrives for the Hike. I'll be stationed at Lake Osprey all day. Tell the kids to meet me there after they register at the Nature Center. Thanks, have a great day. And I'd reconsider the bow saw idea! 'Bye."

Chapter 37

Mercedes naked body lay across the bed. Early morning light bled through the blinds and framed her natural beauty. Mercedes hadn't planned to stay the night, only drop off Thor's stupid Marvel comic strip Halloween costume, Thor the Thunder God, and then drive back to college. However, the two bottles of Chardonnay, the late hour and dreamy, soft music were captivating reasons to stay. At the foot of the bed, Thor stood silently, breathing in her radiance. She was beautiful, perfect in every way. Soft milky white skin, thin delicate features, fine brown shoulder length hair, short nose and a Victoria's Secret body. But it was her insatiable appetite for sex that excited him most, and last night's lovemaking was no exception. It began with a kiss, then erupted into a night of unbridled passion. Her cravings knew no boundaries. Time seemed to stand still as the rhythmic motion of their bodies melted together and climaxed in exhausted pleasure.

Thor felt himself getting aroused and was tempted to jump back in bed, and make love to her one last time, but he had a job to complete. The trap had been set. It was now time to catch the rabbit. Slowly, he pulled the sheet up around her shoulders, and in concert, the bulge in his pants deflated.

Thor pulled a green duffle bag from under the bed, unzipped the top flap and took out his Norse Thunder God costume. He put on the black leather jumpsuit, clipped on the padded chest amour, stepped into his boots, slipped on the two silver gauntlet wrist guards, and locked the silver chain around his neck that held the crimson cape which flowed down his back. Lastly, he pulled out the mystical hammer from the bag, held it high and with one sweep of his arm, rushed out the door.

Chapter 38

One way ticket to paradise. The yellow cab turned off Airport Road into the aviation parking lot and stopped in front of the terminal, "That'll be twenty dollars." Burkhardt reached into the suitcase, pulled out a crisp one hundred dollar bill and handed it to the driver. "Sir, you're my first fare; I don't have change for a hundred. Do you have anything smaller?"

"Keep the change," Burkhardt called out as he pushed open the cab door and walked into the terminal. *How easy it was to be generous with other people's money*, he thought, as the large glass doors automatically slid open. The lobby was deserted, no baggage attendant, no security check points, no ticket agents at the airline counter; it was obvious no other arrivals were scheduled for the morning. The only hint of human activity was the clatter of dishes and hushed laughter from the airport restaurant off the lobby. *Perfect planning on the part of the Bureau*, he thought, *no passengers, no questions and no problems. The FBI thought of everything, well almost everything.* He smiled and hurried through the lobby and out the rear door to the airfield.

Off to his right, he spotted the Gulfstream and two men: Hollister and another man, presumably his co-pilot, walking toward the terminal. Burkhardt studied the two as they moved down the tarmac. Hollister appeared tired and hunched over. He walked with an unsteady limp, the result of an injury, he told Burkhardt during their Germany flight, that he received in Vietnam when his plane was shot down. He spent three months in a Saigon hospital. When able to stand, he was sent home, where another three months in a rehabilitation center outside of Boston finally patched his broken body together. Hollister was never whole again. He was in constant pain, and the combination of medications along with frequent visits to medical centers, exhausted his physical well-being on a daily basis. At sixty-three, he took on the persona of a seventy-five year old man. Burkhardt was confident that Hollister would not be a threat. The co-pilot, on the other hand, was a foot taller and twenty years Hollister's junior. He looked physically fit and walked with vigor and purpose. Each step, in line and stride, only a recent FBI academy cadet would still adhere to. By all accounts, Burkhardt concluded, he was a freshman pilot and receiving on the job flight training from Hollister, a senior Bureau pilot. Burkhardt would pay particular attention to him.

Hollister was first to notice Burkhardt, standing at the terminal gate with only one carry-on and a black leather portfolio case. "Good morning, Agent Burkhardt, good to see you again. You're looking very dapper today." Hollister extended his hand. "This is my first officer, Kent Burns." Burkhardt reached out and was surprised at the strength of Burns' handshake. A sign of an overachiever and an unnecessary display of aggression, the young man would soon regret.

"Pleased to meet you, Burns, first flight with Captain Hollister?" Burkhardt asked, and released his hand.

"Yes, how did you know?" Burns replied in amazement.

"It's my business to know. That's why I'm here today. I observed your movements when you disembarked, the way you positioned your body, your first step. You're left handed correct?"

"Yes, how did you know?"

"I told you, Burns, I make it my business to know. I study everything around me, especially people."

"Speaking of observing people," Hollister interrupted, "Aren't we missing a passenger, Agent Burkhardt?"

"Yes, art thief, Mr. Joseph Jupiter. Unfortunately, Mr. Jupiter was involved in a boating accident last night and won't be joining us in Boston. I have the missing Rembrandt and the $10 million dollars the FBI offered to pay him for the art."

"Kent and I are going to have breakfast before the fight back, care to join us?" Hollister asked, and began to walk towards the lobby.

"No, thanks, I'm good. I'll get on board, stow my gear and call the Bureau. Director Pembroke needs to be updated on the situation concerning Jupiter." Burkhardt turned and headed for the plane.

A crooked smile appeared on Burkhardt's face. What good fortune on his part. Now, with an empty plane, he could plant the bomb without interruption. He bounded up the boarding ramp, two steps at a time, and took the first seat facing the forward galley and cockpit. He unzipped the suitcase, removed a small box and quickly stowed the art portfolio and money in the overhead compartment. He stepped into the cockpit, placed the cigarette-size box containing two glass vials of inhalational anesthesia and a micro C-4 explosive device under the co-pilot's seat. The explosion would vaporize the oxygen level in the cockpit, reducing all neuromuscular functions, and shutting down their breathing, rendering both pilots incapable of any motor functions. Burkhardt took out his cell phone, opened contacts, scrolled down to Gulfstream and pressed call. A muffled ring tone activated the three second timer. He pressed end call, went back to his seat and made another call.

"Gunny, we should be leaving the airport within the hour. Where are you?" Burkhardt whispered into the phone.

"I'm anchored at the pickup location, Commander. Let me double check, right on line, just what you ordered. The GPS doesn't lie."

"Okay, don't get too comfortable out there. I need you moving towards the jet as soon as it hits the water. We must be out of the area before the search and rescue crew from the Clearwater Coast Guard Station show up. What's the visibility like out there? The fog here has just lifted."

"Perfect, sunny, clear skies and calm seas. A boater's paradise and not a ripple on the water. Excellent day for ditching a Gulfstream. I don't see a problem picking you up. Trust me, Commander," Gunny replied, lit a cigarette and picked up his fishing rod.

"There better not!" Burkhardt barked and clicked off.

Gunny sat back in the captain's chair, reeled out some line and let his mind roam back to... Three weeks ago, in this exact spot, he had a *kicking, great, Billy Goat* charter, a day excursion for tarpon and a top of the line fishing trip, and best of all, a two thousand dollar profit in the bank. Everything was included, poles, fresh bait, food, drinks and extra crew to assist all the guests. Fish were plentiful, fishing was challenging and each fisherman had a story to tell.

Rich Swier, a Sarasota businessman and entrepreneur, arranged the fishing trip. Mr. Swier's objective was to build a strong, innovative and technology- based economy in Sarasota, Florida. His latest project was to create a new film capitol in southwest Florida with Sarasota as its main hub. Mr. Swier recently purchased the movie rights to Loud Music, by RJ Coons, a mystery novel that took place in Florida. Swier believed it had the potential to bring money and notoriety to the area. The fishing excursion was designed to convince two Hollywood producers and Danny DeVito to visit Sarasota for a weekend, enjoy the amenities the town had to offer and hopefully, agree to produce Mr. Swier's film project. Swier believed Danny DeVito's star power as Lou Bravo, a major character in the movie, would add tremendous credibility to the film.

If the fishing trip was any measurement for the success of the movie project, then Hollywood would be convinced, hook, line and sinker. Gunny let out more line.

Chapter 39

How could an FBI operation that took fifteen years in the planning go so horribly wrong? Director Richard Pembroke couldn't believe his ears. "You shot Mr. Jupiter, and now you can't locate Mrs. Jupiter? Please explain how something like that happened, Agent Burkhardt!"

"Jupiter got greedy, sir. He wanted the $10 million and the painting. I completed the negotiations and was about to leave with the painting, when he pulled out a gun. I identified myself, told him the FBI had him under surveillance and that he was under arrest. The revelation that I was an FBI agent startled him and when I grabbed for the gun, we struggled, the gun went off and the bullet hit him in the head. I bent down to check his pulse and was struck from behind. When I woke up Jupiter was gone along with his wife and their yacht." Burkhardt sat forward in the seat and waited.

"What about the money and the *Storm on the Sea of Galilee?*" Pembroke barked into the phone.

"The money and the painting are on the plane, sir. I don't know why they were left behind. Maybe the Jupiter's were in a hurry or believed if they left everything, the FBI wouldn't pursue them."

"Well, at least you did something right, Agent Burkhardt. We still can move ahead with the press conference, present the painting to the museum, announce that one of the co-conspirators has been killed and the other is in the process of being apprehended. Perhaps, when this operation is completed, no thanks to you, the Bureau may be able to salvage a modicum of dignity and move forward. I'll meet you at the airport." Burkhardt heard the phone slam down and then silence.

Burkhardt fell back against the seat, loosened his tie, and unbuttoned the top button of his shirt, before he took a long slow breath. He couldn't decide if it was the heat in the cabin or the heat from Pembroke's grilling, but he felt hot and dizzy. Burkhardt closed his eyes and was just about to doze off when...

"You take your coffee black, Agent Burkhardt?" Hollister called out as he boarded the plane.

Burkhardt turned and looked down the aisle, "That's right, you have a good memory. What has it been a month since our Germany flight?" Burkhardt reached out, the heat from the Styrofoam cup warmed his hands and felt comforting. Slowly, he breathed in the steaming hot aroma of the Colombian brew and took a sip. The coffee burnt his tongue, but the robust taste overpowered the pain and Burkhardt took another sip. This time, he was careful not to burn his tongue again.

"Ross, we'll talk after we get airborne. I'm dying to know everything about this so called yachting accident. Maybe, Kent will relinquish the co-pilot seat while you talk and get some flying time in?" Hollister walked into the cockpit and closed the door.

"Some people shouldn't wish for things. They may just come true," Burkhardt whispered to himself and leaned back in his seat. He closed his eyes and visualized the checklist Hollister and Burns had to perform to get the Gulfstream in the air. He pictured the buttons, switches, gauges, toggles, screens, all positioned within the avionics console, and each one essential for a successful flight. *Notify Tampa of flight plan, receive clearance for take-off, set gauge for engines. Engines start.*

Hollister's intercom squawking pulled Burkhardt back down to earth, "We're cleared for take-off on Runway 4. Four will take us out over the Gulf and north to Tampa. You'll have a great view of the water. The different shades of blue are magnificent and maybe you'll see some dolphins?" The intercom went silent and Burkhardt continued with his mental checklist, *set heading indicator, set lift-off speed.* The Gulfstream taxied down the runway. Two minutes later, the intercom squawking rang out again, "Agent, I forgot to mention, if you spot a dolphin and make a wish, ancient folklore claims that your wish would automatically be granted. The Native Americans believed that dolphins were the 'Keepers of the Sea.' That they possessed mystical powers and were friends to all mankind. Their presence in the local waters insured a bountiful harvest and calm waters for all local inhabitants. Dolphins at one o'clock."

Burkhardt looked out the window, and spotted two, sleek, pearl gray dolphins swimming side by side. The graceful mammals rode waves, balancing on the white caps, and then sliding down under the water. They leaped out of the water, turned, raced to the right, then left and narrowly avoided colliding into each other. Effortlessly the pair raced forward and then they were gone.

Burkhardt turned away from the window and thought, "I hope I don't hear another one of Hollister's inane comments." He leaned back in his seat and returned to the mental checklist, *set altitude, auto throttle on, set flaps, turn on lights*, jet lifts off, *set course bring up speed*. Burkhardt scrolled through his contact list on his cell phone and called Gulfstream, *raise landing gear*. A faint ringing sounded behind the mahogany door.

Chapter 40

Burkhardt unbuckled his seat belt, reached into his coat pocket and took out a single stage gas mask. He stood, pulled it over his face and pushed open the cockpit door. The gas had done its job. Hollister was slumped over his seat leaning halfway into the aisle. Burkhardt picked up his hand. He was out cold. Burns, on the other hand, struggled with his seat belt and attempted to stand. Burkhardt reached over, yanked him back into the seat and put his hands over his face. Burns thrashed about, raised his arms, but was too weak to reach his face and moments later he stopped moving.

Burkhardt pulled Hollister out of his seat, dragged him to the galley and propped him up against the refrigerator. He turned off the auto-pilot, set the flaps at 20, reduced speed to 130 knots and began his descent into the Gulf of Mexico. By his calculations the Gulfstream would be over the rendezvous location, in two minutes.

"Gulfstream Flight 617, this is Tampa Air Traffic Control. Your altitude is dangerously low. Immediately climb to 28,000 feet. Over." Burkhardt switched off the radio and pulled back on the throttle. The altimeter read 90 feet. Thirty seconds later, Gulfstream's engines stalled and the jet slammed into the Gulf. Initially, the left wing tip dragged in the water causing the aircraft to swing left away from land. Seconds later, the right wing rested on the water as the jet glided to a stop. The impact twisted the starboard engine, ripping a gaping hole in the side of the fuselage. Ankle deep water filled the cockpit.

The crash wrenched Burkhardt back and forth in the captain's seat, while the seat belt, not adjusted to his height, dug into his body putting intense pressure on his chest and rib cage. Excruciating pain made the slightest movement painful. He could barely move his left arm and with each labored move his bruised ribs cried out in agony. The water was now knee deep in the cockpit.

Each step took a Herculean effort. Burkhardt sloshed through the rising water, picked up Hollister and buckled him back into the captain's seat. He looked out the cockpit window and was surprised that the aqua blue waters had reached the bottom of the front windshield. Waist deep water now filled the cockpit.

It would be only a matter of minutes until the cabin was completely under water. Water touched the bottom of the headrests. Both pilots buckled in their seats, sat motionless with water up to their chins. Burkhardt turned away, stepped from the cockpit and walked towards the rear of the plane. Chest deep water filled the cockpit.

Time was Burckhardt's worst enemy. His greatest fear was to be trapped inside and drowning. Hundred dollar bills floated throughout the cabin. He was swimming through a sea of money, one bill after another. He slipped two bills into his pocket and kept moving to the back. Pulling himself over the tops of the seats, Burkhardt finally reached the rear of the plane and the torn out section of metal. He looked back towards the front of the jet, but only saw water. Water filled the cockpit.

He took three long breaths, held the last one and dove into the water towards the hole. Salt water burned his eyes and ran up his nose, but he managed to squeeze through the opening and out into open water. Slowly, he rose to the surface and bobbed freely in the sunlight. Coughing and spitting out salt water, he gasped for air. Finally, after getting his breath back, he scanned the horizon.

Twenty yards away Burkhardt spotted a large fishing boat rapidly approaching. White spray shot high in the air off both sides of the bow as it plowed through the water and headed towards the Gulfstream. Its outrigger poles bent in the wind and the American flag flapped wildly as the craft made a slight turn towards the jet. On the flying bridge Burkhardt recognized the Captain. It was Gunny, his unmistakable red baseball hat was a giveaway.

"Over here," Burkhardt yelled, and raised his right arm. Instantly, a stabbing pain ripped at his rib cage inflicting such agony he momentarily blacked out. A mouthful of salt water revived him, but the excruciating pain still remained. It was all he could do to tread water and stay afloat.

Billy Goat idled down and slowly circled the Gulfstream now almost totally submerged. After one pass, Gunny pulled up alongside the jet and put the engines in neutral. He spotted Burkhardt clinging to the wing and immediately realized that he was injured. The Commander wasn't his usual boisterous self, ordering people around and demanding something from everyone. He barely looked up. Gunny turned off the engines, jumped down onto the swim platform and threw Burkhardt a line.

"How's my timing, Commander?" Gunny shouted and pulled on the rope.

"Couldn't be better, Gunny." Burkhardt grimaced with each tug of the rope, but managed to reach the boat without passing out. "Be careful, Gunny I think I broke a few ribs when the plane hit the water. My left side is killing me."

"Okay, here we go, nice and easy. One more step and you're out of the water." With one hand under Burkhardt's right arm, Gunny guided him up to the main salon. Burkhardt flopped down on the sofa and wrapped his arms around his waist and rib cage.

"This is where it hurts, my left side. It's killing me real bad. Do you have any pain pills? I need something for the pain."

"I only have aspirin. I'll get it for you." Gunny walked back to galley, took out a bottle of aspirin, poured a glass of water and returned. "I have an idea, my brother lives in Tampa and we're only about thirty minutes from his place. He injured his back five years ago when he was digging up a tree in his backyard. From that day on he had back problems. I'm sure he has pain pills. He has a place right on a canal, nice little mobile home and private. I was there a few times. Maybe we can go to his place and lay low for a couple of days?"

"No, we need to get as far away from the plane as possible. I'm sure the Coast Guard has already sent out a helicopter and probably one of their ships to find the plane. Tampa Airport

Control radioed right before the crash, so they have the last coordinates. Start the engines and let's get out of here." Burkhardt downed four aspirins and walked towards the forward cabin. "I'm going to change into some dry clothes and rest. Wake me when we get to Venice."

Gunny pushed both throttles forward, and the sleek white craft jumped forward and motored south to Venice. Gunny looked back and only saw the horizon on the water.

Chapter 41

Follow the yellow... to Osprey State Park. Lou Bravo stopped the El Camino at the ranger station, rolled down the window and waited. "The yellow brick road is two blocks up ahead on the right," Ranger Diana called out, as she stepped from the office with a big smile on her face. "Good morning, Mr. Lion, Mr. Tin Man, and let's not forget, Mr. Scarecrow, sitting in the back of the truck playing in the hay. Welcome to our All-Trails Hike. Registration is at the Nature Center, just follow the yellow..., only kidding. Take the main road and park volunteers will assist with the parking. Enjoy the day."

"Before we go, we're looking for Dorothy, she left the house early this morning, looking for her cat Romeo. We were told she is the Assistant Park Manager. Have you seen them?" The lion shook its head and gave a halfhearted growl.

"The cat or the Assistant Park Manager? Touché, Blaine Sterling is assisting hikers near Lake Osprey. Sorry, I can't vouch for Romeo. Have fun." Ranger Diana smiled and waved the yellow school bus forward.

"Not a bad ranger, she has a witty sense of humor. You need that when dealing with people. People skills, that's what she has," the Tin Man remarked and waved goodbye.

"She's a hundred times better than the ranger they had last year greeting visitors at the ranger station, what a real ball buster. Every time I came to the park she hassled me. First time, I was dressed as a clown, driving an ice cream truck. She accused me of selling ice cream in the park, a violation of State law FL021 or something and threatened to call the cops. Good thing Blaine was in the truck to smooth things out. The second time, I wanted to donate about hundred books for their library. Again, she stopped me and gave me the third degree. So, I was in a Santa's outfit. It was going to be a Christmas present for

Blaine, a belated Christmas gift. You remember, you were there. Talk about no sense of humor."

"You didn't think we looked a little out of place? After all, it was January." Tony laughed. "Over there, the guy is flagging us over towards the fence."

"Wow, look at those guys!" Lou Bravo pointed to the line of people standing outside the Nature Center. "They're painted green. Their entire body is a hunter green, except for a big, yellow letter painted on their chests. Where's that ranger now? I'll bet she'll hassle those green men big time."

"What do the letters say? Look there's, a lady in a chicken costume. I think it's a lady and she's taking their picture. The green men are lining up. It says 'HIKING DUDES.'"

"Perfect, I think we'll fit in just fine," said Lou Bravo and slapped the Tin Man on the back so hard he crashed into a hiker. Apologies were exchanged and the trio hiked on.

"I know one of those dudes," Hubba Bubba shouted, and pointed to the guy with the green, spiked hair. "He was at that mosh pit at the Van Wezel. Some kind of nature freak. Always hiking Florida parks, camping in the woods, and living off the land. He told me how he eats *road kill,* squirrel, opossum, birds, snake, and alligator. Cuts them up, puts them in his freezer and when he's hungry, cooks one up. Gross, stay away from that dude. He'll turn your stomach inside out."

A group of hikers passed heading toward the Red Trail in hopes of seeing some Florida Scrub-jays. Their leader, a short, stout, gray haired gentleman with *Joe, the Greatest Grandpa* hand stenciled on his yellow shirt, ran up to Lou Bravo. All excited, he asked if he could take a picture of the three Wizard of Oz characters with their hiking group. "I want to send it to my grandkids in Indiana. They made the shirt." They took three pictures and then marched off snapping pictures of everything and anything in sight.

"Let's walk over to the lake and see if we can find Blaine," Lou Bravo suggested and pushed through the crowd in front of the Nature Center. Halfway down the path they passed, a family of four heading towards the foot bridge and the Yellow Trail, and of course, they had to have a picture taken with Oz cast. Everyone stood along the fence with Lake Osprey in the background. A passerby was kind enough to snap two pictures and as the trio turned to leave, Tony spotted Blaine leading a small group of hikers back to the lake area.

"There she is," Tony shouted, pointing past the swimming area. "Down by the lake trail."

"Oh shit, look who's here. That maniac in the Thor costume, it's the guy from the Halloween Dance at the Venice Community Center," Hubba Bubba cried out. "He's dressed in the same black body suit, red cape, blonde wig and that big, silver hammer. See the giant sitting on those blue pipes, back by the woods, behind Blaine."

"Isn't he the guy who had that gorgeous girlfriend? The one Hubba Bubba couldn't stop drooling over?" Lou Bravo joked. "She was dressed as Lady Godiva."

"What do you want from me? That girl looked naked. Her skin tight body suit showed off every curve and bump. Nothing was left to the imagination. What's a guy to do?" Hubba Bubba coughed out. "I wonder if she's here."

"You better pray she's not. That guy threatened to knock your head off with that silver hammer in his hand the next time you looked at his girlfriend!" Tony emphasized with an exaggerated swing of his arm. "Or did you forget that little piece of information?" The imaginary ax crashed to the ground.

"Oh yeah, I forgot."

Lou Bravo looked down at the large figure sitting on the pipes and said "That's the guy Blaine thinks burnt down her house and is trying to kill her. His name is Thor Boltier and his father is Charlie Boltier. Charlie drove the boat when Remi Cole, the former park ranger, shot Blaine. Cole committed suicide and Boltier is now incarcerated at Union Correctional."

"How do you know all this?" Tony asked.

"Blaine called last night and recounted the entire story. Her friend, Star Trek Guy, put a tracer on her phone and they hacked into both Boltier's phones and found out what was going on. Thor said the plan was taking place today, at the All Trails Hike. That's why we're here, to protect Blaine."

"Star Trek Guy?" asked Tony. "Who, or what is Star Trek Guy?"

"Don't ask. He's some kind of computer genius Blaine and Marybeth know. For all I know he could be flying around the park right now. Anyway, let's go tell Blaine we're here."

Unfortunately, at that very moment, the Venice Middle School Marching Band, fifty musicians strong, began to parade along the pathway. A mass of humanity all converged onto one spot and set in motion conditions for the perfect storm. Drums banging, trumpets blasting, saxophones blaring and whistles blowing, disaster struck. A goat pulling a tiny, red wagon with three small children, leaped into the air, and landed between two women walking their pet Shih Tzus. The tiny dogs yanked so hard on their leashes that the two women fell forward and collided with a Friends of Osprey State Park volunteer carrying two boxes of hot dog and hamburger rolls. The boxes flew into the air and rained down bread all along the pathway. Hikers panicked, band members fell out of line and people scattered to escape the chaos.

A few minutes later and after getting their bearings, the Lion, Tin Man, and Scarecrow looked down towards the lake. "Where's Blaine? I don't see her!" Lou Bravo shouted. "He's taken her. That bastard has her!"

"I saw a red flash move into the woods." Tony yelled and pointed to the construction pipes. "Behind the pipes, I bet it was his cape." Pushing people aside, they ran down the pathway and into the woods.

The abduction happened swiftly. Running at full speed, Thor grabbed Blaine from behind and sprinted into the woods. Held in a crunching bear hug, she couldn't move. Her breathing labored, she felt like her ribs were about to break. Struggling, she managed to drag her right foot between his legs and trip him. The two catapulted forward and plowed into the ground.

Blaine was first to stand and instinctively kicked him in the face with such force that the blood from his broken nose splattered up onto her shirt. He rose to one knee and swung at her with the ax. Blaine sidestepped the blow and executed a karate kick that cracked open his left knee. Screaming in pain, he rose and began wildly flailing away with the ax while standing on his one good leg. Blaine whirled and connected a well-aimed kick to the abdomen, ripping the air from his gut and sending him flying backward. Amazingly, the kick didn't send him to ground. Thor stood, defiant, blood running down his face, breathing hard and in pain. Hatred glared from his eyes as he waited for her next slashing kick. She aimed at his groin, but this time he managed to seize hold of her leg, twist her down to the ground and slam the ax against the side of her head. That was the last thing she remembered.

Chapter 42

Bobby Liverpool sat in front of Detective Beale's desk. He squirmed and fussed in the wooden chair, but couldn't get comfortable. He was hungry and could use a stiff drink. However, at nine o'clock in the morning and sitting in the Venice Police Station, he knew he wasn't about to get either one. "So, Bobby, where did you get the pennies?" Beale looked up from his computer, stopped typing and stared at the young man.

"What pennies? I don't got no pennies," the disheveled soul mumbled, looking down at the floor and picking at his fingernails. His curly, unkempt hair hid his dirty, reed-thin face, while the wrinkled, plaid shirt concealed his skinny frame. It was obvious Bobby slept on the beach the night before.

"The bridge tender saw you throwing pennies at the wheels that raise the bridge."

"That's a fucking lie," Bobby shouted.

"Watch your mouth or I'll throw you in a cell right now. Understand?" Beale glowered at him and waited for a reply.

"Okay, but that old bastard can't see that far. I was making a wish." Bobby reached for his shirt pocket, but the flap was torn, "You got a cigarette?" Bobby coughed out.

"There's no smoking in the station. Anyway they're bad for your health. They cause cancer. Don't you read the papers?"

"Do I look like I read the paper? How about a drink? I could use a little pick-me-up."

"Hordowski, can you get this guy a bottle of water?"

"So, Bobby, you were making a wish off the Venice Avenue Bridge? Something wrong with the fountain next to the Venice Theater? What was the wish?" Beale asked, and handed him the bottle of water.

181

"I was wishing for something to eat. I was hungry." Bobby took a big gulp of water.

"One penny would have been enough. Why a handful, Bobby?"

"I haven't had a thing to eat in two days. Thought the more pennies, the more wishes." Bobby took another drink.

"That's bull. The bridge tender saw you do the same thing last week, but this time he called the police. Admit it, you wanted to stop the bridge from coming down. Isn't that right? You wanted to jam up the mechanism. Why?" Beale snapped angrily.

The phone on Beale's desk rang. Beale didn't move. He just glared at Liverpool. Bobby looked at his hands and picked at the sand under his fingernails. On the third ring, Beale reached over and picked it up, "Detective Beale speaking."

"Detective Beale, this is Chief Analyst, Ron Pickett, with the Sarasota County Sheriff's Cyber Communications Unit. I have the information on the phone conversations to Union Correctional your office requested. The provider just faxed over the transcript. I'll e-mail you a copy also, but because of the timeline, I thought it prudent to call you immediately."

"Mr. Pickett, please give me a minute." Beale put the phone down and turned to Hordowski at the next desk. "Take Bobby over to the Church of Good Souls on Venice Avenue. They provide free meals on Saturday. Maybe they can help Bobby's wish come true? They may even let him shower and get rid of the sand raining down on the floor."

"What about the bridge tender?"

"Tell him we took care of it. It will never happen again. That's all he needs to know." Beale turned back to the phone and spoke, "Sorry for the interruption. We had a minor problem, but all is resolved. Now, please read the transcript." Beale took out his notepad.

"The first call from the *No Name* phone to Katie Piper's phone was the picture of a house fire. Second call, from Katie Piper to Blaine Sterling's phone, was the house fire picture and a text message, 'Happy Birthday. Sorry I missed your party, but I am a little tied up at the moment. This is only the beginning. The third call was from the *No Name* phone to Katie

Piper's phone, 'The trap is set, waiting for Saturday's rabbit.' And the last call, from Piper's phone to the *No Name* phone, 'Be patient.' I realize today is Saturday, but I thought you needed the information A.S.A.P."

"'Waiting for Saturday's rabbit.' What does that mean?" Beale thought out loud and underlined the phrase.

"I don't know. You're the detective," Pickett replied. "I'll e-mail your department the papers right away. Good luck, Detective."

"Thanks," said Beale and hung up.

Looking down at the notepad, with lines and circles going in all directions, one recurring thought jumped off the page. "Trap! What will be trapped?" Beale said to himself. "How will the rabbit be trapped on Saturday? Clearly, rabbit is a metaphor for a person, Blaine Sterling!"

"All taken care of," Hordowski blurted out as he entered the office. "By the way, they weren't pennies, but an assortment of coins Liverpool was paid for recycling aluminum cans. The church gave him a meal and will try to find him work and a place to stay. The deacon embraced your suggestion, a shower. What's all that scribbling on your notepad?"

"The phone call, right before you left, was from the Sheriff's Cyber Communications Unit. They just received the data we requested. Take a look at the last phone call." Beale pushed the notepad across the desk. "I circled my take on the call. What do you think?"

"I agree. Everything we have collected points toward Blaine Sterling, Charlie Boltier and his son, Thor. Why Saturday, and how will Thor trap Sterling?"

"I'm not positive, but first, let's phone Ms. Sterling and see what she is doing today." Beale picked up the phone, flipped through his rolodex and dialed. The call was transferred to Blaine's voice mail. "Hordowski, call the park and see if she is working today?" Beale opened his notepad, and wrote in big letters TRAP, CAGE and finally CAVE.

"She's working today!" Hordowski called out.

"We're going to the park. Now!" Beale exclaimed.

Chapter 43

A clump of Saw Palmetto stood approximately three yards from the lake trail. Thick and forbidding, the twelve foot tangle of sharp toothed spines and green, fan-shaped leaves, protected the opening to the cave. "There it is," Lou Bravo yelled, and pointed to a stand of palms a short distance away. "The entrance to the cave is hidden behind all those palms. Follow me."

For an instant, Lou Bravo hesitated. After the death of Blaine's husband, Lou Bravo had pledged that he would look after and protect Blaine and her young daughter, Brooke the memory of Blaine's kidnapping last year at that exact spot churned up a sickening sensation. The realization that again Blaine had been abducted, and most likely imprisoned inside the bowels of the cave, was incomprehensible. Last year, it was the disgraced park ranger, Remi Cole, who delivered this misguided vengeance upon Blaine. Now, it was Thor Boltier executing his father's vengeance upon her.

"Push aside the fronds and be careful of their sharp spines. They can saw through skin like butter," Lou Bravo called out. "Also, watch yourself on these stone stairs. They're a little slippery from all the dead leaves and sand collecting in the corners of the shaft." At the bottom, two massive chunks of stone formed the cave entrance. Wide enough for one person to squeeze through, the entrance quickly opened into a single passageway. A kerosene lantern hooked to the wall, illuminated the high earthen passageway and sandy floor of the dried-up riverbed that disappeared into darkness at the end of the tunnel.

"How are we going to find Blaine?" Tony whispered and stared down the corridor into darkness. "We have no idea where she is."

"We'll follow the light," Lou Bravo answered. "I'm positive these lanterns are deliberately placed throughout the cave to light the way. Most likely, to Blaine's imprisonment."

"Oh yeah, take a fucking look down there, all I see is black. How are we going to follow the light when there ain't no light?" Hubba Bubba spat out.

Lou Bravo turned around, glared at Hubba Bubba, and said, "We won't find out if we just stand here complaining. Let's go."

Large sections of fractured stone, which had fallen from the ceiling, littered the main passageway from the outset. Walking was difficult and on numerous occasions the trio had to crawl under or climb over rocks the size of discarded refrigerators. As luck would have it on the last obstacle, Scarecrow, tired and out of sorts, caught his left pant leg on the jagged edge of a rock. Snagged, momentum flipped him upside down in midair, and miraculously, he somehow landed in Tin Man's arms. "Wow, good catch, Tony," said Hubba Bubba standing back on his feet. "Too bad you weren't at the Van Wezel mosh pit the night those morons didn't catch me and I broke my arm. Thanks, Tin Man, I sure don't need another broken arm."

One hour and two medium sized boulders later, the main passageway curved, and illuminated by a kerosene lantern, opened into a larger passageway filled with columns of stalactites and stalagmites. The huge, limestone sentries fell from the ceiling or rose from the floor and stood silent, protecting the many secrets hidden within the ancient cave. Column after column packed the tunnel leaving only a narrow path to squeeze through. With only a few scrapes and scratches, the trio stepped beyond the sentries, down the passageway and moved deeper into the cave.

Twenty minutes later, the tunnel abruptly ended and opened into a main gallery. Lanterns at the four corners of the gallery illuminated the massive size of the cathedral sized room. The height of the ceiling, too high to calculate, just disappeared into darkness.

"I don't think we're in Kansas, Toto," Lou Bravo said tersely. "Look at the back wall. Do you see a platform? Something is on it. Something big."

"Why is the front half of the room covered with broken stone blocks, and the back section, closest to the platform, cleared?" Tony asked. "Maybe we should follow the path to the platform?"

"This place is far out. Man, just imagine the Heavy Metal band KISS down here. The acoustics would be off the Richter scale. Everyone would go crazy. It would be stratospheric." Hubba Bubba called out in a hushed tone and ran to catch up with the others.

The path led to a massive two-tiered stone platform that stretched across the entire back wall of the stadium. In center stage was a gigantic sculpture of a headless beast, standing on two rear legs with its two front legs striking out at an invisible enemy. "What is that thing?" asked Tony.

"Sick, look at what I found." Hubba Bubba exclaimed, and held up the skull of a twelve-point deer. "It was on the floor alongside the statue. Probably fell off the top? The body, plus the deer skull, this statue has to be at least thirty feet tall."

"That's some big stag!" Tony agreed. "I'd hate to get kicked in the head from that beast. Looks like some type of hunting ritual took place on the platform. The statue, the spears, and those stone blocks placed around the beast, they must mean something? What are you doing up there, Hubba Bubba?"

"It's clay alright," Hubba Bubba shouted, sticking his finger into the figure. "The deer is made of clay, and there are hundreds of holes in the animal's body. Right here is a broken spear point cemented in the beast and on the floor, dozens of spears. I know a guy in Bradenton who collects Indian arrow heads. I bet I can get a couple of bucks for one of these old spears. Bucks, get it, fellas? Deer, bucks, it's a joke, guys. Come on, lighten up, it's scary enough down here. I just thought I'd add a little levity to the party. Hey, there are also some old masks on the stone blocks, maybe they're worth something? You guys want one?" He held one up to his face.

"Quiet, I hear something," Lou Bravo whispered softly. "Over there, in the corner of the back wall, see a light? Listen!"

The three froze, held their breath and waited. What seemed like an eternity, in the loneliness of the cave off in the distance, a muffled sound of metal scrapping echoed along the walls. Then a hushed voice, indiscernible, but clearly the faint sound of words trailed off into the shadows. "Hear it? Someone is down here. It has to be Blaine and that bastard, Thor. Follow me, single file and don't say a word." Lou Bravo reached into his Lion costume and pulled out his Glock.

"Wake up, bitch. I want you to see your new home. Or should I say new prison." Thor shouted and smacked Blaine across the face. The force of the blow jerked her head to the side and almost knocked her off the small table. Awake, but still groggy from the initial blow to the head, she slowly sat up. Her right wrist was handcuffed to a thick metal chain that was tethered to a table leg. Small bird nests were scattered about on the table, and with every move of the chain, a nest fell to the floor.

"What is wrong with you, Thor?" Blaine uttered tersely. "I had nothing to do with your father's incarceration. Why are you after me?"

"Shut up, bitch. My father wants you to pay. That's why you're down here."

"That's absurd! Remi Cole is the culprit. He duped your father, not me. That's why he committed suicide. He finally realized I wasn't involved in his termination. You have to believe me." Blaine pleaded and pulled up on the chain.

"Shut up. I'm tired of listening to your lies." Thor spat out as he pushed his knife against the top button of her shirt. "It's time for a little fun before I leave. If you're nice, I'll leave the kerosene lanterns lit. If not, you'll rot down here in darkness."

After the third button, Blaine grabbed the knife and turned into her attacker catching his free arm with the chain. At that exact moment, a gunshot echoed within the tiny alcove and a loud command bellowed from the doorway. "Drop the knife, Thor, or the next shot will be at your head!" Lou Bravo stepped forward and pointed the gun straight at the target. "I said, drop the knife!" Instinctively, Blaine dropped to the ground and landed on dried bird nests and broken eggs scattered below.

She waited for the next shot. "It's over, asshole. Drop the knife and step forward."

Thor raised his arms, dropped the knife and stepped away from the table. However, in the same motion, his red cape flew into the air and then total darkness. The cape shrouded the lantern's light, and all that was heard were footsteps disappearing down the passageway.

"Hubba Bubba, light your Zippo. That bastard put out the kerosene lantern." A small flame clicked on and the trio walked over to the table. "Blaine, are you alright? Where are you?" Asked the Lion, Tin Man and Scarecrow in unison.

Holding onto the table, Blaine stood and replied, "Over here, I'm fine, but handcuffed to the table. The lantern is on the floor, at the head of the table, right next to me."

Lantern lit, the four gathered for a group hug alongside the table. For the first time that day, a sense of peace and comfort enveloped the strange assembly of characters. Together, their profound courage, loving hearts and clever minds aligned to help defeat evil. In the warm glow of the light, fear and uncertainty melted away and was replaced with a joyous reunion of friendship. Lou Bravo had fulfilled his promise to protect Blaine. Tony was overjoyed that he helped rescue a damsel in distress, and Hubba Bubba was thankful for all the spear points he thought to squirrel away in his pockets. Blaine was the most grateful, because she was alive.

"What a wonderful, crazy group you are. I can't thank you enough for saving my life. He was going to leave me down here to die." Blaine whispered and hugged them tighter.

"It was nothing. We just happened to be in the neighborhood. By the way, did you find Romeo?" Lou Bravo joked and together all four laughed hysterically.

"There's one slight problem. What about these handcuffs?" Blaine held up her right arm, and dangling from her wrist were a pair of silver handcuffs locked to a thick chain. "I'm not going anywhere until we get these off."

"Lou Bravo can shoot them off. Yeah, he can just blast the chain with a couple of bullets and we're outta here," Hubba Bubba called out.

"I wouldn't recommend that if I were you." A voice called out from the doorway. "The bullet could ricochet off the chain or a rock and hit Blaine. Then what would you do while she lay there bleeding? Still handcuffed to the table."

Startled, the four spun around and were surprised to see Detectives Beale and Hordowski, along with a Park Police Officer and two Sheriff Deputies in the doorway.

"Well, do you have a better idea?" Hubba Bubba shouted.

"How about a key!" Hordowski replied, and walked over to Blaine and unlocked the handcuffs. "There you go, Assistant Manager Sterling, free as a bird and no one has been shot."

"How did you find me Detectives?" Blaine asked, rubbing her wrist over and over, until a tingling sensation traveled up her arm.

"We finally heard the phone conversation between Thor and his father, and put the pieces together. Plus, Thor left his costume outside the cave entrance. We just followed the lights and the gunshot. I'll need to take your gun Mr. Bravo, evidence for the kidnapping case against Thor and Charlie Boltier."

"Where is Thor now?" asked Lou Bravo and handed Beale his gun.

"Well, it's obvious he's not in the cave. We have an all-points bulletin out on him. The major highways are all patrolled. The airports and bus terminals have been alerted. We'll find him." Beale said. "I'll need a statement from all of you. Can you come to the station later today?"

"Tony, Hubba Bubba and I have business to take care of on Long Boat Key this afternoon. How about tomorrow?" Lou Bravo replied.

"Ms. Sterling, can you come down to the station today?"

"Brooke and I planned to visit her grandfather in Lake Manatee for the weekend. We'll be leaving as soon as her Brownie Troop returns to the Nature Center."

"Okay, everyone come to the station ten o'clock Monday morning." Beale blurted out in an irritated tone and took out his notepad. He wrote down meeting, ten o'clock, and then drew a picture of Long Boat Key with a big question mark at the end.

No one spoke as they paraded, single file, back through the cavern. Only the echoes of tired footsteps trudging along the trails of rock and stone could be heard. Out in the sunlight, everyone shared their goodbyes and then left in separate directions. Everyone, except Blaine.

Still shaken, Blaine tried to regain her composure by taking long, slow breaths while she buttoned her shirt. She knew that she and Brooke would drive to her father-in-law's house for the weekend after the All-Trails Hike. *Perfect timing for a quiet weekend,* she told herself. Their suitcases, and fresh baked brownies smothered in confectioner's sugar, were packed in the car waiting for the trip out to Lake Manatee. But first she had to get her act together, if not for herself, then for Brooke. She was shocked at the amount of blood on her shirt and slacks. She felt along her stomach, waist and hips, and was relieved that she did not find any puncture wounds. Then, she remembered her hand. She turned her left hand palm over, and although the underside was blood stained and encrusted with tiny, blue, shell fragments, there wasn't any indication of bleeding. In fact, there was no sign of a knife wound at all. Only a faint pinkish line down the center of her hand and crushed remains of egg shells stuck to the skin. Blaine rubbed away the shells and traced the line with her thumb. The pink area was tender, tingled when touched, but no cut. "How can this be?" she whispered and closed her hand.

Blaine walked to the Nature Center to meet her daughter.

Chapter 44

Four quarters equal a dollar, equal disaster observed. "Mr. Younger, I'm going to throw up, please pull over," howled Becky Eberling. Two minutes later, the mini-van pulled off Interstate 75 and into the Skyway Bridge service area in Tampa, Florida. Parking next to the restrooms, Becky threw open the door and raced into the ladies room.

"Okay, I think Becky will need more time to settle her stomach. I suggest we stay here for a half an hour and then continue on to Sarasota. Stretch your legs if you like. There's a fishing pier, concession stand and a beautiful view of the Gulf of Mexico. See you back here at eleven o'clock."

Ken Younger, Director of Forensics, and head coach of Bradley University's Speech Team was not having a good day. The plane ride from Peoria, Illinois, to Tampa, Florida was anything but smooth. Becky, a freshman from Farmington, Illinois and new to the forensics team, didn't handle her first plane ride well. As a matter of fact, it was a disaster. Although all the seasoned members of the team reassured her that flying was no big deal, Mr. Younger feared impending doom was floating in the clouds. Check-in went smoothly. Individual security screening had a few minor bumps, two carry-on containers needed to be discarded. A can of hair spray, tube of toothpaste and Becky's lucky snow globe of Peoria were all confiscated. Boarding and seat assignments went well, that is, everyone had a seat. However, from that moment on, the flight was a nightmare for Becky. The *For Your Convenience Bag* was sticking out of the front seat pocket, a visual reminder that her stomach was churning and about to explode. The flight attendant's lecture on seatbelt use, air bag deployment, and finally seat floatation safety, sent Becky sprinting to the bathroom.

It was over South Carolina, and Becky's fourth trip to the bathroom, that Mr. Younger made the decision that it wasn't humanly possible for her to transfer planes at Tampa and then fly the last leg of the trip into Sarasota, Florida. Physically and mentally, she appeared worn out. Her small body was hunched over and pale with pain. He realized she just couldn't manage another flight, and in good conscience, he couldn't put her through any more misery.

Leaning over her seat Mr. Younger whispered, "Hi, Becky, how are you feeling?" He knew the answer before she replied. Her sunken, teary eyes spoke volumes.

"I've felt better. I'm sorry for embarrassing you, Mr.Younger, but I can't help myself. I feel so sick." Tears cascaded down her face and her tiny body began to shake uncontrollably. "I feel so helpless, Mr.Younger."

"Becky, you didn't embarrass me, and you don't have to fly anymore. I spoke with Mrs. Aronson and we worked out the details for the remainder of the trip. When we arrive at Tampa International Airport, she will take one group and fly on to Sarasota, and I will drive you and four other students to the hotel in Sarasota. How does that sound?"

"Oh, Mr. Younger, that sounds fantastic. Thank you." Becky leaned back in her seat, wrapped her arms around her stomach and closed her eyes. A faint smile crossed her face.

"Let's walk down to the fishing pier and see what they're catching?" Quinton Rimes, captain of the speech team, shouted, as all four students spilled out of the van and headed for the water.

"Remember, be back at eleven o'clock!" Mr. Younger yelled.

The pier was alive with excitement. An angler named Catfish Charlie, a regular at the pier had hooked a 10-foot-long alligator. After walking the alligator halfway down the length of the pier, which took a good hour, a Florida Wildlife Conservation Officer appeared. A crowd gathered around Catfish as he explained what happened, "All of a sudden, there was a tug on my line. I thought it was a giant flounder, I caught a five pounder yesterday. What a fight that was. Well, line starts to go out and then the water explodes right under me, and this here gator jumps out of the water. I've been fighting this monster for over an hour. My arms are killing me."

"We'll take over from here. You know it's a misdemeanor to capture an alligator without the proper permit." The FWC Officer handed the pole off to a local trapper who was called in to assist and eventually pulled the beast to shore.

"Hey, Quinton, do you have a quarter, this viewer takes four quarters." Kaitlyn Hart shouted, looking down at the direction plate on the silver binocular telescope. "I need one more for this to work."

Kaitlyn, dropped in the quarters, swung the viewer around towards the water and adjusted the lenses. "Wow, this thing can see for miles. Oh cool, there's a pelican way out there, just bobbing around in the water. Probably looking for a nice juicy fish to swim by. The water is beautiful, aqua blue, crystal clear, nothing like the Illinois River back in Peoria, except in my snow globe, that is now in the garbage. Take a look."

Quinton lowered his head to the viewer and looked out into the Gulf. "Oh My God, there's a jet plane out there. It just crashed into the water. It literally dropped out of the sky. I don't believe it. Kaitlyn, call 911. It's still floating. Hurry up and call."

Kaitlyn punched in the numbers. "Hello, I want to report a plane crash. It crashed into the Gulf of Mexico, about a half mile from the Skyway Bridge in Tampa, Florida." Kaitlyn turned to Quinton, "The lady wants to know what kind of plane and do we see any survivors?"

"It's a private jet, not that big, and I don't see any survivors. Here, let me talk to her. You take a look." Quinton reached for the phone.

"Wait a minute, Quinton, tell the lady there's a boat coming alongside the plane, a fishing boat, and it looks like someone is pulling a person out of the water. The boat is turning and leaving the area. I don't see anyone else in the water."

"The 911 Operator wants to know if you can read the numbers on the side of the boat."

"I can only make out EO843, but on the back it says *Billy Goat*." Kaitlyn stepped away from the viewer and reached for the phone. "That's it, Ma'am. The viewer ran out of time and so did the plane. It sank."

Quinton and Kaitlyn gave the dispatcher their names, contact information, and mentioned that Bradley University was competing in the American Forensic Tournament at Florida Gulf Coast College. Quinton looked down at his watch. It was eleven o'clock. The two thespians spun around and ran down the dock.

Chapter 45

Joey Banana was always the house, and the house always won at Black Jack, but not last month. As a matter of fact, the house lost big, real big. Joey lost every hand, which was unprecedented, and Lou Bravo and Tony knew something was wrong. It was ten o'clock Lou Bravo remembered, he had enough and threw down his cards. "What's the problem?" he shouted at Joey. "Your head isn't in the game." Lou Bravo never imagined that he wouldn't see his friend alive again.

The El Camino pulled up to the Casa Luna Apartments and stopped. "Hey, Hubba Bubba, go get Donna. Tony and I will wait in the car." Hubba Bubba bounded out of the back, ran across the lawn and into the apartment building. Lou Bravo reached over, opened the glove compartment and took out *Big Al*. Only for emergencies, the Colt 45 packed fire power and an attitude. "Just a little insurance in case Burkhardt shows up."

"Insurance, that thing could stop an elephant at 300 hundred yards! Overkill I would say." Tony just shook his head.

"That's the plan, Tony. That bastard killed our friend, and if given the chance, I'll kill him." Lou Bravo smiled and shoved the pistol under his lion shirt. "Here comes Donna. Get out and let her sit in the middle."

"Hi, boys," Donna called out in a controlled voice and slid into the car. Her greeting was the only thing she uttered until she reached the house. The drive to Long Boat Key was painfully silent.

Forty-five minutes later, the El Camino passed through the open front wrought iron gates that led up to Donna's house. "Looks like the police did a number on your security key pad for the gates, Donna." Lou Bravo quipped. "I guess they forgot the passcode?"

"I wonder what else is damaged. Look at the yellow police tape blocking off the entire house from the driveway, all the way back to the boat dock, minus the boat. Just park the car in front of the double glass doors. We'll need my key, or should I say, Sam's spare key, unless our neighborhood police broke the lock and left the door wide open." Donna reached inside her purse and handed Lou Bravo the key.

"Donna, I think it would be a good idea for you to stay in the car while we check out the house, just in case that bastard is inside. I don't want you to get shot." Lou Bravo reached under his shirt, and pulled out the Colt 45. "Meet *Big Al.* I use this bad boy for special occasions and Donna, I believe today is a very special day!"

"I'm going! That monster killed my husband and tried to kill me. I'm not hiding in the car and that's final!"

The four walked down the white pavers, pulled up the yellow tape and stepped up to the glass doors. Donna unlocked the door and their footsteps echoed down the foyer as they walked across the marble floor. "Tony, you take the upstairs. Hubba Bubba you check the garage and backyard. Donna and I will take the downstairs. We'll meet up in the study."

Ten minutes later, everyone was back in the study with no sign of Burkhardt, and to Donna's relief, the house wasn't ransacked. "So this is where you guys play cards? Not much of a room compared to the rest of the house. All that's in here are shelves and shelves of books," carped Hubba Bubba.

"That's why it's called a study, numb nuts, but you probably don't know how to read," snapped Lou Bravo. "Now, Tony, if I'm not mistaken, Joey said a book with an eye on its jacket, on the spine of the book. That's where the camera was hidden."

"Is it the physical eye, human, animal or insect eye, or the pronoun I?" asked Donna.

"We didn't ask. Let's look for both," Lou Bravo answered and walked towards the wall of books behind the desk.

Ten minutes later, Tony called out, "I found it, Tiger Eye. It's not an animal, but a gemstone. Take a look." There, in the center of the back bookshelf, about five feet off the ground was a nondescript, thin brown book with a picture of an egg shaped rock on its spine. In the middle of the golden brown gemstone, carefully concealed within a swirl of the tiger eye stone, was a tiny camera lens. "If we weren't looking for a camera, there's no way anyone could spot it."

"That is so cool. Who knows how long that little fucker has been there?" Hubba Bubba blurted out.

"Hey, watch your mouth," Lou Bravo shouted and smacked him on the back of the head. "Get out of the way. I need to take a look at the camera."

"Two years, that book has been on the shelf for two years. We took a trip to South Africa two years ago, and in Cape Town, Joey bought me a beautiful, handcrafted, 14 karat yellow gold, tiger-eye ring. As a gift, the jeweler gave us the book, said the stone had an enchanting history and that we would marvel at the details surrounding the gemstone. Supposedly, the stone brings the wearer good fortune." Donna replied. "We went on an amazing safari excursion through Kruger National Park, rode elephants, photographed lions, giraffes, zebras and rhinos. We slept out in the desert in tents one night, and also visited Nelson Mandela's prison cell on Robben Island. I'll never forget that vacation. I wear the ring all the time, here look."

"Okay, I found the camera and it appears to be positioned to film the bookshelf behind the desk. What's so important about a shelf of books?" asked Lou Bravo, as Donna sat down at the desk, ran her hand along the underside of the desktop and pressed a button. Immediately the bookshelf separated in the middle and an empty wall appeared in its place.

"Rembrandt's the *Storm on the Sea of Galilee* hung there. I had no idea Joey had this camera installed. He never mentioned anything about recording the room. All I know is that he would go into the study once a week, work on his computer and then leave." Donna pulled open the left side drawer and lifted out a laptop computer.

"If anyone is interested, this is a wireless high-definition video monitoring camera with state of the art home security surveillance and worth mucho big bucks," Hubba Bubba called out. "This baby is high tech all the way, motion activated, zoom lenses, one month storage capacity, and I bet locked into that PC on the desk."

"Well go over there and pull up the recording for Friday. Let's take a look at what happened when Burkhardt showed up." Lou Bravo instructed. "Donna, will you be able to look at the footage?"

"Yes, I'll be fine," and joined the others around the computer.

A few clicks later, Hubba Bubba scrolled down to Friday, and the recording began with Joey and Burkhardt entering the room. The bookcase opens up and the Rembrandt appears in all its splendor on the wall. Burkhardt examines the work of art and Joey counts money. Burkhardt turns and shoots Joey in the head.

"Okay, that's enough. Shut it off, now!" Lou Bravo shouted. "We don't need to see anymore. Donna told us the rest of the story at Patches."

Donna cried uncontrollably. Tony reached over and held her in his arms. He rocked her back and forth, and whispered in her ear that Burkhardt would regret ever coming to Florida. He promised her that he and Lou Bravo would make him pay for killing her husband and their friend.

"Donna you have to call the police. They have to see this tape," Lou Bravo snapped angrily, and handed her the phone. "And the FBI, they need to know about that bastard FBI agent."

"I don't think that call will be necessary," Hubba Bubba shouted. "Take a look out the window!"

Chapter 46

Billy *Goat* slowly backed into slip #18. Gunny masterfully manipulated the throttles, back and forth, and effortlessly the twin screws pulled the thirty-eight foot yacht into its berth. Engines cut, bumpers set out and dock lines secured, he called down to the stateroom, "How about something to eat, Commander? The Crow's Nest has a great little tavern and the burgers are to die for!" Gunny took a long, slow drag on his cigarette, and thoughtfully watched the smoke float across the helm deck and out the window. He needed one last nicotine fix, and quick. Gunny wondered *if the No Smoking sign plastered across the reception desk or the abrasive receptionist who chastised him for entering the building with a lit cigarette, would still be there. How could he forget?*

"Sounds good, and we can discuss the Art Center project," Burkhardt replied, as he hobbled up the steps into the main salon.

"You still look a little beat up. Would you rather go back to your apartment and rest?"

"No, I'll be fine. Anyway I'm starving, and I want to hear about the bridge details and security systems before Fish and his crew arrive Sunday morning." Gunny opened the door and Burkhardt walked through. "Two for lunch, a booth by the window would be nice." No sign, and the cute little hostess was as sweet as sweet could be.

"Who is Fish?" Gunny asked, and picked up his menu. "I know what I'm having, my usual, a burger, fries and a cold, draft beer. What about you, Commander?"

"Red meat, greasy fries and alcohol. Gunny, I'm sorry to say, that is a meal for an early grave. Oh, and let's not forget, the cigarettes." Burkhardt opened his menu just as the server appeared.

"Hello, gentlemen, what would you like to drink?" Asked a cheerful, young waitress with short red hair, freckles and black plastic glasses.

Gunny immediately zeroed in on her and answered, "I'll have a draft beer, Budweiser, a burger medium rare and fries."

The server looked over at Burkhardt, who looked up from his menu, and replied, "I'll just have water, and a Caesar salad, topped with blackened chicken. Thank you." The server left, along with Gunny's attention.

"Okay, Gunny, tell me what you have."

"I have the keys to the three bridge tenders' houses. The KMI and the Circus Bridge houses have a locked fence out front. One key opens both locks. I have the time schedules to raise the bridges. At eleven fifty-five every cop is off the island, all on their way to Denny's for dinner. The KMI Bridge goes up at eleven fifty-six, Venice Bridge eleven fifty-seven and the Circus Bridge at eleven fifty-eight."

"How do you know every cop is off the island?"

"I sit in a room for ten hours a day, five days a week, one hundred and eighty-five days a year, for the past thirty years and you ask me how I know! I have thirty hardcover, composition books filled with bridge schedules. I've written the time, date, description of every police vehicle, fire engine, postal truck, armored car, commercial delivery truck, and a half dozen private cars that routinely crossed the bridge. If all I did was look out the window at boats, I would have gone mad a long time ago."

"What about the security system at the Venice Art Center? The Dali Festival starts Monday morning." Burkhardt stated. "Plus, today and Sunday the museum will be setting up the exhibits for the grand opening. So what's happening with the security system?"

"Wait a minute, Commander. Take a look at the television over the bar. It's that reporter from the Bayfront fire, Bryce Faceman."

A close-up of the Channel 6 reporter filled the screen. In the background was a small panoramic view of the Skyway Bridge and the fishing pier jutting out into the Gulf of Mexico. "Hello, viewers, this is Bryce Faceman reporting live from the

Skyway Fishing Pier in Tampa. Hours ago, a private jet crashed into the waters directly behind me. As you can see, the Coast Guard, Tampa Marine Police and Tampa fire departments, as well as the FBI, are on the scene. I was told two college students from Bradley University, located in Peoria, Illinois, were looking through the telescope viewer behind me and observed the jet crash into water. They also identified a sole survivor, a tall, slim, white male rescued from the wreck and taken away in a large fishing boat. At this time, authorities are not releasing an explanation for the crash, the identity of the survivor, or the circumstances surrounding the fishing boat. Reporting from Tampa, this is Bryce Faceman, Channel 6 News." The camera pans to the aqua blue water, fades out and then returns to the regular broadcast. A picture of the local weather forecast occupied the screen and in big bold letters, Cold Wave Next Five Days, chance of frost.

"I don't believe it. What are college students from Peoria, Illinois, doing on that fishing pier, at the exact time I crash the jet into the Gulf of Mexico and you show up in your boat. What are the damn chances? Ten-to-one, a hundred-to-one, a million-to-one?" Burkhardt took one last bite of salad, pushed the plate forward and in pained voice asked, "So, tell me about the security system."

"I have breached the Art Center's security system and have begun to migrate all security commands. Performance Max Heating and Cooling Company installed and operates the heating and air conditioning system for the Art Center. They monitor and adjust the building's temperature remotely from their office. I inserted a malware virus into Performance Max's software program that in turn, enabled me to hack into the Art Center's entire security system. The virus is designed to replicate the security codes and send a flow of commands back to the creator. The creator being my computer or when I give you the disc, your computer, Commander."

"What does that mean?" Burkhardt growled and looked at the bill the server just dropped off.

"What it means Commander is that all security alerts go directly to your computer before it goes to the Art Center, to the security monitoring center or the police. We manipulate the security codes to all clear and no communication goes any further. That means you walk into the Venice Art Center Wednesday night, take the paintings and walk out undetected." Gunny sat back in the booth pleased with himself and waited.

Burkhardt smiled, threw down two twenties and stood, "When do I get all this information?" Both men walked out into the sunlight. Gunny sat down on the bench along the entrance walkway and lit a cigarette.

"The proprietary codes are on a disc for your computer person, along with the keys, schedules, boat rental, tide tables and all my information, which is in a manila envelope in my kitchen." Gunny took another drag on the cigarette, reached into his pocket and handed Burkhardt his car keys. "I'm back to work tonight, so I won't see you until Wednesday when you tie me up in the bridge tender's office at 11:56 p.m. I want to hose off the boat so take the car. The apartment key is on the ring. Take the envelope and leave the keys on the kitchen table. See you Wednesday."

"How are you going to get into your apartment if I have the keys?" Burkhart growled as Gunny walked down the dock.

"I have an extra set on the boat. When I'm finished, I'll bike back to the apartment and get ready for work."

Gunny didn't wash off the boat. Nor did he polish the brass fittings along the wheelhouse windows or wipe the salt residue from the stainless steel railings. Instead, he reached over the transom and peeled off the black vinyl letters he pasted on the boat to appease the Commander. He slapped on the official name, *Gone Fishin'*, and smiled for the first time since lunch. He then removed the E, Z, 8, and 6 from the registration numbers on both sides of the boat revealing original registration numbers FL60362FH. With everything secured, Gunny lugged his silver folding bike up from the rear salon, and out onto the dock. A light rain started as he biked down Venice Avenue.

Burkhardt didn't drive back to the apartment. Instead, he parked against the curb at the intersection of Harbor Drive and Venice Avenue.

Chapter 47

Confectioners' sugar fell like snowflakes on the girls of Brownie Troop 265 seated at two picnic tables alongside the Nature Center, drinking juice and devouring Blaine Sterling's homemade brownies. Not a single brownie shirt was free of the surgery white circles, especially Brooke's, who managed to consume three before her mother walked up to her table. "Hello, girls, how was your hike?" Blaine Sterling asked, controlling an urge not to burst out laughing at the collage of confectioner sugar shirts all in a row.

"It was fantastic," all the girls called out in unison. "We saw two Scrub-jays perched high on a tree. We think they were trying to pull off acorns to eat. That's what Mrs. Farrell said. She had the binoculars. And thank you, Mrs. Sterling, for the delicious brownie snacks."

"You're welcome, girls. Thank you for participating in the All-Trails Hike. Brooke, we need to go, don't want to keep your grandfather waiting."

Brooke said goodbye and the two walked out to the parking lot. An ambulance pulled away, its red and yellow flashing lights reflecting off the green palms as the vehicle disappeared down the road. John Forrester walked over, "We sent the hiker from the Big Lake to the hospital. He was in a lot of pain and his ankle was quite swollen. The paramedics thought it was broken, so for his own well-being, they took him to Sarasota Memorial."

"How did it happen?" Blaine asked and rubbed her hand again.

"Mr. Cottontail had a costume malfunction," Forrester chuckled.

"Peter?" Blaine laughed.

"Close, Bernie, but his anthropomorphic name was Kitty Cottontail," said Forrester with an embarrassed expression.

"What is an anthropomorphic name?" asked Brooke.

"I guess you could say it is a fancy word for animal name. On our ride back to the Nature Center, Mr. Cottontail, still in his rabbit's costume, explained that during the Furrie Hula Hoop race, where two contestants run inside a hula hoop, his head piece shifted, blocking all vision. Sightless, he tripped over his partner, Rocky Raccoon, fell and twisted his ankle. The ranger station was contacted and ranger Dan and I were dispatched to Big Lake."

"What was a man dressed in a rabbit's costume doing at Big Lake?" Blaine asked praying the answer would not frighten her daughter.

"It appeared that Mr. Cottontail, belonged to 'Furries', a club that believed humans have a connection with animals. They dress in costumes of their favorite animal, role-play and socialize. They scheduled to meet the day of the All-Trails Hike and rendezvous at the Big Lake for a day of celebration. Twenty-five 'Furries', showed up and the party started."

"Furries?" Blaine asked.

"That was the name of their club," Forrester added sarcastically. "There were all kinds of furries, raccoons, bears, wolves, foxes, one squirrel, a tiger and some bird type costumed people at Big Lake. All of the costumes looked realistic and were probably very expensive. The spot was alive with activity, bears walking hand in hand, animals picnicking, lions and rabbits fishing and animals swimming minus their fur suits." John gleefully pointed out.

"John, Brooke and I are about to leave to visit her grandfather. You must secure the cave today. After the police have finished their investigation, no one must be permitted down inside the cave. It is imperative that cave remain undisturbed. Take a look at this." Blaine opened her left hand and held it up for Forrester to see.

"So, it's a hand. Very nice. Needs to be cleaned, but what am I looking for?"

"Brooke, would you take the keys and go wait in the car for Mommy. I'll be there in a minute, sweetie." With a frown, Brooke grabbed the keys and stormed off into the parking lot.

"Adult talk again, when will I ever get to be a part of the conversation?" Brooke yelled, opened the car door and jumped in.

Running her finger across the palm of her hand, Blaine said, "That's the point. Thor slashed my hand with his knife. Look at my shirt, my slacks. That's my blood, John, but my hand is healed! And the only indication of a wound is an itching along the wounded area."

Forrester reached out and took her hand. He felt around the entire palm, slowly moved his index finger along the life lines that crisscrossed her hand, no separation. He couldn't feel a slit, an indentation or even a new scab forming. The hand was whole. Only a faint, pinkish discoloration down the center of the hand, but beyond that the hand was whole. "How is that possible, Blaine? What happened down there?"

Blaine retold the entire story, the warnings from Star Trek Guy, the meeting with Detectives Beale and Hordowski, information about the cell phone call from Charlie Boltier and the connection to his brother Roy, whose company was installing the Park's new sewer lines and detailed how Thor abducted her. Then how Lou Bravo, Tony, and Hubba Bubba and the police recused her. Finally, the most astonishing aspect of the story, was Blaine's account of the twelve nests of eggs and their curative effect on her wound. "John, when I get back Monday we need to go back down into the cave."

"I agree. See you in two days."

Chapter 48

Noxious gasoline fumes choked the air with a foul smell so thick you could taste it with each breath. Drivers closed their windows, and turned their air conditioners up to maximum to escape the offensive odor. Northbound traffic crept along at a snail's pace as cars merged from three lanes into a make-shift single lane along the center median. I-75 literally turned into a huge parking lot, with vehicles backed up for five miles or more.

Hours earlier a fuel tanker carrying 8,000 gallons of gasoline and traveling south, collided with a pickup truck, careened across the median, then turned over in a ditch on the north side of the highway. Over 7,000 gallons of gasoline spilled out of the ruptured fuel tank, filling the ditch with a lake of petroleum. Firefighters blanketed the tanker, truck and gasoline ditch with foam to control the gas fumes and the fire. Police detoured traffic onto Bee Ridge Road as firefighters contained the fire, an ambulance transported the driver to the closest hospital. Hazmat teams and crews from the Environmental Protection Agency all worked to remove the tanker, contain the spill and pump out the contaminated gasoline. Sandwiched within the traffic jam was a red and white Mini-Cooper.

"What happened, Mommy?" Brooke asked as the car came to a complete stop. "Why are there so many fire trucks and police cars blocking the road?"

"It looks like some kind of accident up ahead. I'll turn the radio on to the Highway Advisory Channel and see what is causing the backup."

All northbound lanes on Interstate 75 are closed between Bee Ridge and Fruitville Road. A fuel tanker overturned and environmental crews are on the scene. Clean-up will take 10 hours. Avoid I-75 northbound from mile marker 207 to 210.

"Looks like we're in for a slow trip to Grandpa's, sweetie. Good thing I have my Patti Highland tapes. Nothing like a little bit of country to soothe the pain and ease the ride." Blaine added with a smile and pushed in a CD.

"Give me a break," Brooke groaned, put in her ear buds and turned on her new I Pod.

Traffic inched forward a few car lengths. Up ahead, police diverted vehicles off the highway and down the Fruitville exit ramp. Blaine joined the parade of cars down the incline, through the flashing red light to begin the serpentine route to circumnavigate the accident and then back to I-75. "Brooke, please call Grandpa Dillon. Tell him we're caught in traffic and that we'll be a little late."

Brooke took her mother's phone, punched in the numbers and waited. "Hello, Grandpa. Mommy wanted me to tell you we're in traffic and we'll be late."

"I figured as much. The news is covering the accident on every channel. I can't believe the mess. Don't worry when you get here, you get here. By the way I have a surprise for you when arrive."

"A surprise, what kind of surprise, Grandpa?" Brooke sang into the phone.

"It wouldn't be a surprise if I told you, would it?"

"Well give me a hint Grandpa, please," Brooke pleaded.

"Okay, one hint, it's a riddle: `I have four frogs, but don't croak and always sleep with my shoes on. What am I?' Good luck. Say hello to your Mother. Love you, 'Bye."

"What do you think it is, Mommy? Four frogs and sleeps in shoes. Maybe it's a pet? Grandpa has cats, but cats don't have shoes. Maybe it's a doll? That's it, he carved me a doll. He's a woodcarver. Dolls have shoes. But what about frogs croaking? I don't know. I'm so confused." Exasperated, Brooke leaned back in her seat, put in her ear buds and looked out the window. A light drizzle fell, countless beads of water ran down the length of the glass clouding the outside view. Trees and buildings passed as a blur, but a large I-75 sign caught her attention as the Mini Cooper turned right and up the entrance ramp.

"That wasn't too bad, twenty-five minutes. Maybe we can make up some time on the Interstate." Blaine turned on the GPS, eased into the center lane and accelerated.

Eight minutes later the GPS announced, "Exit 220 1.4 miles, turn east onto Route 64." Blaine moved into the right hand lane and a few minutes later exited onto 64. The rain-soaked, two-lane country road was challenging, especially when an approaching SUV, traveling at a high rate of speed passed and splashed up water engulfing the Mini Cooper. Temporarily blinded, Blaine gripped the wheel with white knuckles, steadied the vehicle and drove guardedly towards Lake Manatee.

"That was some bath, Mommy. Too bad that guy didn't throw in some soap." Brooke giggled. "I have an idea. Why don't we put a soap dispenser on top of the car, so when it rains and a car passes, you press a button, soap covers the car and we get a free car wash? What do you think?"

"I love it, sweetie. Why don't you write BMW with your idea? Also, draw a picture of our Mini Cooper, the soap dispenser and you looking out the window. You're a good artist. Who knows, maybe they will pay you for your invention?" The big smile on Brooke's face was priceless.

Six miles down the road the GPS chirped, "County Road 675 one half mile. Turn left onto Rutland Road."

As the rain stopped, Blaine could see the Old Myakka Fish Camp and General Store off in the distance. It was a squat, weathered cedar shake building with a wraparound porch nestled in a stand of ancient oak trees. Blaine eased up on the accelerator and turned onto a shell covered parking lot. "Look at that sign, Brooke, 'Canoes for Rent.' Let's reserve a canoe for tomorrow. We can go fishing, paddle around the lake and maybe go for a swim? What do you say?"

"Really, Mommy, that's fantastic. Is that my surprise?" Brooke shouted, jumped out of the car and raced up the front steps and onto the porch. "Come on, Mommy, hurry up. We don't want them to run out of canoes. Hurry."

"I don't think we have to worry about that, sweetie. Look at all the canoes lined up along the stream leading down to the lake. They also have row boats. Would you rather rent a row boat? I think they come with a small outboard engine. What do you say?"

The Old Myakka Fish Camp was a fisherman's paradise. Every imaginable piece of fishing equipment filled the large showroom from the floor to the ceiling. Poles, reels, tackle boxes, hooks, lines, hats, waders, buckets, nets, sinkers, anything and everything under the proverbial fishing sun was for sale. And if they didn't stock it, they could order it online. Also a small, country food and drink concession was set up featuring home-cooked selections that changed daily. Barbecue ribs and fried chicken were local favorites, delicious and reasonably priced. Aisles of cleaning supplies, paper products, canned goods, pet food, and other sundry items for the home or campsite lined the major part of the floor space in the back section of the store.

Tucked in the far corner, four paces from the rows of grocery products, was an eight-foot, wood crafted, antique, green slate pool table. Bequeathed by the original owner, Willie (The Cue King) Mombo, a billiard aficionado, and long-time pool hustler, the billiard table represented a piece of local history that made the Fish Camp unique. Many a fish story was recounted, overstated, fabricated, or painted in glowing colors over a friendly game of pool. However, when Assistant Park Manager Blaine Sterling and her daughter entered the building, a large man hastily rolled his pool cue to the side of the table, crouched down behind the shelf of paper towels and listened.

"Hello, ladies, and welcome to The Old Myakka Fish Camp. How can I help you?" Behind the front counter was Boaty Johnson, owner and longtime fisherman. At seventy-two, Boaty fished, rowed, sailed and motored every piece of fishing ground along the Florida Coast. If he wasn't building a boat, repairing a boat, buying a boat, then he was fishing off one; hence, the amiable nickname *Boaty*.

"We would like to reserve a canoe for tomorrow," Blaine announced. "For the day. We'd like to go fishing, do a little sightseeing and maybe some swimming."

"Well, young lady, you've come to the right place. We have everything you'll need for a lovely day out on the lake. Canoe rental is eighteen dollars a day. That includes life jackets, two paddles and an anchor. We also sell live bait and have a large selection of fishing gear available for rent." Boaty pulled out the rental form, scribbled Full Day on the top and handed it to Blaine.

"My father-in-law, Dillon Connelly, lives on Old Oak Knoll Place, said he had all the fishing gear we needed. Do you know him?" Blaine took out her credit card and handed the form back to Boaty.

"Yes, everybody knows Dillon. He's a good man and a great woodcarver. He's doing a huge project for a town back in New York, restoring an old carousel for their town square. I was just up at his barn last week and from a distance some of the horses looked alive. It's a shame about his wife. She was an unbelievable artist and the sweetest lady I ever met. The cancer came so fast. It's so sad." Boaty checked the form, initialed the bottom and looked up at Blaine and said, "You do have a fresh water fishing license? Can't fish without a license, unless you want a fifty dollar fine. Could be more depending on how many fish you caught."

A glazed look covered Blaine's face, *Of course you needed a fishing license. That's what she told everyone at the park. How could she forget?* "No, I don't have one."

"No problem, Ms. Blaine Sterling. Just fill out this application, pay seventeen dollars and you're legal. Your daughter is under seventeen, so she doesn't need one." Boaty took her credit card, ran it through the machine, checked over the application and handed her the fishing permit. "You can pay for the canoe tomorrow, and you'll need bait, minnows are best for bass. See you tomorrow." He handed her back the credit card, placed all the paperwork in a drawer and waved goodbye.

"I didn't know Dillon had a son," a voice called from behind the paper towels.

"Man, you scared the beejesus out of me. I thought you left. So you heard the whole conversation? Dillon didn't know he had a son until a few months ago. The Florida Highway Patrol was investigating an accident along State Roads 64 and 674 when a news helicopter spotted a car in the woods a few hundred feet from the accident. Turned out to be the car that belonged to Dillon's son, whose adoptive surname was Sterling. Disappeared eight years ago." Boaty pulled out the paperwork from the drawer and froze.

"So Blaine Sterling married Dillon's son?" Thor growled.

"Was married, he's dead." Boaty handed him the fishing application. Thor quickly glanced at it and threw it back down on the counter.

"Put this gas can on my account. I have a hot date tonight." Thor pushed open the screen door, took out his cell phone and rushed down the stairs to his truck. "Dad, I have some good news and some bad news. What do you want first?"

The voice on the other end said, "Bad."

Thor took a deep breath and carefully detailed how he kidnapped Sterling, dragged her into the cave, chained her to the table, how he was shot at and finally how he escaped. Thor then reported that he saw Sterling at Lake Manatee, that she is staying near their cabin and that he was going to burn down her father-in-law's barn and shoot her during the confusion.

"Call me when it's over." The phone went silent.

Chapter 49

Rain has a way of chasing people indoors. Even a light drizzle can frighten away the hardiest of tourists and send them scurrying to the movies or T.J. Maxx. Rain is the bane of every shop owner in downtown Venice. All the outside tables stood empty. Only puddles of water filled their seats. The basketball courts, shuffle board lanes and tennis courts on the corner were abandoned. The cherished parking spots beside the Post Office were unoccupied. This part of Venice was a proverbial ghost town. Burkhardt smiled and thought, *just the way he wanted it*. Nothing moved, except a bicycle.

Burkhardt turned on the engine and with one movement the wiper blades cleared the water droplets and condensation that clouded the windshield. Approaching the intersection, a bicycle sloshed along in the rain. Hunched over the handlebars, a hulk of a man laboriously peddled, a cigarette hung from his lips and his rain-soaked, red baseball hat appeared ready to fall off his head. "You stupid bastard, you can barely peddle a bike and you're smoking a damn cigarette!" Burkhardt screamed and slammed down on the accelerator.

The red Chrysler lurched forward from its parking spot at the curb and raced for the intersection. The impact was murderous. The huge man, still holding on to the handlebars, was catapulted forward and down onto the pavement. Dragged for over a block, Burkhardt heard the scraping of mangled metal and then a muffled thud as the wheels mashed over the body and the silver bicycle. Burkhardt glanced in the mirror as the lifeless body wrapped around pieces of bent silver came to rest against the curb.

The car didn't stop. No one screamed. No one called 911. No one cried for John `Gunny` Mousser. The car turned onto Tampa Avenue, passed the Post Office, the water fountain, slowly past the Center Mall and into Gunny's parking lot off St. Augustine. Burkhardt took the elevator to the second floor. The apartment key read 234. He turned right and walked to the end of the hallway. Inside, Burkhardt walked into the kitchen and on the counter found the manila envelope. He poured the contents out on the slate counter and guardedly inspected each piece of paper. Everything in order, he wiped off his prints, put the keys in his pocket and left.

On his short walk across the parking lot to his apartment, Burkhardt thought he heard, off in the distance, sirens wail. He didn't stop to listen. He opened the apartment door, placed the envelope next to his computer, took a pain pill and went to bed.

Chapter 50

Horseshoes don't have laces and they certainly don't have Velcro straps for easy removal. Once on, they're to remain on, until replaced.

Brooke's face lit up like a Christmas tree on Christmas morning. A big grin, from ear to ear, gave away all her secrets and any hint of mystery vanished in her angelic smile. "I solved the riddle! I know what the surprise is," Brooke shouted as the car drove into the parking lot that fronted Grandpa Connelly's white farmhouse and art studio. Blaine parked up against the white split rail fence that bordered the entire parking lot and the brick pathway that lead up to the house. "Look at the fences. What do they all have?"

"Wood, white paint and horseshoes." On the tops of all the fence posts, squarely in the middle, painted white, sat a horseshoe. On the entire line of fence, from one side of the parking lot to the other, a horseshoe adorned each post. "I don't get it? What does the fence have to do with the riddle? The horseshoes, feet up, symbolize good luck. Most likely placed there to wish people arriving at the house good health and happiness during their visit."

"That's cool. I didn't know horseshoes brought good luck. Maybe Grandpa will give me one and I'll put it up in my new room. Anyway, the riddle said, 'I sleep in my shoes.' People don't sleep in their shoes, but horses do. Horseshoes don't come off, they are nailed to the horse's hoof. So I think Grandpa carved a horse for me. That's the surprise. What do you think?"

"That's amazing, Brooke. I guess it was your good fortune that I parked in front of this fence post. Maybe I should get some credit for helping you solve Grandpa's riddle. What do you think?" They rolled out of the car laughing, gathered up their belongings from the back seat and walked up to the house.

On the front porch, Dillon Connelly waved. "Hello, you finally made it. You must be exhausted. Let's sit on the porch and have some light refreshments." Along the back corner of the porch a tray of finger sandwiches and a large pitcher of lemonade sat on a white wicker table. Two wicker chairs and a love seat complimented the social setting. A beautiful array of palms and colorful hanging plants filled the tiny alcove with a lush green color and the scent of jasmine. Connelly poured three glasses of lemonade while Blaine passed the sandwiches and Brooke reached for the chips.

Blaine had to pinch herself every time she looked at Grandpa Connelly. The resemblance to her late husband, Troy Sterling, was uncanny. The physique, blonde hair, brilliant brown eyes, and warm smile was a mirror reflection of her husband. But of course, he was the father. The realization that Troy was gone still ached, but for Blaine and her daughter the reunion with Dillon Connelly put in motion a journey of healing. Three lives were delicately together healing as one. Blaine knew that their sorrow would turn to joy before long.

"Grandpa, what are those men doing over at the barn? Are they painting it for you? I hope they don't change the color. I like red," Brooke blurted out and pointed at the five men dressed in coats.

"Oh, those men are..." answered Dillon, but was cut off in mid-sentence when Blaine's phone rang.

"Hello, yes. Hi, how are you? What, another call to the prison. From where? Here in Lake Manatee! I don't believe it. Tonight! I will. I'll call right after I hang up. I promise. 'Bye, and thanks." Blaine put the phone down and looked up at Dillon and Brooke. Her stare was not one of fear or terror, but of concern and anger. Composed and in control of the situation, she carefully crafted her words so that an adult and child could both comprehend the gravity of the message. She took a deep breath. "That was my friend, Star Trek Guy. He said that Thor Boltier, the man that tried to kidnap me at the park, is going to burn down your barn tonight. Also, during the chaos, he plans to shoot me. He said that I should call

Detective Beale and the Sheriff's Department." Blaine slid next to Brooke and hugged her tight.

"Blaine, I know about Thor. I was about to tell you, but your phone call interrupted my announcement. Boaty Johnson called. He's the owner of the Fish Camp and a good friend of mine. He warned me that Thor was planning on burning my barn tonight. I had no idea he planned to shoot you. I notified the Sheriff and Fire Department." Connelly took a drink of lemonade and looked out at the firefighters spraying the sides of the barn. "Oh, and Brooke, the men spraying the barn aren't painters. They're firefighters, spraying a fire retardant on all the walls to slow down a fire, just in case there is a fire. The barn is still going to be red."

"I have to call Detective Beale. He's searching for Thor and I need to tell him what Boltier plans to do tonight." Blaine punched in the number. "Hello, Detective Beale, this is Blaine Sterling. Thor Boltier is in the Lake Manatee area and is planning to burn down my father-in-law's barn tonight and attempt to shoot me. You know? The operation has been coordinated. You'll see me tonight. What? Okay." Blaine turned off the phone, sat back in the love seat and watched the firefighters leave in an unmarked pickup truck. "It's not all coordinated when it comes to my family. I do the *organizing* and it's coordinated when I say it is coordinated!"

Connelly stood, picked up the pitcher of lemonade and said, "Let's move into the kitchen. We'll have more privacy and I need time for tonight's dinner." During the next half hour, Blaine dissected every tangible piece, part and aspect of the police and fire departments' course of action. SWAT teams had been deployed to the area, sharpshooters stationed with 360 views of the barn and house. Firefighters from the surrounding counties were placed on alert. Dillon listened, prepared and placed the Chateaubriand in the oven, while Brooke peeled the potatoes. He whipped up a tangy Béarnaise sauce, washed off the fresh broccoli and made a fresh garlic and olive oil marinade to steam the vegetables in.

Next Blaine outlined a strategy for the family, a survival protocol from Blaine's Ranger Academy training that would ensure their safety. The five basic techniques to control a

219

threatening situation, remembered as DICKS. Her instructor, Knut Chestnut, drilled it daily into the cadets with a big grin on his face. Develop a plan, identify the situation, control the situation, keep focus on the situation and secure the situation. *The Situation: Boltier attempts to enter the house.*

"We have a safe room, in case of a hurricane or a break-in," Donnelly interjected from the sink. "When we designed the kitchen we instructed the architect to add a safe room behind one of the custom mahogany cabinets. Behind the wine column, a hurricane-proof fake door, leads to the safe room. The back room is completely self-sufficient, equipped with an air filtration system, running water, auxiliary power, a communications network, living furnishing, sleeps six comfortably and stocked with one month's supply of food/water. I'll show it to you later."

"Perfect. We'll remain in the kitchen after dinner and if we need, retreat to the safe room if the situation outside deteriorates. More than likely, Thor will make his move early, while Brooke and I are up and moving about." Blaine reached across the kitchen table, squeezed Brooke's hand and looked her in the eye. "Everything will be fine, sweetie. You will be safe, I promise."

Connelly turned off the water and walked over to the large, polished mahogany and glass back door. He grabbed the brass knob and turned around, "Now that we solved the security situation. On a happier note, Brooke, did you solve the riddle?" Grandpa Connelly called out.

Brooke perked up as any seven-year-old would do, especially when the topic of conversation was a surprise present for her. "I did, it's a horse of course. Only horses sleep in their shoes, because they wear horseshoes. Am I right Grandpa? Please tell me I'm right," Brooke implored.

"You are, my dear. Now let's go see your horse while we still have daylight." Connelly pulled open the door and the three of them marched off to the barn. Instinctively, Blaine scanned the perimeter as they followed the brick path down to the barn. Twenty yards from the house, Blaine spotted two camouflaged individuals dug-in the underbrush, a marksman in an orange tree along the tree line, which looped behind the barn and back down to the main road. Confident that law enforcement had secured the area, Blaine would now fully concentrate on her action plan to protect her daughter.

Halfway to the barn Connelly turned to Brooke and asked, "What about the frogs? Did you figure out why they don't croak?"

"Mommy looked it up online. They're on the horse's feet, or something? She also helped with the riddle when she parked in front of the fence post. That's when I saw the horseshoe and figured out the riddle. Grandpa, could I have a horseshoe, so I have good luck?"

"Sure can! I have a barrel full of lucky horseshoes for smart little girls, but first help me push open the barn door."

Together the three pushed opened the door, Connelly walked inside, switched on the lights and magically the entire barn was transformed into a kaleidoscope of carousel horses. Horses of all different sizes, colors and shapes filled every corner of the barn. Jumping white horses, kicking brown horses, red bucking horses, horses with long flowing manes and short tails, or horses with short cropped manes and long flowing tails. Each beautiful and unique in its own way. "Now, let's find your horse, Brooke," Grandpa announced, took her hand and together they marched through a maze of Mustangs and Mares to the center of the barn. There on a golden platform, eyes blazing, hooves in the air, every buckle glistening in the spot light, *Black Beauty*, the franchise carousel attraction stood. And standing on the floor, in front of the majestic steed, a smaller, replica model waited for Brooke.

"Go ahead, Brooke, get up on the saddle. Your *Black Beauty* is strong enough. Actually, your carousel horse is a half-scale duplicate in every feature and I'm certain your *Black Beauty* will fit in your new bedroom."

"He's beautiful. I love it. What a magnificent surprise, Grandpa." Brooke jumped on her horse and hugged his neck as tight as she could. "Thank you, thank you, thank you, Grandpa, I'll always remember this awesome day. Mommy, please take a picture of me with *Black Beauty* and Grandpa." Brooke smiled. So did Grandpa Connelly. So did Troy Sterling, Blaine believed.

"We need to get back to the house. It's getting dark and I have to finish preparing dinner. And thank you, Brooke, for cleaning and slicing the potatoes. You'll love my special recipe for potatoes au gratin, delizioso. The two of you can take your suitcases upstairs to the guest room and then get ready for dinner. Don't forget to bring down the brownies!" Together they held hands and marched back to house.

Chapter 51

An explosion of search lights illuminated the entire backyard and front façade of Connelly's barn. A silhouette of a large man danced back and forth along the length of all the red boards. Splashes of liquid splattered up against the old wood revealed reckless lines of scribble and marks across its surface. "Sir, put the gasoline can down and raise both your hands," screamed a voice from the darkness. Stepping into the light, the deputy again shouted into the bullhorn, "Sir, drop the gasoline can and raise both hands."

Standing at the window, Blaine and Connelly saw the gas can sail through the air and slam up against the barn door. A dark liquid splattered against the wood and dribbled down to the ground. In an instant, the arsonist raised his left arm and in his hand a small flame flickered. A single rifle shot pierced the night sky, the silhouette collapsed and a parade of law enforcement/fire personnel stormed across lawn to the barn. The small fire was immediately extinguished and a crowd of officers surrounded the crumpled body that lay on the ground.

An hour later, after the lights went dark and the procession of vehicles and equipment departed, there was a knock on the front door. Standing in full camouflage attire, jackets, pants, boots, gloves, hats and green/brown painted faces, were Detectives Beale and Hordowski. "Hello, Mr. Connelly, I'm Detective Beale and this is Detective Hordowski," announced one of the camouflaged officers. "May we come in?"

Connelly led them back to the kitchen where Blaine and Brooke were seated. A half-eaten dinner remained on the table, cold and unappetizing. The gourmet dinner Dillon promised Brooke had been unceremoniously interrupted and sadly ruined. Blaine sensed his disappointment and only hoped dessert would bring a modicum of pleasure back to the table.

"Detectives, can I get you a cup of coffee?" offered Connelly as he walked over to the coffee machine. "We have a fresh pot and were about to have dessert in an attempt to salvage what little pleasure remains from the meal. Homemade brownies prepared by my daughter-in-law, please join us."

"I'd love a cup and one of Blaine's brownies sounds perfect," Beale answered and stuffed his hat in his back pocket.

"Yes, I'd enjoy a cup and dessert," said Hordowski and took his hat off also.

Over four cups of coffee, one hot chocolate, a plate of brownies and five shirts covered in confectioners' sugar, Beale and Hordowski detailed the scheme Charlie Boltier, from prison, mapped out for his son, Thor, to execute. First, Thor had to firebomb Sterling's house, so Charlie could gloat over and claim responsibility for the arson. Secondly, work in the park. Unbeknownst to Boltier's brother, Roy offered Thor the opportunity to open the cave and put in motion the abduction and subsequent demise of Blaine. Lastly, Hordowski spoke about the fire and how Thor planned the shooting as an afterthought, concocted from the Fish Camp encounter. Poorly conceived, both detectives believed the plan was just a desperate attempt to appease his father for bungling the cave kidnapping.

Ten minutes later and still talking, Beale's phone rang. The caller ID read 'Medical Examiner.' He excused himself and walked over to wall of windows that looked out on the barn and orange orchard in the distance. "Hello, Detective Beale, yes. Just now, I see. Thanks for the update. `Bye." Beale turned, "That was the Medical Examiner, Thor Boltier just died on the operating table. I believe that brings the case to a close, Ms. Sterling. We can cancel our Monday meeting. If we need any additional information, I'll call. Good night, everyone, don't get up, we know the way out."

Beale and Hordowski were halfway across the kitchen when Blaine called out, "Should I tell Lou Bravo that our meeting has been cancelled?"

"I don't think that will be possible. Mr. Bravo, Mr. Lilly, Mrs. Jupiter, and some character called Hubba Bubba, are being interrogated by the FBI." Detective Beale snapped, "We're now headed to the Sheriff's Department in Sarasota."

"FBI!" gasped Blaine. "Why are they being questioned by the FBI?"

"I don't have all the facts, but they were found in your friend's house, Donna Jupiter. Something connected with her husband's death, a Rembrandt, missing FBI agent and possibly a hit-and-run death this morning in Venice." The detectives said goodbye and left.

"Who wants the last brownie?" Blaine announced in a cheery voice, hoping to defuse the tension brewing in the room. Two hands simultaneously shot into the air. "Well, folks, we seem to have a tiny problem here at the contest table. One mouthwatering, confectioners' sugar-covered brownie and two hungry participants. What a conundrum tonight at the *Brownie Bowl.*"

"Mommy, I have an idea. Think of a number, one to ten, and the closest guess wins." Brooke jubilantly proclaimed.

"Without going over!" Connelly reminded everyone and motioned that he was putting his thinking cap on. "I have one." And wrote it down on a piece of paper.

"Brooke, you go first since you're the youngest. What's your number, sweetie?"

"Two."

"Grandpa what's your number?"

"Five."

Seconds agonizingly ticked away, still Blaine didn't turn over the paper. The contestants held their breath and waited. Slowly, Blaine pushed the paper to the center of the table and stopped in front of the plate with the one remaining brownie. She flipped the paper over and to everyone's surprise, no number was written down.

"What a rip-off. What's the winning number? I don't see a number, just words, three and see," a confused little girl uttered.

"That's right, sweetie. I thought we'd liven up the dinner party by having some fun. Voila, the *Brownie Bowl,* where no one leaves hungry and everyone is a winner." Blaine reached over, cut the brownie into thirds and handed out the prize.

Everyone laughed and spilled more confectioners' sugar on their clothing.

After the last bite, Blaine leaned in and whispered to Dillon, "Brooke and I need to go home after breakfast. I can tell she is upset. She's overly quiet, detached and most probably, agonizing over tonight's experience. She needs the security of her own home, even if it is a yellow trailer." A faint smile appeared to ease her pain.

"I agree. She's just staring out the window. Poor thing." Dillon stood and walked over to the sink. "I'll leave with you. I have to go to Punta Gorda and deliver a Santa sleigh to your friends' father, Don Maiello. He wants to put it on his roof for Christmas. I'll also put Brooke's horse in my truck. It will give you a little more room and better visibility out the windows."

Blaine took her daughter's hand and they walked towards the doorway. Before leaving, Blaine turned and said, "Please explain to Boaty that we're sorry we need to cancel our canoe trip, but under the circumstances, he should understand. Tell him we'll definitely go next time." From the hallway Brooke called out, "Good night, Grandpa. Thank you for my beautiful horse."

"Sleep soundly, my beautiful Granddaughter."

Dillon walked down to end the hallway, sat down at a small table and picked up the phone and called Greg Butterworth. Greg was organizing Blaine and Brooke's Homecoming surprise that was to take place Sunday afternoon. Greg, a retired Maryland State Trooper now living in Venice, started a new delivery business, *Have Pickup Will Travel*. With his connections he was able to arrange everything for the Homecoming Party. "Hello, Greg, this is Dillon Connelly. We have a problem. Blaine wants to leave tomorrow, right after breakfast. Will you have enough time to complete all the Homecoming Party arrangements?"

"No problem. They took the trailer away this morning. I put up the banner, the house has been cleaned, food and drinks are refrigerated and all the presents are in the living room. We're good to go. All I need to do is inform the neighbors to be ready in the morning."

"Wow, that's a relief. See you tomorrow morning."

Blaine bent down, kissed her daughter good night and smiled. "Sweet dreams, sweetie." She turned off the light, lay back on her pillow and stared up at the ceiling.

From across the room a tiny voice whispered, "I love you Mommy. I'm not afraid anymore."

Chapter 52

First year ranger, Trish Cox, hated early morning gate duty. For the record, she disliked all things early morning: meetings, conference calls, canoe trips, bird walks, but most of all, early morning gate duty. Rising before dawn was never fun and was the bane of her existence from an early age. Her parents owned a dairy farm in West Alexander, Pennsylvania. Two hundred Holstein cows, all of which had to be milked twice a day, four in the morning and six o'clock in the evening, seven days a week, three hundred sixty-five days a year. As the eldest child, Trish was responsible for dressing, preparing breakfast and getting her three younger siblings off to school, five days a week and one hundred eighty-five days a year. On the weekends, she worked in the barn milking cows. So any respite from an early morning assignment was welcomed.

However, today's gate duty was the exception. This morning, Ranger Trish, enthusiastically embraced her assignment. As a matter of record, she volunteered to replace Assistant Manager Blaine Sterling who was scheduled to be on gate duty. It was just happenstance that Sterling, after the attempted kidnapping, was off campus and recuperating at her father-in-law's house.

Trish woke early, dressed and hurried down to the gatehouse. For three months she envisioned how this momentous day would unfold and how she would be the ranger to welcome the affluent guest to Osprey State Park. The reservation, for Mr. Jasper Fishbourne, from Boston, Massachusetts was for two campsites to accommodate his Poseidon motorhome, which was a camper's dream come true. The Poseidon 49S, at $900,000, was one of the most expensive luxury motorhomes in the world. Rarely, if ever, seen in state parks, today's encounter would be a chance of a lifetime to view and possibly step inside the mansion on wheels. Trish Cox had to be the ranger to experience the moment.

At 8:35 a.m. in the morning, the Rolls Royce of motorhomes pulled up to the gatehouse and stopped. The sleek, gold vehicle towered over the gatehouse like a prehistoric creature hovering over its prey. Its oval front bumper, circular-shaped front window and dark, Z-shaped tinted windows that ran the length of the motorhome cast a shadow of mystery like some alien spacecraft. Two minutes later, the driver's side window slid sideways and disappeared into the body of the beast. Ranger Trish stepped outside. She could hardly contain herself.

"Good morning, Mr. Fishbourne and welcome to Osprey State Park." She looked up as a large tattooed arm appeared and rested against the open window sill. A hulk of a man leaned out. His dirty blond hair, pulled back in a ponytail, hung down past his massive broad shoulders and thick meaty neck. He filled a sleeveless, white T-shirt like he was poured into it that revealed a hellish barracuda tattoo that covered the entire length of his muscled shoulder line. A knife edge nose, steely gray eyes and a weathered face wasn't what Trish perceived a person who owned a million dollar motorhome would look like.

"Call me Fish, everyone else does. I have a reservation for two adjoining campsites abutting South Creek."

"Yes, campsites 69 and 70, but first I need to complete a checklist of requirements for the State Park system, an inspection of your vehicle and a list of the people in your party." Trish handed Fish a folder of papers, walked to the back of the motorhome and began the measurement documentation, all the while in awe of the vehicle's grandeur. Completing the license and dimension verification check, she moved to the passenger side of the vehicle, attempting to look inside through the tinted windows, but without success. Suddenly, a side panel separated, a row of red carpeted stairs dropped down and Fish walked out. "I need to inspect the lower compartments along the side of the motorhome," Trish announced, pointing to the row of handles along the bottom of the motorhome.

Clicking a remote, the stairs disappeared back into the motorhome, another click and the compartments opened. A final click and to Trish's amazement, a ruby red, Lotus 3Z slid forward from inside its compartment. Showroom perfect, the sports car glistened in the sun and oozed with opulence. "When we need something from the store. Can't be driving the motorhome all over town, can we?" Fish stated smugly and handed her the forms.

"No, of course not! Can't have that, can we? I now need to see, I mean inspect, the inside," red-faced, Trish attempted to regain her composure with a cursory check of the papers. Unfortunately, the attempt fell short and her retort, "I believe these papers are in order," didn't fool anyone.

"Is it absolutely necessary to inspect the vehicle? I can assure you, we are not transporting any drugs, firearms, exotic animals, illegal aliens or anything hazardous to a person's health and wellbeing. Unless, if you classify fishing poles as health hazards? We're avid fishermen, travel cross country fishing in every state and submit articles about our experiences to a national fishing magazine. We're in Southwest Florida to do some Tarpon fishing. *Fishing News*, the holy grail of fishing, wrote that this is the premier area for Tarpon fishing, so we arranged a charter out of Sarasota tomorrow morning. All we have inside is fishing paraphernalia. That's all." Fish crossed his arms, two open jaw sharks bulged out from his tattooed biceps, a posturing technique he used many times to intimidate rivals.

Ranger Trish took a step back. "Mr. Fish, last year an individual visited the park in a brand new Airstream camper. He had kidnapped the owners, drugged the husband and forced the mother and daughter help him cook up methamphetamine. Something went wrong, the camper exploded and burnt to the ground. Fortunately, no one was injured. Because of that incident, the State issued Regulation 495-B, requiring all vehicles entering Florida campsites to be inspected, inside and out."

"Okay, I guess I can't fight City Hall, step right in." Fish moved aside.

The view was breathtaking. Sleek and clean, the interior resembled an elegant nightclub, minus the crowd. Polished, oak flooring extended the entire forty feet from the driver's cockpit all the way to the master bedroom creating a sense of endless spaciousness. Silver-gray leather sofas, captain's chairs, mahogany tables and three separate seating ensembles complemented the sleek modern look throughout the space. A beautifully crafted kitchen with stainless steel appliances, granite countertops and finished with custom walnut cabinetry appeared to blend luxury and utility. Juxtaposed to the luxurious interior throughout the motorhome and directly off the entrance, recessed into the wall, was the fishing cabinet. Packed with poles, reels and fishing equipment, it just seemed out of place.

"Ranger Trish, as you can see, the fishing equipment may appear thrown together in a haphazard manner, but I can assure you, there is a system in place." Fish opened the glass door and pulled out a fishing pole. "This pole is a Jim Payne rod, the best fly fishing pole in the world. Handmade, this beauty has a price tag of $3,500.00. Here, hold it. Light as a feather. I caught many a fish with that rod and plan to hook more here at Osprey State Park."

Past the fishing cabinet was the first slide-out room, when pushed out from the motorhome, it added an additional three feet of living space. An elaborate computer station with hard drives, laptops, monitors, modems, keyboards, printers and wireless boxes filled every inch of space. Seated in the center of all the technology was Estaloba Church Osekbarto or Echo for short. In her early thirties, slender, short black cut hair, dark eyes, medium height, Echo was a hacker. She was in the initial stages of breaching Performance Max's computer network, the air conditioner company for the Venice Art Center, when Fish walked up with Ranger Trish. Echo hit a key and turned around. "Echo, I'd like you to meet Ranger Trish. Ranger Trish, this is Estaloba Church Oserbarto. Now you know why she is called Echo." The two exchanged greetings.

"I see you have tide charts, navigation maps and weather forecasts for the week on the three monitors. Planning a trip?" Trish asked.

"Echo is our computer guru. She's working on our Tarpon trip tomorrow and arrangements for the move up to Georgia." Fish interjected and pointed to the living room where three men were gathered around a 50" television shouting and laughing at the chaos unfolding on the screen. Each man had a remote and one after the other flailed away at the destruction taking place in video land. "These fine gentlemen, playing Mortal Combat for the millionth time are *Chipper, Bruno* and *Buster.*" The three looked up, gave a nod and went right back to the mayhem. "Don't mind them. They have zero personalities, but they're strong and can haul a three hundred pound Marlin up on deck without breaking a sweat."

They didn't look much like fishermen, Trish thought, *and with names like Chipper, Bruno and Buster they looked more like the biker thugs.*

Moving past the kitchen and into the master suite, Trish almost was knocked over when the bathroom door swung open and a short, stocky man rushed out. "Oh, I'm sorry, I didn't realize we had a guest," Captain Ringer exclaimed shaking Trish's hand.

"Captain, this is Ranger Trish Cox. She is making an inspection of the motorhome. We are finishing the tour, or should I say the inspection, with the master suite, my bedroom." Fish pushed open the door. A king-size bed, heated marble floor, walk-in closet, 40 inch wall television and entertainment center, private bathroom and sauna, all complemented the extravagant lifestyle of the rich and famous. All the luxuries of home, but on wheels. Trish was speechless. Her bedroom, plus her bathroom and most of her kitchen would fit inside the master suite, with room to spare. She didn't want to leave. "So did we pass inspection?" Fish barked out. "Last room, end of tour. So is..." Fish's phone rang. He read the caller ID, Burkhardt. "I need to take this. Hello, yes, we're at the park. Campsites 69 and 70. Two o'clock, fine. See you then."

"Inspection completed Mr. Fishbourne. I don't see any complications and if you would sign at the bottom of the form, I'll be out of your way."

"By the way, Ranger Trish, what's the fishing like in the park?" asked Fish.

"In South Creek we have bass, snook, an occasional redfish and snapper. In the lake, sunnies, bluegills and an occasional alligator." Trish smiled and walked back to the ranger station and watched the motorhome drive off. Something just wasn't right. What it was she couldn't say, just an uneasy feeling about the new visitors. Call it ranger intuition. Trish put an asterisk next to Fishbourne and wrote: *talk to Assistant Park Manager Monday.*

Chapter 53

Abracadabra. Now you see it. Now you don't. Brooke was first to notice, or should one say, not notice. Her curious eyes scanned the block as the Mini Cooper turned onto Serpentine Lane. It was gone, absent from the location that for months was known as home. The banana yellow trailer was missing.

"Mommy, someone stole the trailer. It's gone. Look, our house is finished. It looks brand new. It's beautiful."

"I love the color, a soft cream. No more yellow for the Sterling family, hurray. Look, sweetie, there's a banner hanging from the roof. Can you read it?" Blaine pulled into the driveway and turned off the engine.

"Welcome home," Brooke shouted and raced up to the front door. "Hurry up, I want to see my room," she called with one hand on the doorknob.

Together they opened the door and stepped inside. Instantly, a thunderous roar screamed out, "Surprise, welcome home," and all the neighbors jumped out from their hiding places and welcomed Blaine and Brooke home. Greg Butterworth stepped forward and handed Blaine a bouquet of flowers and Brooke a big, yellow greeting card in the shape of a banana, signed by all the neighbors. Brooke happily waved the banana card in the air, to the joy of everyone and ran off to inspect her room. Everyone else marched into the dining room to enjoy the potluck buffet the neighbors provided.

"Help yourselves, we have plenty of food," Butterworth announced. "Don't forget to leave me a piece of my wife's sweet potato pie. It's beauty on a fork, but heaven in the tummy."

An hour later, the front door flew open and in rushed a Lion, Tin Man and a Scarecrow. The trio danced around the room shouting, *Welcome Home, Welcome Home, Blaine and Brooke.* After five minutes of utter chaos, the costumed characters flopped down on the couch, exhausted and hungry. Blaine pushed in, sat next to the lion, handed him a piece of cake and asked, "Where have you been?"

"We've been to see the wizard and he has a very big problem. One of his most senior FBI agents is missing. His jet crashed into the Gulf, the stolen Rembrandt remains missing and the wizard's $10 million dollars in cash is unaccounted for. I would say that is a major problem." Lou Bravo took a bite of the cake and continued. "We turned over a video that captures the missing FBI agent murdering Joey Jupiter, stealing the Rembrandt and walking off with the $10 million in cash. I would say the wizard is having a very bad day."

"How is Donna?" Blaine asked.

"She's shaken up. The video was traumatic, but her friend Sam is helping her cope. You know Sam, she owns Luna's Restaurant in Venice."

"Yes, I met her last year at a fundraiser for the Venice Book Fair. She was hosting an author seminar at her restaurant. She's a terrific person. I'm positive she will be a comfort to Donna. I noticed how she had a way of solving problems, maybe it's the business component of her life. Yes, she will able to bring Donna some closure..." Blaine was about to finish when Brooke raced into the room shouting that everyone had to come see her room.

All the neighbors put their plates of food down, walked back into Brooke's room and there in the corner of the room was Brooke's *Black Beauty*. Standing on a golden pedestal was the magnificent horse. Hooves in the air, head held high, eyes blazing, the black stallion came to life. It was a magnificent sight, everyone struck speechless by the beauty of the sight before them. "It's beautiful, Grandfather, thank you so much," Brooke cried out and raced over to Connelly and jumped into his arms. Everyone clapped and gathered around the steed to confirm it was indeed a statue.

Blaine lifted Brooke onto the horse and turned to the neighbors and said, "I want to thank everyone for this wonderful homecoming, especially Greg Butterworth for organizing the affair. But it is getting late and tomorrow is a school day for Brooke. Thank you and we'll see you all after everything is unpacked."

Blaine grabbed Lou Bravo's arm and pulled him over to the horse. "Thank you for saving my life and giving Brooke a mother back," she whispered and hugged him.

Chapter 54

Money is the great equalizer. The old adage, *money talks*, was all too familiar to him. As a teenager, delivering newspapers along the streets of Beacon Hill in Boston, Burkhardt witnessed how people with money lived the good life. The big houses, fancy cars, lavish parties, all the perks society offered, went to the entitled people with money. As a young man, starting out in business, he was confronted daily by the harsh realities that business transactions were made with a handshake, behind closed doors and between individuals with deep pockets.

The promise of a big payoff was the carrot and that was exactly what he promised Fishbourne and his fishing party. One million each at the completion of the Venice Art heist. Burkhardt embraced the money philosophy and understood if he needed people to accomplish a task, they had to be paid. Not friendship, nor threats, or a superior product; money spent in the end was the determining factor.

Burkhardt felt generous as he stuffed his attaché case with $1.5 million dollars, $250,000 for each co-conspirator. A surprise bonus, compliments of John *Gunny* Mosser, who would not be counting his million dollar pay-off. He was dead. Burkhardt slipped in the manila folder with all the plans and his Glock for extra security. A quick scan of his room and he was off.

The KMI Bridge was up and a large, two-masted schooner was passing through the raised spans of the structure when Burkhardt stopped. "Lucky bastard," Burkhardt thought as he watched the yacht slowly motor north up the Intracoastal Waterway. "Possibly headed to Sarasota and brunch at Marina Jack," he mused. Burkhardt checked his watch, quarter to two, four minutes elapsed between the gates lifting and traffic proceeding over the bridge. "Just like Gunny reported, four minutes. Bridge up, bridge down, all bridges, perfect timing," Burkhardt shouted and pushed down on the accelerator.

Fifteen minutes later the red Chrysler turned into the Park and stopped at the Ranger Station. This time Ranger Diana was on duty. Ranger Trish was somewhere in the park regaling the other rangers about her morning adventure with the Poseidon Motorhome. The only thing missing from Trish's travelogue were pictures which she planned to acquire during their stay. "Good afternoon and welcome to Osprey State Park," said Diana and stepped towards the car.

"How do I get to the campground," Burkhardt barked out and handed Ranger Diana a twenty dollar bill.

"You take the second road on the right. If you are planning on staying overnight, you will need to register before the Park closes. What campsite will you be visiting?" Diana handed back the change and nonchalantly studied the driver.

"Campsite 69 and I'm not intending on spending the night," he gruffly remarked and closed his window.

"Have a nice day..." Diana, trailing off mid-sentence, called out as the car pulled away.

Burkhardt did not notice the natural beauty of the park. He couldn't appreciate the ancient oaks, with their long arms spreading across the road shielding all visitors from the oppressive heat, nor did he behold the delicate beauty of the Spanish moss hanging from branches like gigantic spindly spider webs. And of course, Burkhardt couldn't enjoy the quite hush of the park, buffered by the lush greenery that filtered out the hustle and bustle of a harried world, because his radio was playing *Rachmaninoff's Symphony No. 2*. He sped past the entrance to the boat launching dock and didn't slow down until a large colorful painted sign with animals of all sizes and shapes and *Campground* in big, block letters jumped into view. He crossed the bridge and followed the one-way lane to campsite 69.

"Where the hell is Fish?" Burkhardt screamed slamming his briefcase down on Echo's computer table. "I told that son-of-a bitch I would meet with everyone at two o'clock. It's now two-fifteen. Where is he?"

"He went fishing," Echo said quickly and shut down her computer.

"Call him on his cell. Tell him he has five minutes to get his ass back here or he's off the payroll." If looks could kill, Burkhardt was ready to explode and everyone in the motorhome took notice.

"Fish, Burkhardt is here and he's pissed. You need to get your ass back here in five minutes or you're off the project." There wasn't a reply. Echo clicked off.

"Okay, let's sit down in the living room and wait," Burkhardt pointed to the first seating area. "Guys, turn that damn television off."

An hour earlier, Ringer had unhooked the trailer hitch and parked the Escalade in lot #70 and positioned the motorhome on lot#69. When Chipper, Bruno and Buster removed the two Jon boats from the Escalade's roof, Fish decided to do a little fishing. The mention of bass and bluegill excited his fishing curiosity and afforded him the excuse to put to use his Jim Payne fly rod. Fish gathered up his gear and marched down the road toward South Creek.

Five minutes down the road Fish stopped dead in his tracks. Before him loomed a campsite in purple. An old beat-up purple trailer with a purple awning that covered a purple picnic table stood in the center of the lot. A purple VW bus from the `60s, a purple bicycle, purple wagon and purple folding chairs all complemented campsite #87. Standing on a half broken wooden ladder, painted purple, was a woman attempting to hang a strand of purple lights over a palm tree. Wobbly as the ladder appeared, she managed to complete the string of purple lights and stepped down to the ground. What planet, was another story? *What was with that purple hair?* Fish thought, *and why was she surrounding herself with all things purple?*

Standing no more than five feet tall, thin, in her forties, with short curly purple hair, she turned and her restless purple-green eyes stared directly at Fish. "You like what you see, mister?" She said, and rested her hands on her small hips.

"I sure do," replied Fish and walked up to her. "My name is Jasper Fishbourne, but my friends call me Fish." Fish stuck out his hand.

"Nice to meet you Fish. My name is Vardi Zammiello, *the Purple Lady*, but my friends call me Miss Vardi." They both laughed.

"I get it now, that's why all the purple," Fish answered. "That's not what caught my attention, Miss Vardi, it was the tattoo. The purple rose on your leg."

Vardi put her leg up on the picnic bench and ran her finger lovingly over the rose. "This is my favorite, my first! You know what they say about your first. It may not be perfect, but you always remember it. You remember your first, Fish?"

"Yeah I do. She was a cheerleader and it was in the back seat of a Chevy." Fish grinned and puffed up his chest.

"You pig, I was talking about your first tattoo." Vardi smacked his arm flirtatiously and smiled.

"It's a work of art and from a distance, the petals, appear to pop, almost in 3-D. Plus, up close, there are three, maybe four different shades of purple. It's beautiful. The tattooist was a master," Fish uttered and stepped back to take in the total view.

"You think the rose is beautiful, what do you think about these tattoos?" *The Purple Lady* whispered, and pulled off her sweatshirt. A bouquet of flowers cascaded down from the top of her left shoulder, across her breast and down to her stomach. Hundreds of purple flowers flowed up and down, sideways and across her body. A collage of purple shapes and designs all flowed together in an emblazon collage of nature. Particularly striking was a large daisy with pedals radiating from the left breast and Vardi's pink nipple sticking up from the center. Fish felt a surge of excitement, and reached out and cupped her breast. His erection hardened, as Vardi's hand reached down and slowly stroked his manhood. He pulled her closer and their bodies began to move slowly in rhythm. "Let's go inside," she whispered. "Don't want to upset the neighbors."

Fish reached for the screen door when Echo called, "Burkhardt, is here and he's pissed. You need to get your ass back here in five minutes or you're off the project."

242

"What time is it?" Fish barked into the phone.

"It's quarter past two. You better get over here fast before this guy does something crazy."

"I'll be there in four minutes," Burkhardt shouted and let go of the door. "Sorry my delicious purple flower, but something else has come up and not in my pants. I need to go." He turned and sprinted down the road.

Chapter 55

Fish kill. If looks could kill, one exhausted fisherman caught his last fish.

Everyone was seated in the living room when Fish burst through the door. Out of breath, he gasped, "Sorry I'm late, but I completely lost track of the time. I was appreciating a lady's flower." The three muscle men high-fived each other, the Captain smiled, Burkhardt just glared. "Sorry, won't happen again."

Burkhardt cleared his throat, "Okay, there's been a change in plans. We're going to hit the Art Center tomorrow night, not Wednesday as planned. So you all need to pay attention while I outline the new schedule. But first, I have a surprise. A bonus, on top of the million, each of you will receive after the job is completed." Burkhardt reached into his attaché case, took out six envelopes containing $250,000 each and handed them out. Flipping through the bills everyone's spirits soared, while Burkhardt's command increased a hundred per cent.

"Why the magnanimous gesture?" Fish asked sheepishly.

"Let us just say, my fortune, is your good fortune. The foreign buyers are anxious to acquire the merchandise. To show their appreciation, a bonus was forwarded. They would appreciate the artwork sooner, rather than later. That's the reason for new date and the bonus. Now, let's get down to business."

Burkhardt passed out a folder to each member of the team detailing the timeline of the operation and each individuals' responsibilities. First, Echo explained how she breached the Venice Art Center's security system. She hacked into the Center's heating and air conditioning company portal, which was connected to the Art Center's computer system. Next she inserted a rogue program that infected the encryption algorithms enabling her to access all proprietary codes from the Art Center's computers. With the codes and passwords, she routed all the security commands through her laptop and back to the Art Center. With a tap of a key, Burkhardt had the ability to bypass the alarm network, walk into the Art Center and rob the gallery undetected.

"Great job, Echo. Moving on, a colleague of mine placed a red buoy at the headwater of South Creek and Dryman Bay. Dryman Bay empties into the Intracoastal. This afternoon, Chipper and Buster will take the two Jon boats out to the buoy. Leave one and return to camp. Understand?"

"Sure, no problem, boss," the two answered in unison.

"Tomorrow morning, Fish, you and the captain drive over to Marker 4 and pick up the boat. It's a 25' Bayliner, reservation #42375625, with a three-day rental and paid in full under your alias, Ringer. Tie up at the buoy and take the Jon boat back to the park."

Burkhardt looked down at his notes and circled three names, Chipper, Bruno and Buster and asked them to take out the key in their folder. He told them that their key would open the bridge tender's office. Once inside, they need to force him to open the bridge and then kill him. Leave the office, make sure the door is locked and climb down to the Intracoastal and wait for the Bayliner.

"How long do we have to wait for the boat?" Chipper asked. "Won't there be people all over the place, pissed that the bridge is up and no fucking boat. What about the cops?"

"Good questions, Chipper, at least one of you Neanderthals is thinking." answered Burkhardt. "Next to your name is a bridge and a time. What everyone needs to understand is that this operation is driven by a time schedule. In order to succeed, we must follow the schedule. If anyone screws up the timeline, the entire operation will fall apart like a house of cards. Do you understand?" Everyone answered in harmony.

Burkhardt picked up his paper and continued." At 11:50 p.m., Monday evening not many people are out and about. Most of the shops close at 5:00 p.m., and the four or five restaurants serving dinner shut down around ten thirty or eleven o'clock. More importantly, at 11:50 p.m. the evening police shift ends and all patrols leave the Island. There is a four minute window before the next shift cross the bridges, so all bridges must be raised at 11:52 p.m."

"Gentlemen, please check your list, Chipper, you have the Venice Avenue Bridge; Buster, the KMI Bridge. Fish will drive you both to your destination. Bruno, you have Circus Bridge. The Captain will take you to the Bridge and wait until the bridge is raised. The two of you will then pick up Fish and Echo at the marina." Burkhardt reached into his attaché case and took out four pictures, held them up and announced, "This is the prize, ladies and gentlemen. Four of Salvador Dali's most treasured paintings: *The Burning Elephant*, *The Young Virgin*, *The Lobster Phone* and *Basket of Fruit*. Echo, you have the first two paintings; they're directly forward in the main gallery. Fish, your paintings are on the west wall, off the main entrance. Here take these. All of the artwork is secured to the walls. You will need to cut the paintings from the frames. Next, Chipper will be picked up and finally Buster. All of you will cruise back to the Jon boats, and then back to camp. Any questions?"

"I know the cops can't drive over the bridge, but can't they walk to the bridge tender's office, lower the bridge and arrest us?" Fish asked.

"No they can't!" Burkhardt barked. "The bridge tender is dead and cops don't know how to operate a bridge. They'll have to call the Department of Transportation to get someone to lower the bridge, which should take at least thirty minutes. Plus, who are they going to arrest? No one is on the bridges. No crime has been reported. We're just a bunch of good ol' boys floating down the water, cruising out into the Gulf to do some night fishing."

"When do we get paid," Buster blurted out. "How about when we get back to camp?"

"No! Fish, will drive everyone out of the park in the motorhome. Leave the Escalade, Jon boats and outdoor camping equipment behind, and rendezvous with The Lone Star Vehicle Transport trailer on Tamiami Trail. Fish will drive the motorhome into the transport and the transport will drive to Sarasota where I will be waiting with your money and six Corvettes."

"That's bullshit, man. I don't see why we can't get paid in the park and leave," Bruno shouted.

"Because I said so. If you don't like it, get out." Burkhardt slammed his fist down on the desk, reached into his attaché case and glowered at all six. No one said a word. "That's more like it. I'll see you tomorrow night." He closed his attaché case and walked out.

Chapter 56

Old rocks tell a new story. Blaine pulled up to the gate, punched in the security code and waited for the chain link fence to slide across the road. All clear, Blaine shifted into first gear and slowly drove into the Park. Up ahead, a light went on in the Ranger's Station and Blaine spotted Diana organizing the office for the day.

"Good morning, Diana, getting an early start?" Blaine called out and smiled.

"I wanted to talk to you before you started your day. I had a feeling you'd be early, so here I am. Ranger Trish checked in an unusual camper yesterday, a Mr. Jasper Fishbourne and party. The motorhome by itself was unique, a Poseidon, you know the RV millionaires drive around in. Wait until you see it." Diana handed Blaine her phone. "Take a look. I drove by their campsites yesterday afternoon. That's right, they have two sites. The RV is so humongous nothing else could squeeze onto site #69, so everything else is on site #70."

"That is some motorhome. So, what's the problem?" asked Blaine.

"Flip through the rest of the pictures. Do they look like millionaires?" Diana quizzically interjected.

"No, but what does your typical millionaire look like nowadays? They appear to enjoy fishing. I still don't grasp the issue?"

"The problem is with their Jon boats. They started fishing with two, now there only one. Where's the other one?" Pointing to the boat floating in the water alongside their campsite. "Plus, launching a boat from a campsite is a park violation."

"Diana, you're right, it is a violation. I'll speak to them later today. About the mystery of the missing Jon boat, I'll try to get an answer. However, I have a meeting with Park Manager Forrester that may take up most of the day, so you may not have an answer until tomorrow. How does that sound?" Blaine handed Diana back her phone.

"Before you leave, I put together a folder on the motorhome and its occupants. You may want to verify some of the information listed on their registration forms."

Blaine put the folder on the passenger's seat, said good-bye and drove off. *What a magnificent motorhome. Oh, to be rich,* she thought.

Forrester was waiting outside Blaine's office when she arrived. Next to him was a Florida style Indiana Jones, complete with a red flowered Tommy Bahama shirt, khaki shorts, Timberline boots and the iconic Indy fedora. The Club Car was packed with lanterns, rope, water, collection bags, first aid kit and backpacks.

"Good morning, Blaine," Forrester called out. "I'd like you to meet Ryan Murphy, Sarasota County Archaeologist." Blaine stuck out her hand and they exchanged greetings. "I thought Ryan would be an asset to our investigation. He has extensive knowledge of the Native Americans that inhabited this area and could possibly help identify some of the artifacts in the cave. He was also museum curator at Spanish Point, and when I revealed the purpose of the undertaking, and the possibility of a Spanish Point connection, he was eager to join the team." The trio jumped in the Club Car and drove off.

The cave entrance was still concealed by a thick clump of palms and patches of thorny briars. Blaine was first to push away the vegetation and climb down the rock stairs. She switched on her lantern and squeezed between two hulking rocks that marked the tunnel entrance. The main passageway was a dried-up riverbed of pebbles and sand that curved down into the hollows of the cave and disappeared into darkness. The trio stopped and looked into the foreboding abyss.

"Twelve steps," said Murphy. "The number twelve has cultural significance throughout history. The twelve tribes of Israel, twelve Apostles, twelve constellations, and let's not forget the twelve Clans of the Calusa Indians. These steps could have been chiseled out over five hundred years ago, maybe more." Murphy snapped a picture.

Thirty yards into the passageway, immense stalactite and stalagmite formations oozed downward from the ceiling or rose from the floor. These immense columns of limestone blocked sections of the tunnel presenting a challenge for the group, especially Forrester. At times, the Park Manager had to stabilize the prosthetic leg, and with the help of team members, hoisted himself over the large rock inclusions that littered the floor. With only minor cuts and bruises, the trio squeezed through the large columns of limestone and continued along the pathway. Murphy snapped a picture.

"Look at this," Murphy called out. Holding up his lantern against the earthen tunnel wall, he pointed to the different parallel lines that fell from the ceiling down to the floor. "Notice the difference in color, some stratification lines are darker than others, some thicker and some appear wavy. These earthen lines record the past. Tell geologists how many years old this cave is. Like tree rings, they denote a sequence of years. This cave could have been gouged out by rivers of water, as the sea level rose, ten thousand years ago, maybe more." Murphy snapped a picture.

"That's amazing, but we need to move on. There's more to see," Blaine instructed and walked down the tunnel.

Twenty minutes later, the passageway ended and opened into an immense chamber the size of a football field with a cathedral ceiling that disappeared into the darkness. Their lanterns scanned the gallery, revealing large chunks of stone that littered the cave floor and a narrow pathway which appeared to lead to a platform in the rear of the chamber. Murphy snapped a picture.

"We need to follow the path," Blaine said and marched down the footpath that wound its way between massive pieces of broken rocks.

Halfway down the path, the chamber was clear of all broken stone and terminated at a two-tiered platform. Forrester called out, "Why is only half the gallery cleared?"

Murphy reached into his backpack, took out his compass and turned until the compass arrow pointed north. "Because, the sun sets in the west," Murphy answered. "Many ancient cultures believed their gods lived beyond the setting sun, in the west; ergo, they wanted to get as close to the gods as they humanly could. This platform is due west. Most likely, significant ceremonies took place upon the platform." Murphy snapped a picture.

"What on earth is that?" Forrester shouted and pointed up to the platform. In the center of the platform, a huge sculpture of a headless beast, over twenty-five feet tall, standing on two rear legs, with two front legs kicking out at its attacker. Alongside the statue, the skull of a very large stag lay, fallen from the top of the statue long ago.

Murphy was first to step up onto the platform and circle the beast. The rest of the team followed. They all pushed and poked at the statue. "It's clay. Blaine, to your knowledge, are there any clay deposits in the park?"

"Not deposits, but there are layers of clay under the Mesic Pine Flatwoods. That's about sixty percent of the ground surface in the park." Blaine pulled at a broken arrow shaft, it wouldn't budge. "The clay helps retain some of the water that percolates down from the sandy surface soil. Thus extending the water supply for all the plant life in the park."

"Then, this clay was dug up here, transported to the cave where the statue was constructed and finally, I believe, a very important hunting ceremony took place on the platform we're standing on now. Look at the spear and arrow holes on the statue." Murphy picked up a broken spear point. "These holes were made from spears identical to this one, maybe even this one." He pushed the spear point into the puncture. It fit. "Also the flaking technique and the notching at the base of this spear point is similar to arrow heads and spear points found in the midden at Spanish Point. There is clearly a connection between Spanish Point artifacts and what we have here in this cave." Murphy snapped a picture.

"What do you make of these twelve stone blocks topped with masks that circle the stag?" Forrester asked. "Just look at these masks. The human faces are a bit scary, but beautifully crafted. And the colors, red, black, blue, brown and white appear to be recently painted, but that can't be possible." He picked up one, turned it over and brought it to his face. "A perfect fit, what do you think?" Murphy snapped a picture.

Blaine picked up another mask, carefully looked it over and pointed to the back wall. "Look at the mural. I believe the answer is in the drawings." Behind the statue, the entire back wall depicted a large hunting scene. Vivid colors of black, red, white, brown and blue highlighted men standing with long spears, men running with spears, men spearing deer, groups of men shooting arrows at deer and killing them.

"Magnificent," Murphy called out. "This mural is a paramount archeological discovery, as important as the Lascaux cave paintings in France. To my knowledge, this painting is the only depiction of an ancient hunt that took place in Florida. This is an archeologist's dream come true." Murphy snapped a picture.

Blaine walked to far end of the platform and held her lantern over her head. Beams of light touched the end of the mural revealing a small alcove tucked away in the back corner of the cave. "Over here, gentlemen," Blaine called out. "This is where I was held captive, and why we are here today."

The tiny room, the size of a small apartment kitchen, and unlike the organized platform, was in shambles. Wooden chairs were overturned, bird nests were thrown about the room, or piled up on a large wooden table. Dirt, grass, twigs, crushed nests and broken egg shells littered the floor. The back wall was painted a sky blue, with twelve cerulean blue and gray crestless birds circling what appeared to be a red sun.

"Twelve stairs, twelve masks, twelve stone blocks and now twelve birds circling the sun," Murphy declared. "There has to be a connection somewhere, but where."

Forrester started to brush away the debris from the table. One side at a time beautifully carved images of animals appeared. A deer, alligator, owl, raccoon, Scrub-jay, tortoise, bobcat, osprey, panther, fish, eagle and otter. Twelve animals in total, circling the four sides of the wooden table. "You're not going to believe this, but there are twelve etchings of Florida animals carved into the table." All three looked down at the intricate carving before them. "Clearly, a master woodworker painstakingly cut out all the images. I wonder if there is an order, or sequence connecting the carvings to the mural?"

"Who has the Scrub-jay carving?" asked Murphy. Blaine raised her hand. "What month does a Scrub-jay lay eggs?"

"It takes place from February through June."

Murphy looked at his compass, pointed around the table and said, "Blaine, I theorize that the animal to your left is born in March and the animal to your right in January." Murphy waited.

Carefully, Blaine wiped off both images, looked up and smiled. "You're correct, Sarasota Archeologist, Ryan Murphy. It's a calendar. These ancient people created a twelve month calendar, based upon the life cycle of the local animals. And, they fashioned their recordings around the only fulltime resident of Osprey State Park, the Florida Scrub-jay. Remarkable."

"Very good, Assistant Park Manager Blaine Sterling, but further research must be conducted to prove all of this," Murphy added pedantically and aimed his camera towards the wall mural.

"No pictures!" Blaine said quickly and blocked his view with her hand. "From this point on, everything that transpires in this room stays in this room." Blaine reached across the table and pulled a battered Scrub-jay nest over to her side. She then took out her Swiss Army knife, opened the blade and dragged it across her open palm. Blood gushed from the incision and puddled in her cupped hand. Forrester reached over with his handkerchief, while Murphy froze, horrified at what just transpired. Blaine reached into the nest, pulled out a dappled gray-blue egg and broke it into the wound.

"What just happened? Are you people psycho? I'm outta here." Murphy jumped back from the table and started for the door when Blaine shouted.

"Before you leave, Ryan, look at my hand." Blaine slowly opened her hand, placed it down on the table and wiped off some of the broken pieces of eggshell.

Murphy's eyes popped wide open. He grabbed the edge of the table and stuttered, "What happened to the wound? The bleeding has stopped and it looks as if the cut has healed. All that is left is a pink line. How is that possible?" Murphy bent forward and guardedly ran his finger along the palm of Blaine's hand.

Afterwards, Blaine rubbed her hands together, smoothed away the last remaining shell flakes and said, "It itches for about a week, and the pink line where the incision was made, disappears a week later." She held her hand up for all to see.

Forrester, reached over and took Blaine's hand, "So, you believe the Scrub-jay egg has some form of healing power? Amazing! The bleeding stopped, the wound sealed, and the only indication of an incision is this faint pink line down the center of your palm, which, you say, will disappear in two weeks."

"Correct, that is why it's imperative no one outside this room should know. The threatened Florida Scrub-jay is in a fight for survival. Just last week, Sandy Cooper, our park Scrub-jay coordinator, reported that the Scrub-jay population has decreased from one hundred birds a decade ago, to nineteen birds today. If news of the healing power of Scrub-jay eggs was public knowledge, poaching of the eggs would decimate their population overnight. Not just in our Park, but all over Southwest Florida." Blaine stopped talking and took a deep breath. The silence was chilling and time seemed to stand still until she said, "And we cannot be the catalyst for such a catastrophe."

Forrester was first to reply, "I agree, the Scrub-jay population could never survive such an onslaught. It is our professional responsibility, at this time, to keep this information confidential. It is possible that in the future, when their numbers are robust, we could make a public announcement."

"I don't know," Murphy interjected and picked up an egg from one of the nests. "As a scientist, I believe I have the responsibility, maybe even an obligation, to investigate, hypothesize, conduct research and communicate my results to the scientific community, not conceal an important discovery."

"You also are obligated, as a scientist, to help preserve the living creatures in our environment. If you reported that Scrub-jay eggs have a chemical proponent to heal wounds, you then

255

could possibly be responsible for the elimination of a species. Who knows what the ramifications could do to the balance of nature in this region? Do you want that condemnation?"

Blaine, didn't wait for a response, she opened her backpack and sweep all the eggs and nests on the table and scattered about the floor into it. "I'm going to lock this backpack in my office safe," said Blaine. "When the time arrives, that the Florida Scrub-jay is removed from the Threatened Species List and I pray it does. Then, and only then, will I hand over to you, Mr. Ryan Murphy, the contents of the safe. At that time, you may announce to the world your scientific results. Is everyone in agreement?"

The trio made their way back to the surface and went their separate ways.

Chapter 57

Fish tales, ponytails and a big fat fairy tale. Blaine dropped Forrester and Murphy off at the office, turned the Club Car around and headed for the campground. Forrester said he would contact the District Office in the morning, request a directive on the cave and e-mail Murphy the particulars regarding a possible archeological dig. He also wanted to convene a meeting with all the park rangers after he received confirmation on the cave.

A steady stream of campers with cameras, talking on cell phones or tweeting feverishly passed Blaine as she approached Fishbourne's campsite. Bob Wyllie, a long-time Osprey Park camper and this year's camp host, walked up to Blaine and said, "What an amazing motorhome. I've never seen a more luxurious RV in my life. Has to be a million bucks, maybe more. You're in for a real treat."

Standing in the middle of the road was a giant of a man, covered in tattoos, casting into a bucket. With one fluid motion he pulled the rod back, flicked his wrist and moved his arm forward. The fishing line exploded from the reel and hook, line and sinker arched upward twenty feet in the air and splashed into the bucket. "Catch anything?" Blaine shouted and pulled the Club Car in front of campsite #69.

"I've had a few nibbles, but I think I'll hook the big one tonight." Fishbourne reeled in the line, turned and faced Blaine. "My friends call me Fish, and you are?"

"I'm Assistant Park Manager Blaine Sterling. Welcome to Osprey State Park. It appears you have drawn quite a crowd. Hope the entourage of curiosity seekers hasn't interrupted your focus on fishing, especially if tonight is the night." Blaine smiled, stuck out her hand and said, "Nice to meet you."

"The pleasure is all mine," Fish answered and shook her hand.

"That's a nice bamboo pole you have there. A Jim Payne fly rod if I'm not mistaken, pricey!" Blaine added at the end.

"Yes, to both questions, $3,500.00, not including the reel. I love to fish and can afford the best. Fished all my life. My father was a fisherman. His father and grandfather lived on the water. You could say it is in my blood. Take a look, every fish I ever caught is tattooed on my body. I'll be adding a Florida Tarpon tomorrow."

"I'm not a big fan of tattoos," Blaine replied tersely.

"Would you like a tour, Assistant Manager Blaine Sterling?" Fish added with a solicitous grin and a wave of his arm announcing the grand tour.

"Thank you no, but I do need to talk with you about your Jon boats. Park policy prohibits launching any form of watercraft from a campsite. I notice you have one boat tethered on South Creek next to your campsite. Please haul out the boat today and future launches must be made at the canoe dock." Blaine handed him a copy of the regulation with the fine schedule highlighted in yellow marker.

"Sorry, didn't realize it was a problem. The boat will be hauled out tonight."

"There is one other matter, Mr. Fishbourne. Where is the second Jon boat? I was informed that you had two boats when you arrived Sunday morning." Blaine looked Fish straight in the eye and waited.

"Oh, that Jon boat. I lost it in a bet. Some kid in a red baseball hat was fishing along the creek and I bet him, if he could cast into the bucket on the front of the boat, I'd give him the boat. If he missed he'd have to jump in the creek with all his clothes on. I even said, he could have three tries. He was about thirty feet away. There was no way anyone could make that cast. Especially, a punk kid." Fish looked down at his feet and kicked at an imaginary rock sending it up thirty feet into the air.

"Was the boy about twelve year's old, had big ears?" asked Blaine.

"Yeah, that little bastard had big ears and sunk his cast right into the bucket, the first time!"

"You were snookered, Mr. Fishbourne. That was Ethan Forrester, the Park Manager's son. All that boy does is fish. They live at the Park and every day I see Ethan fishing. Sometimes at the lake, other times on South Creek. He has won every fishing contest at the park and a half dozen tournaments in the area." Blaine smiled.

"I'll be damned. That little hustler. Oh well, a bet is a bet," Fish exclaimed and slapped his leg.

"The Forresters are at Busch Gardens for the day. A reward for Ethan receiving all A's on his report card. I'll talk to the Park Manager tomorrow when I start work. I'm sure he'll make Ethan return your boat."

"If it's no trouble, but I can live with being snookered." Fish smiled, pleased with his little fairy tale.

Blaine said goodbye, jumped into the Club Car and drove down the road. She stopped in front of the restrooms and wrote on Diana's folder: *John Forrester doesn't have a son. Why is Fishbourne lying?*

Chapter 58

Monday night is mac and cheese night, a long revered family tradition. Blaine's grandmother made it, Blaine's mother made it and Blaine makes it every Monday night. Cheddar cheese, milk and elbow macaroni, simple ingredients for a grand comforting meal.

"Hello, I'm home," Blaine called out as she walked inside the house. "Who knows what day it is?"

From the kitchen voices answered, "It's mac and cheese night. Hooray." Seated at the kitchen table were Brooke and Mrs. Bretch. Brooke jumped up the moment she saw her mother, ran over and gave her a big hug. A neat pile of homework papers, books and class folder covered the table. "Brooke finished all her homework. Her class folder has a field trip permission form and this month's lunch menu. I'll be going. See you both in the morning. `Bye."

Dinner was perfect, macaroni and cheese. Who could ask for anything more. "So, Brooke, tell me about your class trip. Where are you going?" Blaine pulled out the permission slip and quickly scanned the paper.

"We're going to the Venice Train Depot and learn about trains. We're studying transportation, so Mrs. Cordas thought it would be a good idea to see a real train and depot. I can't wait. Can you come? You could help chaperone." Brooke grabbed her mother's hand and looked up at her with pleading blue eyes. "Please, Mommy."

"I'd love to, sweetie, but first I need to check my work schedule. I'll write a note to your teacher on the permission slip and I'll call her tomorrow. Now you need to take your bath and then head off to bed. I'll be in to kiss you good night, now off with you. I have some work to do." Blaine finished cleaning up the kitchen and headed for the study.

"Once a liar, always a liar. What are you hiding Mr. Jasper Fishbourne?" Blaine mumbled to herself and powered up her computer. One minute later, she logged on to Google Street View.com, punched in Fishbourne's home address on the park's registration form and waited for the picture.

"Mommy, I'm in bed," a voice echoed down the hallway. "Can you read me a story?"

Blaine finished reading *Berenstain Bears Get Stage Fright*, Brooke's favorite series, kissed her good night and left.

"Liar, liar, pants on fire Mr. Fishbourne," Blaine exhaled. She doubled checked the park's form, with the photocopy of his Boston license, both addresses matched. "Living in an abandoned warehouse, I think not sir." She phoned Florida Park Police dispatch. They ran the motorhome and Escalade's license plates through DMV with the same results. She wrote on the folder: 721 E. Back Bay Boulevard, Boston, abandoned warehouse.

"What are they up to? A million dollar motorhome, a computer expert, a boat captain, three muscle bound gorillas and a smooth talking fisherman who doesn't know Tarpon fishing is best in May and June. The mix of people doesn't make sense for a fishing expedition. They're fishing for something all right and it isn't Tarpon. I'll speak to Forrester in the morning," Blaine thought and powered down.

Chapter 59

The graveyard shift sucks. A detective's entire body clock gets all scrambled up and only after a week's readjustment to daytime work can a person feel normal. Beale and Hordowski were working on the John Mousser hit and run when the call came in at ten o'clock in the evening. Beale picked up the call on the third ring. "Detective Beale, how can I help you?"

"Beale, this is FBI Director, Richard Pembroke, Boston division of Art Loss investigation. I believe our agency may have valuable information that will assist you with the Mousser hit and run case, which in turn will aid us in locating our missing FBI agent, $10 million dollars and a Rembrandt."

"Good evening, Director, I'm all ears," Beale replied.

"It appears our agent Ross Burkhardt, and John Mousser were in Vietnam together. In fact, they were in the same helicopter division, nicknamed *Billy Goat battalion*. Burkhardt was in Venice under the pretense to purchase the Rembrandt, arrest Mr. Jupiter and return to Boston. Burkhardt hasn't returned."

"A lot of men were in Vietnam," said Beale. "That doesn't necessarily mean that these two men reconnected here in Venice. Mousser lived in Venice for forty years, was a bridge tender and hadn't even gotten a parking ticket. Doesn't sound like a man involved in anything illegal."

"Well, the plane that crashed into the Gulf of Mexico last Saturday, off the Skyway Bridge in St. Petersburg, was the jet Burkhardt was on. We also have information that a fishing boat picked up someone from the wreck and the name of that boat was *Billy Goat*. Mousser has a fishing boat." Pembroke waited.

"That's right. Our CSI team went through Mousser's boat from top to bottom. Nothing incriminating turned up. We also checked his condo, nothing. Only thing remaining to check are the paint chips left from the automobile that ran down Mousser. The report should be on my desk sometime today."

"We believe Burkhardt and Mousser were working together on a project. The painting is missing, the $10 million is unaccounted for, Mousser is dead and Burkhardt has vanished. With this new lead, would you go back to Mousser's condo and check again? There has to be something." Pembroke waited.

"Okay, Detective Hordowski and I will turn the place upside down. If there's something to be found, we'll find it."

"Thanks, Beale. We are sending a team down to Tampa tomorrow to help assist in the recovery of the plane. Keep me posted on your Venice connection."

Beale and Hordowski put on their jackets and left the police station.

Chapter 60

A full moon hung over the piney flatwoods as the black Escalade left the Osprey State Park for the last time. Orange moon shadows danced through the branches lighting patches of road under the dark hammock of green. A red fox sprinted across the road, followed by her two kits and together they quickly disappeared into the undergrowth.

Fish had made the drive many times before, twenty-five minutes to the KMI Bridge, two minutes to the Venice Avenue Bridge, and four minutes to the Venice Art Center. Island police shift change, eleven fifty in the evening, bridges begin to rise at eleven fifty-two and access to Venice Island is completely blocked at eleven fifty-five. Fish and his passengers, Echo, Chipper and Buster, all had the schedule memorized. The Captain and Bruno left for the Circus Bridge at ten o'clock.

Buster was dropped off first. The Escalade made a rolling stop, the back door jerked open and a large man jumped out. Dressed in black, he slowly moved up the sidewalk bridge as the Escalade drove over the bridge and disappeared. "Don't run," he mumbled to himself. "That's what Burkhardt said. You don't want to attract attention to yourself. You're walking home, that's normal."

Halfway across the bridge, a car sped by. The girl in the passenger's seat stood up, took a drink and tossed the bottle into the air. Buster froze, and helplessly watched the bottle sail across the bridge and explode against the office wall. The bridge tender ran to the window and looked down as the tiny convertible disappeared into the night. Buster took a deep breath, inched his way up to the door, pushed the key into the lock and turned. The door opened. Gun in hand, he walked inside. "Sit down in the chair and you won't get hurt," Buster ordered. Without hesitation, the startled bridge tender did as he was instructed. Buster looked down at his watch and barked a second command, "In three minutes, I want you to raise the bridge. That's all you have to do. I'll tie you up and leave. Do you understand?" The man shook his head in compliance. Buster looked at his watch again. The seconds ticked by slowly. Buster checked his watch again. "Okay, walk over to the console and raise the bridge." A single shot rang out and the old man tumbled to the floor. Two more gun shots echoed down the Intracoastal Waterway that night.

Echo tapped a key on her laptop and activated the security blocking program as the Escalade pulled into the Art Center's parking lot. Fish stopped at the entrance doors. The engine was still running. He walked straight to the Center's front door, pushed a metal suction cup against the glass, turned the cutter clockwise and released the metal cup. A perfect circle hollowed out from the glass adhered to the device which he unhooked and placed in his tool bag. He reached through the opening and pushed open the door. The security alarm was silent. Echo handed him a flashlight and his leather art portfolio as they walked in.

The Art Center was a cornucopia of Dali's surrealist paintings. Thirty-five masterpieces spread throughout the rooms and hallways of the gallery were a dream come true for all art lovers in Florida. When the exhibit opened, over five thousand people lined up to view the paintings. Venice police had to divert traffic to the Venice High School for extra parking and shuttle the throngs of art lovers back to the Art Center. The front page of Venice Journal Star pictured Mayor John Holic and Mary Morris, the Director of the Art Center, cutting a big red ribbon officially opening the start of the Celebration of the Artist in Florida. It was a historic opening day for the city of Venice and an infamous night for all partisans of the Arts.

Echo's two paintings, Dali's most important works in the exhibit, *Basket of Fruit* and *The Clock*, were in the main gallery. She panned the room from left to right with her light and on the second pass found them. Fish, on the other hand, had to walk to the far side of the gallery and down a hallway to find his two, *The Young Virgin* and *The Lobster Phone*. Echo just finished removing her second painting and was about to place it into her portfolio case when...

Chapter 61

Beale pulled onto Venice Avenue and drove towards the Island. At eleven o'clock at night, not a soul was on the road. "That's a great boat Mousser had, perfect for fishing or just cruising around." Hordowski uttered. "I'm sure the Sheriff impounded it and as soon as he is able, he'll put that beauty up on the auction block. I think I'll buy a boat. What do you think?"

"I think you're insane. Let me tell you a few things about boat ownership, my friend," Beale snapped. "I had a Thompson, 24 foot inboard/ outboard, bow rider when I lived on Long Island. It was a great boat when it was running, but it was a money pit. Always needed something repaired, cleaned or removed. My best two days of boat ownership were the day I bought the boat and the day I sold it."

"There's a police auction up off Fruitville this Saturday. The newspaper said they had cars and boats for sale. I think I'll go. Why don't you come with me, to show me the ropes? What do you say?"

"What do I say? It's your freakin money, why not? But, don't come crying to me when you need money to fix your boat. Here we are. Parking for KMI condo residents only, that's what we need. I see a spot under the carport."

The back entrance door was locked. Beale had Mousser's keys, unlocked the door and stepped inside. Hordowski walked over to the elevator and pressed the button. "I'll take the stairs," Beale announced. "I have a thing about elevators. Try to avoid them as much as possible, especially when I'm on the job. See you upstairs."

The yellow police tape still blocked the door to Mousser's condo. Beale opened the door, stepped under the tape and was looking into the hallway when Hordowski approached and said, "So what are we looking for?"

"Anything that can connect Mousser to Burkhardt. You take the kitchen and bedrooms. I'll take the living room, hallway and bathrooms."

For the next forty minutes the two detectives methodically dissected each room one square inch at a time. From top to bottom, side to side, front to back, every piece of furniture was inspected. Every drawer was opened, pulled out and turned upside down. Every kitchen cabinet, food pantry and cleaning closet was emptied and then put back to its original placement. Nothing.

"It's no use, Beale, there's nothing here. The place is like a museum. Everything is neat and tidy. Nothing is out of place. Both bedrooms consist of: one bed, two night tables, two shell lamps, one television and three flower paintings. The kitchen, everything stored neatly on shelves, drawers or closets. Counters, clear of clutter. The hallway, six framed pictures of his boat."

"I believe you just solved the case Detective. This guy was a neat freak. Everything had a place and there was a place for everything. Look around, what's out of place?" Beale crowed.

Confused, Hordowski called out, "A couch, two end tables, two lamps, coffee table, television, two fish pictures, a mirror, two more fish pictures and a small bookcase."

"So what's out of place, Mr. Detective?" Beale added sarcastically and walked over to the mirror. "The mirror. It's too close to the fish pictures. Mousser put the mirror here for a reason. Take it down."

Taped to the back of the mirror was an envelope and on the front was written, To Venice Police. Beale took out his pocket knife, opened the envelope and read:

To whom it may concern:

If you are reading this letter, you undoubtedly are aware of my untimely demise. My only regret is that my death occurred before I could enjoy the one million dollars Burkhardt promised

270

me. Payment for participation in the Three Bridges art heist, which will take place on Wednesday at 11:56. At that time, all three bridges will rise, blocking access to Venice Island and all scheduled police patrols. The Dali exhibit, at the Venice Art Center, will be robbed. Burkhardt has the Rembrandt, the FBI's 10 million dollars and is staying with his goons in a motorhome at Osprey State Park.

I'm sure he either killed me or orchestrated my death.
John Mousser

"This is it. Mousser gave us a blueprint to take this guy down and prevent another major art disaster. We have two days to coordinate with the FBI, Sheriff's department and the Park police. First, we need to go back to headquarters and update the Chief."

Chapter 62

The bridge spans stood skyward, unmoving and stoic. The gates were down, red lights flashed and the caution bell clanged. The Venice Avenue Bridge was raised when Beale applied the brakes. "What the hell! The bridge is up. I don't see any boats. Hordowski, get out and look down the Intracoastal."

Hordowski ran across the road and looked up and down the waterway. "No boats, the KMI Bridge is also up," he yelled.

"What time is it?" shouted Beale.

"Twelve o'clock."

"It's tonight, the robbery is tonight! They changed the day! Mousser, was likely murdered before the change. That's why he wrote Wednesday. We don't have two days. It's now. I'm going to the Art Center. You run up to the bridge tender's office and see if you can get the bridge lowered. We have to get cops on the Island."

Hordowski sprinted up the sidewalk leading to the bridge tender's office. The door was locked, but with one kick, the wooden frame splintered and flew open. A gray-haired woman was duct taped to a chair in the middle of the room. Slumped forward towards the floor, her frail, tired body pointed to a pool of blood that puddled in front of her feet. Hordowski checked for a pulse. There was none.

"Dispatch, this is Detective Hordowski, badge number 34292. We have a dead bridge tender at the Venice Avenue Bridge and I suspect the two bridge tenders from the KMI and Circus Bridge have also been shot. All bridges are up and there's no access to Venice Island by car or foot. You need to contact the Department of Transportation to get personnel out here to lower all three bridges ASAP. I tried pushing a few buttons, but nothing happened. We also have a robbery in progress at the Venice Art Center. The Dali art show is there.

Those paintings are worth millions. Detective Beale is on route to apprehend the thieves." Hordowski hung up and looked down at the dark water below.

Chapter 63

An unlocked door is an invitation for trouble. An unlocked door and a disabled security system is a recipe for burglary. Beale cut the headlights on his Crown Vic, rolled into the Art Center's parking lot and pulled over on the grass. A large SUV stood at the entrance to the Art Center, its engine still running. *This guy is pretty cocky to keep his engine running or just plain stupid, like most criminals*, Beale thought and reached through the window and removed the keys.

Slowly, Beale squeezed through the entrance door, stepped into the foyer and listened. The sound of ripping or cutting echoed from inside the main gallery. Large banners of Dali and his clock-melting painting, announcing *The Year of the Artist,* hung down from the ceiling everywhere. Between the separation folds of the banners and directly in front of him, a single beam of light illuminated a painting. Beale waited for his eyes to adjust to the dark and then stepped out from behind the surrealistic banner. Gun in hand, he shouted, "Police, put your hands up and step away from the painting!"

In a matter of seconds, the silence of the Art Center was turned into a beehive of hysteria. Echo let out an ear piercing scream, spun around wildly and tumbled to the floor. Her flashlight fell from her hand and skated across the room in convoluted circles. Over and over, beams of light shot up in all directions spotlighting surrealistic tigers, swans, elephants, virgins and many other bizarre treasures about the gallery until it bumped up against Beale's foot. Flashlight in hand, he aimed the light straight ahead and again commanded, "Get up and drop the box cutter. Now!"

The sound of metal on concrete vibrated far along the floor and down the hallway where Fish was working.

"What's your name?" Beale shouted and took a step towards his prisoner.

Barely discernable, the girl said, "Echo."

"Echo what," Beale snapped angrily and pointed the light directly in her face.

A defiant young woman stared back at him ensconced in a frame of white light and self-reliance. She put up her hand to block the glare and answered, "Just Echo."

"Well, just Echo, didn't your mother tell you it's against the law to steal? People go to jail for that offense. Believe me, you'll be one of them, shortly. By the way, any accomplices tonight?"

Before Echo could answer a muffled pop sounded and immediately a burning pain ripped through Beale's right shoulder blade. The sudden impact threw him forward, spun him around and slammed him head first onto the floor. He lay on his back, motionless, arms twisted above his head. He still held onto his gun. Blood puddled around his head and coated his hair in a black gooey mess. Beale closed his eyes.

"Where the fuck did this cop come from?" Fish barked out and kicked Beale's gun across the room. "Won't be needing that anymore, asshole! Looks to me like the only thing you will need is a good mortician."

"Maybe we should call 911?" Echo stammered and looked down at the lifeless figure.

"What, are you crazy? Finish your last painting and meet me in the truck. If you call anyone, I'll break your neck. Understand!" Fish picked up his portfolio and walked outside.

Two minutes later, Fish ran back into the gallery shouting, "I can't start the truck. That bastard took the keys!" He knelt down and frantically rummaged through Beale's pockets. Finally successful, jiggling them in the air he yelled, "Found them, let's get the hell out of here."

The Escalade turned onto Tamiami Trail and headed south for the marina. The road was deserted, no cars in front and a quick glance in the rear view mirror proved the same. Fish smiled and thought, *so far so good*. He looked down at the speedometer, 45 mph and laughed. "Old habits are hard to kick," he whispered out loud.

Echo picked up her laptop, checked the screen and turned to Fish, "Why did you shoot him? You could have just hit him over the head with your gun. He wasn't moving when we left."

"Too fucking bad. I didn't like his attitude and plus, he was a big guy. I didn't want to bother with a fight, too messy. He was collateral damage. Grow up! It's all part of the business." Fish shot her a menacing stare and slammed down on the accelerator. The Escalade jumped forward and raced down the block past the hospital.

"Pull over, I'm going to be sick," screamed Echo. "Now!" Fish jerked the Escalade to the shoulder and slammed on the brakes. Echo jumped out and barfed all over the sidewalk and a wall mural of circus animals where she rested her hand for support. Fish threw her a towel and motioned for her to get back into the SUV.

A few minutes later the SUV pulled into the marina and headed straight to the gas dock where the Captain and Bruno waited. Fish picked up the two art portfolios, his satchel of tools and jumped onto the boat. Echo looked down at her laptop, held her finger over the keyboard and tapped the Esc key. Off in the distance an alarm rang. She smiled and ran to the boat.

Chapter 64

Night painting or is it a surrealistic fishing trip? Bruno threw off the last bow line that tethered the Bayliner to the gas dock as Captain Ringer eased the craft forward away from the marina and out into the Intracoastal. Moonlight danced on top of the water providing a natural light from bank to bank. The water was smooth as glass, not a ripple on the surface, clearly a boater's dream night for cruising. Two feet off starboard, a fish jumped out of the water and made a big splash. Too dark to identify, Fish could only kick himself for not bringing his rod. Ringer pushed on the throttle and the boat effortlessly cut through the water towards the Venice Avenue Bridge. A white frothy wake splashed off the bow of the boat and rippled sideways towards the bank as the vessel picked up speed. Not another boat plied the water that night, only a yellow Bayliner, out for a little night fishing, glided cautiously down the Intracoastal.

Off in the distance, the shadow of the Venice Avenue Bridge loomed huge and menacing. Its spans open and unyielding, stood as a reminder that technology if not used properly sometimes brings life to a standstill. Flashing lights on both sides of the bridge illuminated a chaotic scene unfolding above the Intracoastal. A line of police vehicles on the west side of the bridge stretched all the way back to Tamiami Trail waiting for the bridge to close. Police officers helplessly stood by, their vehicles ready to move on to the Art Center as soon as the bridge lowered. On the Island, firefighters removed the body of the bridge tender and transported her to the hospital.

Twenty feet from the bridge a small light flashed three times. "Look, Chipper's signal," Ringer called out. "There along the bank. Go up on the bow and help him climb on board."

With the precision of a master captain, Ringer eased the craft to the bank, held the craft steady and waited motionless for Chipper to jump aboard.

A few minutes later, the Bayliner passed under the bridge and was nearly blindsided by a Venice Police boat cutting across their bow towards the Island. Its huge wake rocked the smaller Bayliner and almost threw Chipper and Bruno overboard while walking along the deck. Ringer turned into the wave, cut through the wall of water and steered back away from the racing police cruiser. The police boat drove up against the embankment and unloaded three officers with bicycles. Dressed in SWAT uniforms, the trio picked up their weapons and rode off in the direction of the Art Center.

Ringer maneuvered the Bayliner into the middle of the channel and headed north for the KMI Bridge. Three flashes of light signaled Buster's location on a small dock along the waterway at the foot of the bridge. Police and firefighters marched up to the bridge tender's office only to report that, Bruce Donaldson, a bridge tender for over forty years, was dead. People from Marker 4 Tiki Bar, a local restaurant near the bridge, gathered in the parking lot and speculated as to how long it would take to lower the bridge. Speculation ranged from ten minutes to two days. However, after twenty minutes, most of the patrons became bored, got in their cars and drove away, leaving only the police and firefighters standing on the bridge waiting for it to close.

Ringer motored up to the dock, pushed the throttle into reverse, held the Bayliner steady and waited while Buster stepped on board. "All accounted for," Fish yelled. "Let's go collect our million dollar payoff." Everyone cheered as Ringer pushed the throttle forward into cruising speed and headed for Dryman Bay and channel marker #28. Fish looked back at the two bridges, still up and motionless. Their silhouettes, in flashing lights of red, blue, yellow and white, splattered across the night sky, a surrealistic canvas befitting their night's shocking masterpiece. *Dali himself would be amused by their caper.* Fish thought, and leaned back in his chair and watched the pageant fade into darkness.

The Bayliner cruised along the Intracoastal, past Roberts Bay, maneuvered around Dona Bay, across Lyons Bay and finally into Dryman Bay. Checking his electronics, Ringer yelled back to Fish, "Tell Echo to turn on the mooring beacon. We've entered Dryman Bay, should reach the mouth of South Creek and the Jon boats in ten minutes." Ringer scanned the waters for a flashing light.

"She's watching the local news. Some reporter, a Bryce Faceman, is reporting on the bridge openings. There's a close-up of this jerk, in a boat, splashing around under the Venice Avenue Bridge. This bozo is more concerned about his hair getting wet than the bridge now closing," shouted Fish. "Wait a minute, he said they found the cop I shot. Firefighters transported him to Venice Hospital. I guess he's not dead, thanks to little Miss Heartfelt and her computer. Beacon on!"

Off the starboard side, a flashing light blinked, on off, on off. An outline of two boats floating side by side appeared. Two sleeping pelicans, startled by the approaching craft, lifted off from the nearest Jon boat and disappeared into the night. Ringer powered down and slowly headed towards the light and the waiting boats tethered to the mooring. Fish reached overboard and secured the Bayliner to the mooring, while Ringer shut off the engine. Bruno, Buster and Echo climbed down into one boat. Chipper, Ringer, Fish and the two art portfolios in the other. Low in the water, the flat bottom boats idled down South Creek to the campsite at a leisurely 3mph. Bruno and Chipper manned the spotlights and tentatively scanned the water from bank to bank, while gripping the side of the boat in a viselike hold. A family of raccoons on the far bank, gnawing on fish, scampered back into the undergrowth as the two boats crossed downstream and docked at campsite #69.

Chapter 65

The Poseidon's headlights sliced through the night and slowly inched forward from campsite #69 and out onto the campground road. An overhanging branch from a large oak snagged the top rung of the rear roof ladder and snapped off with a loud clap. The late night disturbance caught the watchful eye of a great horned owl who turned its head and shook out its feathers. The motorhome stealthy maneuvered through the campground and out beyond the main gate. Fish turned right and drove north on Tamiami Trail.

A quarter mile up the highway, a black enclosed truck transport trailer waited on the shoulder of the road. Its driver, Baxter Cuttings, lit a cigarette, took a long slow drag and turned the emergency flashers on. He jumped down from the cab and walked into the woods to relieve himself. After completing his business, Cuttings walked to the rear of the trailer, opened the two metal doors and lowered the loading ramp. He lit another cigarette and looked inside. "What a crazy world this is! I love it," he yelled into the cavernous trailer.

Two weeks earlier, out of nowhere, Cuttings got a call to pick up an empty trailer in Boston, drive to Osprey, Florida and pick up a motorhome. Then deposit the trailer in an empty warehouse in Sarasota, Florida, collect his money and drive back to Alabama. The caller promised twenty-five thousand dollars up front and another twenty-five when the drop-off was completed. Two days later, a Fed Ex package arrived with the money; Baxter was out the door of his Huntsville, Alabama, home and headed north.

The first leg of the trip wasn't bad, but the drive down from Boston was a nightmare. Rain all the way to Georgia, with accidents on almost every overpass, continually backed traffic up for miles and forced hours of lost time to be made up sleeplessly. But he made it and with time to spare.

Cuttings, took a final drag on his cigarette, flicked the crimson butt to the ground and crushed it out with his boot. He looked up and followed the headlights approaching off in the distance. A moment later, a spacecraft like motorhome appeared and pulled over to the shoulder. The driver slowly inched the futuristic vehicle up the ramp and into the trailer. Cuttings immediately engaged the loading ramp motor and pushed the doors closed. Lastly, he turned a small chrome valve on the side of the trailer that would stabilize the air circulation system inside the trailer.

Four police cars, lights flashing, sped by heading south, as Baxter Cuttings shifted into first gear and eased the black trailer onto Tamiami Trail. He smiled as the flashing lights disappeared around the curve in the highway and darkness returned to the road. "Perfect timing," he shouted and banged on the back window as if to inform his passengers of their good fortune.

Ten minutes later, the black transport trailer turned down School Avenue and disappeared into a dilapidated warehouse. Abandoned for years due to a depressed real estate market, the out of state owner made repairs only when forced by the City of Sarasota, to keep the structure from falling down. A perfect, undisturbed location, for a clandestine operation to transpire.

Dangling from a steel rafter at the far end of the building was a manila folder, and written in big red letters was the name, Baxter Cuttings. Cuttings inched the truck forward until the letters on the folder pushed against the windshield. He turned off the engine, reached out the window and pulled the folder inside. Frantically, he tore open the package and froze. The last thing Cuttings saw were strips of newspaper flying from his hand as a bullet from a Glock 23 shattered his brain.

Burkhardt pulled open the trailer's side doors and pointed a remote opener at the motorhome. Instantly, the gold door moved sideways into the body of the motorhome and a stairway unfolded down to the ground. He slipped on a gas mask and climbed the steps. Inside, Burkhardt stepped over Fish sprawled out on the floor, fishing pole in hand. Moving into the living room, the three muscle bound morons, lay on the couch in front of the television where a video game was still in play. Echo and Ringer sat in the kitchen area. Slumped forward in chairs, their arms stretched out across the table and cradled their resting heads. A bottle of champagne and two half-finished glasses bubbled in front of them waiting for the next celebratory toast. Resting on an empty chair, across from the pair, were the two art portfolios.

Burkhardt removed his mask, picked up the portfolios and grabbed a glass of champagne. He held the glass up and bellowed, "Cheers." In one quick gulp, he consumed all the bubbly, threw the glass to the floor and walked out.

The drive back to the apartment was uneventful. Not a single police car or fire emergency vehicle on the road. The flashing lights and blaring sirens were all but a memory as the Chrysler cruised over the KMI Bridge and down into Venice. Exhausted, he would get a good night's sleep and make his Boston call in the morning.

Burkhardt had just parked the Chrysler in its usual spot and was about to open the car door, when a torrential rainstorm exploded overhead. "I don't believe this," he shouted at the sky. "The meteorologist said Tuesday! That the cold front would push in early Tuesday and bring heavy showers in the early morning hours. Hello, it is Monday!" Burkhardt looked down at his watch. The time read: 2:22 a.m. in the morning. "Okay, I was wrong, kill me!"

Portfolios in hand, Burkhardt raced across the street and into his apartment. Soaking wet, he turned on the wall heater, removed his wet clothes and jumped into the shower. Five minutes later, dressed in his very best Riviera gold silk pajamas, Burkhardt removed all the Dali paintings from their portfolios and placed them about the room. He walked over to the refrigerator and took out a bottle of champagne. Dom Perignon, 2004, nothing but the best for such an auspicious occasion. He popped the cork and poured himself a glass. He stood, raised his glass and toasted himself. "To my dearest Diane, it has taken twenty years to find *Storm on the Sea of Galilee* and punish the family responsible for your death. Rest in peace." Burkhardt savored the moment and all the magnificent masterpieces that enveloped the room with all their heady magic. Burkhardt finished the bottle, turned off the light and climbed into bed. Woozy, he closed his eyes and fell asleep with visions of masterpieces dancing in his head.

Chapter 66

A man's best friend is his dog. A woman's best friend is a brown and white Pekingese, named Peekie. Sam and Peekie arrived at the restaurant at around eight in the morning. She had a meeting with a new vendor and wanted to complete her inventory balance accounts before they sat down to draft a new contract. No sooner had Sam opened the truck door, little Peekie jumped out and ran around to the front of the building.

Sam followed the barking and spotted Peekie scratching frantically on her tenant's apartment door. Peekie had never acted in such a manner before. Usually she would race around to the front, do her business and wait for Sam to open the restaurant. This morning's behavior was quite unusual. "Peekie, come here girl." called Sam. "Peekie, come over here, right now!" Peekie continued to scratch at the door.

Stepping up to entrance alcove, Sam immediately smelled the distinct odor of gas. She took out her keys and pulled open the door. The pungent odor pushed her back out of the doorway and onto the slate patio. She took a deep breath, covered her mouth and nose and ran into the room to shut off the gas heater. Out of breath, she peered into the bedroom and then raced back outside gasping for air. A few minutes passed for Sam to collect her energy and breathe normally. She gazed up from the patio chair and stared into the apartment and almost passed out. Inside, and directly beyond the entranceway, she saw a table, a champagne bottle and five paintings.

Sam collapsed back in her chair, still gazing at the amazing works of art she tried to compose herself and make sense out of the picture unfolding before her eyes. With shaking hands, Sam reached into her pocket, took out her cell phone and dialed. "This is Sam. I'm at the restaurant. You have to get over here now!"

On the other end of the line, a groggy voice pitifully answered, "I'm still asleep, Sam. I'm not dressed to go out. What time is it anyway?"

"Donna, I don't care if you drive over naked. You have to get here right away. I'm looking at the *Storm on the Sea of Galilee*. It is here at my restaurant, along with the four Dali paintings."

"I'll be right over."

Anyone who knows Donna Jupiter understands there is nothing in her vocabulary that infers: *I'll be right over*. Donna has never been right over, her entire life. Getting dressed for any affair, no matter how insignificant the venue, has always been a Herculean journey and one that took time and purpose. Donna had her own flight plan for dressing and never wavered from the First Class preparations.

First, Donna takes a hot, steaming, hydro-tub bath filled with bubbles and oils to soothe the body and the mind. Next, a body moisturizer is administered to illuminate and add vitamins and antioxidants to the skin. Donna believes that the eyes are the windows to your soul, so particular care is essential when outlining the eyebrows and eyelashes with a pigmented Gucci waterproof liner and mascara to highlight her dark brown eyes. An all-day foundation to smooth away redness, a light dab of powder and a little blush for the natural look makes for a perfect face. A thin spray of mousse, a quick brushing and a touch of hairspray transform a beautiful head of hair into a coiffure's masterpiece. Also, a glossy lip color, to coordinate with her nails, and then a designer outfit from Neiman Marcus, Bergdorf Goodman or Nordstrom's almost completes the ensemble. Let us not forget shoes. Donna Jupiter, is a shoe maven. A separate, walk-in closet off the master bedroom is just for her, with over one hundred pairs of shoes. Included in the collection were five pairs of Stuart Weitzman boots, very expensive and extremely difficult to obtain. Jewelry, matching purse and a splash of Beautiful perfume and an hour later, Mrs. Jupiter was prepared to leave the building.

However, there's an exception to every rule and for Donna Jupiter it happened after one phone call. Within a span of fifteen minutes, the matriarch of meticulous wardrobe coordination was dressed, out of her house and speeding down Gulf of Mexico Drive at 70mph. The yellow Bentley circumnavigated St. Armands Circle with ease and motored over the Ringling Bridge onto Tamiami Trail towards Venice.

A record for any normal driver, Donna pulled into Luna's back parking lot in a breathtaking twenty-nine minutes. Peekie greeted her as she stepped out of the car with a customary lick and together they walked into the restaurant and found Sam sitting at the bar. "Where is it?" Were the first words out of Donna's mouth. "I have to see my painting, please, Sam." Her second request, in a conciliatory tone, was more like the Donna she loved. They hugged and walked back to the apartment.

"I left the door open so the gas would dissipate. It was impossible to breathe in there when I first went in. The gas heater must have leaked fumes into the room and that's what probably killed him."

"So, he just fell asleep and didn't wake up," Donna spat out in disgust. "That was too easy a death for that monster. He deserved to die a thousand deaths for what he did to my Joey. I saw the bullet hole in my husband's head. I relive the agony every day and this monster just goes to sleep. That's not justice."

"You're right, let's go in."
Immediately, Donna approached the Rembrandt. She bent down and cradled the masterpiece it in her arms as if she was about to rock her baby to sleep. Her entire demeanor changed in a matter of seconds. Transformed into another person, in a different time and place, she spun around humming to herself in quiet joy, keeping her eyes fixated on the Rembrandt and only the Rembrandt.

The bedroom door was ajar. Sam walked in and she stepped up to the bed and gazed down at Burkhardt stretched out under the covers. His eyes were closed, hair neatly combed and a peaceful glaze enveloped his face as if he had just fallen asleep. Sam touched his neck. His skin felt cold. He wasn't asleep, he was dead.

Suddenly, gun shots rang out and three bullets exploded into Burkhardt's forehead. Blood splattered over the white pillow case, on the headboard and up onto Sam's shirt. Horrified, she spun around and there standing behind her stood Donna with a silver gun pointing down at the bed. "Oh my God, Donna, what have you done? Why did you shoot a dead man? This is not good." screamed Sam.

"I promised that monster that if I had a chance, I'd put a bullet in his head, just like he did to my husband. I did it for Joey."

"Alright, let's go sit at the table and think this problem out, but first put the gun back in your purse. We don't need you shooting anyone else." Sam took Donna's arm and led her to the table. "I'm not a lawyer, but I don't think you can be charged with murder if the individual is already dead. However, I believe you will be charged with something. What, I don't know. That's for the court to decide."

Donna reached into her pocketbook and pulled out her cell phone. "I'll call my attorney and have him come over here right now," Donna whispered as if not to wake anyone.

"No, not yet I have a plan," Sam answered. "Put the phone away and listen."

Over the course of the next half hour, Sam and Donna organized the steps they needed to follow to successfully navigate their predicament. Donna was to call her attorney, explain what had transpired and have him come over to the apartment. Next, she was to call the FBI, inform them that she had possession of the *Storm on the Sea of Galilee* and claim the $5 million reward. Sam was to call the news station, then the Dali Museum, explain that she had the four Dali paintings stolen from the Venice Art Museum and petition for their $4 million reward. Lastly, she was going to call the police. The final piece to the artistic puzzle was the disposition of the Claire Chase carry-on behind the sofa containing 10 million dollars.

"Good morning, this is Bryce Faceman broadcasting live from the Casa Luna Apartments in downtown Venice, Florida, where a bizarre twist of fate brings to a conclusion the mystery of a missing FBI agent, a stolen Rembrandt and last night's Dali art heist."

The television camera pans out across the front of the apartment building and a line of police and fire vehicles blocking the entire street; then to a close-up of Bryce Faceman. "This reporter has credible information from a reliable source that the FBI Agent, Ross Burkhardt and the paintings... Wait one moment, behind me, at this time, you can see EMS rolling out a body on a gurney and into an ambulance. There appears to be a sheet over the individual, and that confirms my informant's tip that Agent Burkhardt died last night from carbon monoxide poisoning due to a faulty gas heater in the apartment."

Moments later, FBI personnel wearing white gloves carried out five paintings to a waiting truck and drove off. Two police detectives escorted a woman in handcuffs out the front door and into a white Crown Victoria. The camera moves back to Faceman and he reports, "Police have just taken into custody Mrs. Donna Jupiter, whose husband I was told, was killed by Agent Burkhardt. Reporting from downtown Venice, Florida, this is Bryce Faceman saying good-bye." The camera holds a close-up of Faceman and then fades away.

Chapter 67

Bandana rocked the night away. Charismatic lead singer, Butch Gerace, had over sixteen requests to sing their signature tune, *Woolly Bully*, which they obliged and belted out twenty times, interspersed with Lil` Red Riding Hood and all their other rock and roll melodies while the guests danced under the stars. Three months had passed since Joey Jupiter was laid to rest and what better way to honor her husband than to have a memorial party in his own backyard. Over one hundred friends, business associates, politicians and celebrities were invited to the party.

In true Joey Banana tradition, Donna Jupiter was the queen of entertainment. Her entire backyard was transformed into a sea of banana yellow. Yellow Tiki huts, yellow palm trees, yellow tables and a crystal, yellow banana-shaped champagne fountain in the center of the yard. Yellow lights glistened up and down all the beautifully manicured trees and bushes, while additional yellow lights twinkled along the pathway leading down to the dock. Waiters and waitresses, dressed in yellow, gracefully moved about with trays of hors d'oeuvres and drinks all evening long.

The hostess, dressed in an exquisite yellow evening gown by Christian Dior, was first to address the party. Her brief speech thanked the guests for attending the memorial and most of all, for being loyal friends to her husband over the years. Next, local officials praised Mr. Jupiter as a friend to the community, an esteemed businessman and a pioneer in philanthropic endowments. Unexpectedly, the final speaker, was FBI Director Pembroke. He lavished great praise for Mr. Jupiter and his daunting assistance in obtaining evidence that finally implicated a corrupt agent and the dismantling of a ring of art thieves responsible for criminal activities in Boston and most recently in Venice. Director Pembroke also announced that the FBI now has in their possession all the stolen paintings from the Isabella Gardner Museum and now with the recovery of the *Storm on the Sea of Galilee*, the paintings will be returned to the museum at the end of the month. In addition, Pembroke concluded that the FBI was presenting Mrs. Jupiter, the medal of valor posthumously for Mr. Jupiter's work in the line of duty.

With the completion of the last speech dinner was served, a culinary masterpiece second to none. The buffet, which filled four large catering tables, was an endless gastronomic delight that satisfied the more finicky of diners one course at a time. After dessert, Blaine left the table and walked down towards the dock where she bumped into, not quite by accident, Detective Beale.

"Hello, Blaine, enjoying the party?" Beale asked with a cheery smile on his face.

"Who wouldn't? Just look around, I don't see a single frown. Yes, I'm having a great time. By the way, how are you feeling?" Blaine said and pointed to his arm.

"I'm fine. My shoulder has healed. Only a small scar to add to the other collection of gunshot wounds. Occasional headaches now and then from the concussion, but I'm good. Thanks for asking." Beale's cell phone rang. He looked down at the message, punched in a response and put the phone back in his pocket.

"Blaine, I wanted to inform you that I received a call from the Attorney General's office today. The court ruled, because of his involvement in your house bombing, that an additional ten years will be added to Boltier's sentence. I thought you'd want to receive the news as soon as possible." Beale looked a little uncomfortable, but smiled.

"Thank you. My daughter and I will be able to sleep a little more comfortably knowing he most likely will spend the rest of his life in prison. Thank you for the news." Blaine reached out and touched his hand. "I was more astonished to hear the news that Joey was working for the FBI. I also didn't hear Director Pembroke mention the $10 million? Does the FBI know where the money is?"

"I don't think anyone can put a monetary value on a person's life. Can you?"

After what felt like an eternity of awkward silence, Blaine asked, "Are you going down to see Donna's new boat?"

"I was, but I just received an urgent message and I have to go. A break in the missing former Venice City Council member case. `Bye."

Following a stream of partygoers along the path down to the boat dock, Blaine stopped by a bench and rested. At first, she just looked out at the water, serenely glistening in the moonlight. She shifted her gaze dockside at the grandeur of Donna's new yacht. It was beyond description. Completely restored, the 1960 Christ-Craft Constellation was identical to her old yacht that was destroyed in Sarasota Bay, but looked brand new.

"Quite a boat," a voice announced from alongside the bench. "May I sit down?" Disregarding a response, and with a swish of a yellow gown, the hostess sat down beside Blaine.

"Oh hi, Donna, I was just daydreaming. What a fabulous party, thank you for inviting me and your new boat, amazing." Blaine turned and together they fixated on the floating gem a few feet away, but miles away in their fantasies.

"It's a beauty alright, cost me a million dollars to keep that piece of machinery at my dock. Worth every penny, if I can relive how Joey loved to cruise around in that old boat."

"Speaking of money, I read in the paper last week where you and Sam donated five million dollars to help save the Venice Circus. I was wondering if you and Sam would be as generous and donate another five million to help save the Florida Scrub-Jay at Osprey State Park." Blaine was surprised at her bold request, but desperate times call for desperate measures.

"I read the same article, but that the donors were anonymous," Donna snapped. "Whatever gave you the idea Sam and I donated millions of dollars for the preservation of the Venice Circus?"

"The name of your new yacht, ANONYMOUS." Blaine stood and pointed to the stern of the boat and smiled.

295

"Clever woman, Blaine Sterling. Let's go on board and talk to Sam."

Available at www.amazon.com and www.bn.com

RW

Made in the USA
San Bernardino, CA
29 May 2015